ACCIDENTAL GANGSTER

Dutch Schultz and Me

Harriet Goodman Grayson

OBP
Ocean Breeze Press

Westerly

www.oceanbreezepress.net

Accidental Gangster: Dutch Schultz and Me
By Harriet Goodman Grayson

© Copyright 2022

ISBN: 9798419796843

Published by Ocean Breeze Press

Cover photo credit: family photos

Cover and interior design by Ricketts-White Design
www.rickettswhitedesign.com

Dedicated to my grandfather, Goldy

Chapter 1
Prohibition Begins

The sky was the brightest blue. A few drifting clouds covered her resting body. She yawned, her wide mouth fully open, the sharp teeth exposed to the sunlight. The scratchy sandpaper tongue helped to clean her shiny fur. Raw fish heads were responsible for that glossy sheen.

Everyone on the fishing boat heard the car come to a stop. The stones of the gravel driveway ricocheted against the tire's wheel covers. The tiny gray rocks haphazardly thrown into the air. The furry beast scattered and dove beneath the deck, her three kittens running behind.

Two burly men in fancy suits emerged from the long, black sedan. They walked across the wooden planks of the dock. When they reached the largest boat, the biggest one shouted out, "Goldy Goldfarb."

Goldy looked down at the strangers from his boat's top deck. She returned to protect her protector. He heard his furry champion hissing at them. "I'm Goldy," he told them.

A boy of 14 watched nearby studying his father's reaction. "Stay here Izzy." The man with the golden colored brown hair walked towards the boat's ladder.

"What can I do for you gentlemen?" He signaled for his son

to move into the deck below.

"Our boss wants to see you."

"Who's your boss?"

"Get in the car and you'll find out," the short, fat man told him.

"Izzy," he whispered. "Izzy, as we leave try and get the car's license number."

"Papa, you're not going?"

"When we leave, get the license plate number. Gather up Fluffy and her kittens. Stick them in a crate. Go find Caesar and put him in a crate. Then bicycle home. Get Zayde to help you to collect the cats."

"Why?"

"Just do as I say."

The voices grew louder and more insistent. "Goldy, get your ass down here!"

The biggest one was about to climb onto the ladder.

"I'm coming." He turned to son. "Remember what I said."

Goldy climbed down the ladder to the waiting car. "Where we going fellows?"

"Get in!" he said, rather roughly. They pushed him into the back seat of the new sedan.

As the car backed up, the gravel flying in random directions, Izzy ran to write down the license number.

Goldy turned his head as the car drove down the beachfront road. "Nice car," he said, smiling as they drove off. "Heading to the Island or are we going to Brooklyn?"

"Just shut up and watch the scenery."

Goldy looked out the big rear car windows as the smell of

the ocean and the gulls disappeared. He was so tempted to speak, but remained quiet trying to figure out where they were taking him. It looked like Brooklyn not too far from the ocean. He thought he saw the amusement park in Coney Island in the distance. It was hard to miss. He swore it must be the Wonder Wheel. His five kids loved that place and only a nickel on the newly constructed subway to get there.

The car stopped on an ordinary street. It could be any metropolitan town. Hands reached for him to get out of the car. The three of them entered the rear door of a restaurant.

A man was sitting alone at a table waiting for him, "Sit."

Goldy obeyed.

"Do you know who I am?" The man was younger than the two burly guys and looked a decade younger than Goldy.

"Yeah, I read the papers, you're Dutch Schultz."

"Yeah, you got it. How about a drink?"

Goldy saw that he and Schultz were the only ones sitting at a table. "Sure."

"How about a whiskey?"

"Fine," said Goldy. The shot glass appeared and was filled to the brim.

"L'chayim," Schultz said, as Goldy raised his glass. Both men emptied their glasses with one giant gulp.

"So what can I do for you Mr. Schultz?"

"Call me Dutch. You like steak?"

"Sure," Goldy answered.

"Got to be Kosher?"

"No, I'm real liberal about food. Why am I here?"

"I never heard of a Jew who was a fisherman."

"Wasn't Jesus a fisherman?"

"No, he was a carpenter."

"Well you need to be a good carpenter to be a fisherman," Goldy smiled while Dutch laughed.

"I like you Goldy," Dutch tapped his elbow. "Funny guy. What's with the name Goldy, short for Goldfarb?"

"People think that, but really it's my golden brown curly locks. It was my mother's nickname for me."

"Your mother alive?"

"No, she died a couple of years ago."

"My Papa knows your Papa from the old country. Right, Polacks from Bialystok."

The steak was served to Goldy and the glasses refilled to the top. "Thanks," said Goldy.

"Ess," Dutch stabbed the steak with his knife, "ever eat such tender meat?"

"Delicious," Goldy tasted it. "Food and whiskey, wonderful. But why am I here?"

"Prohibition is about to start. First rate booze in Canada where it's perfectly legal. I need to bring that booze from Canada to America. I need your boats."

"OK. You want me to take my boats to Canada?"

"No, no, no. I need you to take your boats just beyond the international border. There you will be met by a boat from Canada. You transfer the booze from the Canadian boat to your boat."

"OK and where do I deliver the booze to?"

"Somewhere in the Rockaways. Different location for each drop. It's a wild place those Rockaways, miles of shoreline.

Who goes there at night?"

"I get it. Might need my rowboats to transfer once we're near the beach. My fishing boats need a dock or stay 50 feet away from the shore. Else their bottom gets scraped. Big maintenance problem. Understand?"

"Goldy Goldfarb, I will make you a rich man. Are you afraid of the police?"

"Pogroms you fear. The Cassocks you fear, but the US government? Never. What's the worst, I get arrested? My cousins have gotten arrested for union protests. In jail you get free food. They beat you up a little, get a black eye. It's OK. Pogroms in Bialystok, they attack your family. Lock the women and children in the synagogue and set it on fire. Burning to death I fear, but not this American government."

"A Jew who understands. I like you Goldy; we're going to make lots of money together."

"When do we start?"

"I'll let you know. Are you finished eating?"

Goldy swallowed the last of the steak, "OK."

The big black sedan pulled up in front of the house. To greet him was Esty's parrot Polly, who was actually a male bird. The colorfully feathered parrot screamed out, "Papa home, Papa home."

Izzy and Zayde ran outside to greet him. The younger children ran to the front of the house.

"Papa, Papa, "Izzy screamed out, hugging him so tightly he could step no further.

"Goldy, Goldy," Zayde cried while he ran his fingers

through his son's thick wavy hair.

"Goldy, Goldy," Esty ran to greet him, lavishing his cheeks with wet kisses.

"What happened? Who were those men?" his father asked.

Goldy was shaking his head. "It is too crazy. I'm OK. Really, I'm fine." He managed to free himself, walk onto the large front porch, and sit on the rocking chair.

"Papa home, Papa home," Polly screamed.

All the younger children jumped on top of him. Little Gladdy was clinging to his feet.

"Papa," she cried. He picked her up.

He kissed each of his four younger children and again his wife, Esty.

"OK. I am fine. Let me speak alone to Zayde. OK?"

Slowly, the five children went back to play in the big fenced in backyard where their canine babysitter was waiting. Ruby watched them return. Gladdy at two, and the youngest, fell on top of her. She licked the child's face.

"What a reception? You think I was gone for a couple of years," Goldy said.

"We were worried. Was it the police?" his father asked.

"No, no, no. This you would never guess."

"Tell me, what happened? Nu?" his father demanded to know.

"You recognize the name Dutch Schultz?"

"The punk gangster. Maybe 19 years old? Him?"

"That's the one. Says you and his father know each other from the old country. Bialystok boys!"

"I don't know him. That's not his real name. But I got

6

friends who may know him. I don't think he's from Bialystok. Maybe? So what does he want?"

"To use my boats to transfer booze from Canada. He has some connection with the Jews in Canada that manufacture the real whiskey."

"I suppose they think this Prohibition is going to last," his father said.

"New ways for gangsters to make money."

"And you said?" Zayde asked.

"Why not. What can happen? I go to jail. Better than the 1902 Bialystok pogrom. Not likely to burn to death."

"You're right, but don't think this booze running is without risks. And I don't mean from the cops or the government," Zayde was a clear-headed man.

"I understand. It will be you and me. Leave out Esty and the kids," Goldy told his father.

"What about Izzy. He's 14 and can be very useful."

"Let me think about that. He should be still thinking about school."

"You will need a gun."

"A gun?"

"Yes, these are dangerous people. This squawking parrot is no protection. And the German Shepherd dog can be shot. You need something more threatening and lethal."

"Do you got a gun?"

"I'll get one from your Cousin Mo. He was in the war."

"Didn't they give them back their guns when the war was over?"

"Yes, U.S. issued stuff. He got one off a dead German. I'll

buy it from him."

"You think this is a good idea?" Goldy was still feeling hesitant despite his words.

"I don't think you had a choice. Better to be on the good side of Dutch Schultz and his associates. Let's go with it. See what happens," the older man said.

"He told me he'd make me rich."

"Let's hope we all stay safe and alive."

That afternoon was the first meeting between Dutch Schultz and Goldy Goldfarb. So began their fifteen-year relationship.

Goldy and his father readied the fishing boat for longer clandestine voyages in the open sea. More supplies and fuel were brought onboard. The boat was painted and the barnacles scraped off the bottom. Hard work was required, but the financial gains appeared unlimited. Dangerous? The open sea presented challenges. Goldy kept his German gun by his side and Zayde bought a hunting rifle.

Chapter 2

Three Years Later

Despite Prohibition, it seemed there was a speakeasy on every corner. More people died from alcohol poisoning than traffic accidents. The bathtub versions were completely unregulated and potentially lethal. Not with the stuff from Dutch Schultz and friends. They offered pure Canadian booze, literally right off the boat—Goldy Goldfarb's boats.

Father and son worked most nights and slept all day. The cats were their constant companions since they lived the same schedule. All they needed was extra fuel, but they wanted to appear busy selling fish. Goldy went to his suppliers professing to need more supplies. It was the Roaring Twenties and there was supposedly a huge demand for fresh fish.

"I'm going over to see Rivka," Goldy told his father.

"Good, nice you see your sister. Never thought I would see her being useful. But times are crazy."

"Well, later, we'll go to their house for a party for Moishe. First college graduate in the family. "

"You're responsible. I hope he doesn't forget who got him through college."

"I'm sure he knows. I'm walking over there now." He rose

from the porch rocking chair and walked towards the sidewalk.

"Papa leaving, Papa leaving. Go Papa," screamed out Polly.

Esty opened the front door.

"Where's he going?" she asked her father-in-law.

"Going to see Rivka."

His sister, a widow, with two children, lived three blocks away. She was part of his small team. Being trustworthy was the key attribute of team membership. That meant only family members were involved in the business. Esty was too emotional; she was afraid. So his wife remained a good cook and housekeeper. His sister was good at the books. Her dead husband was a terrible businessman. But she was careful with the money.

She was sitting at the kitchen table with her twenty-one-year-old son. The new graduate stood up when his uncle entered the room. A cup of hot tea was waiting for him.

The young man hugged his uncle. "Thanks so much for everything."

"A pharmacist. You are now a professional man," his uncle congratulated him with a slap on the back.

"He's very grateful to you, Goldy. Without you we would be penniless and on the street."

"No drama, my dear sister. Moishe earned those good grades."

"He's a pharmacist, a pharmacist, what a great profession, my baby boy," she kissed her son.

He winced and smiled at his uncle.

"Who guided you to this profession? Who paid for your schooling at Brooklyn College of Pharmacy?" his smiling uncle asked.

"You, of course."

"And, why was I so enthusiastic about this kind of schooling?"

"I thought Zayde told me about someone back in the old country," the new graduate answered.

"Yes, but what does a pharmacy possess that other businesses never keep?"

The young graduate stared at his uncle and then his mother.

His mother spoke, "Alcohol."

Goldy pointed his finger at his sister, "Correct. Alcohol. Every pharmacy stores alcohol for medicinal purposes."

A light bulb went on in the young man's brain. "You want me to help you in the bootlegging business?"

"Yes, but not what you may be thinking. I certainly do not want you selling alcohol, however, you can store my booze. Everything is above board. Alcohol is legal."

"I've been searching with your uncle to find you a store. Probably somewhere in Far Rockaway," his mother replied.

"Convenient for people to walk into from the street. Near a bus stop. We can take you along see what you like. It's going to be your store. Your mother's going to own it. I am the investor. Your silent partner," Goldy explained.

"You know besides alcohol pharmacies also sell more potent drugs," Moishe suggested.

"No, no," he slapped his nephew on the arm, forcefully enough to create a swirl of air.

"I was just saying. Morphine, cocaine, I can legally sell

those products."

"Never. That's for the guineas and shvartzes, not for a nice Jewish boy from Rockaway. You hear me," Goldy wasn't smiling.

"OK. You know it's all part of what makes a pharmacy so useful."

"I catch you selling drugs, morphine, cocaine and anything else like that," he paused, "I'll kill you myself. You understand. This is not a joke."

"Of course uncle, I'm so sorry. Just a stupid thought," he apologized.

"Go outside, I want to talk to your mother."

Moishe left the adults to discuss other things. When he was gone they spoke.

"I don't know where he got the idea of the drugs."

"Someone told him about the drugs. Probably someone at school. You make sure he doesn't get involved. Those dagos are dangerous. I know. Booze is bad enough, but the drugs, nasty, nasty. Make sure he stays away."

"OK, I will. He's a good boy. He'll listen."

"I hope so."

"The smartest one in the family is your Silvia," Rivka told her brother.

"Yeah, always good in school. And what a throwing arm. If only she was a boy. I'd get her to try out for the minor league baseball team."

"Better she goes to school. Ask her if she wants to go to pharmacy school. You can open a store on the outer side of Rockaway near Belle Harbor."

"I'll talk to her. Now let's take a ride. You can drive that old car in the garage. I know you love to be in control. It needs a running," he told her.

"Oh, great. I drive. You sit and don't give me instructions. Where we going?"

"I won't give you instructions, just directions," he laughed at her excitement.

"Let's go, come on," she took the car keys from the hook near the front door.

"OK. First, get out of the driveway and onto the street."

"Where are we going?"

"To Brooklyn. Keep your hands on the steering wheel and your eyes looking straight ahead."

She gently jabbed at his head, "No instructions just directions."

He directed her to McDonald Avenue in Brooklyn. There were more horses and carts than cars in the early 1920's. Rivka was not accustomed to driving a car when her husband was alive. Now she was on her own. Goldy bit his hand to stifle any words of criticism about her driving.

"Stop here!" Goldy yelled.

"What? Washington Cemetery. We going to visit Mama? She would be so proud of Moishe."

"Be careful where you step," Goldy guided his sister to their mother's grave.

"You got a book to say Kaddish?"

"Here," he said. They shared the tiny book while praying over the dead.

"That's nice," his sister said between sighs, "want to visit other graves."

"No, not yet. Let me show you something."

He walked to the headstone.

"Be careful, you don't want step on her dead body."

"Come here," he told her while she tiptoed towards him.

"What are you doing? Desecrating her grave?" She was angry.

"Come here," he pulled her closer to him.

He kneeled by the stone. "Look here." He pulled up a piece of the granite monument.

"What are you doing?"

"Come here. Look." He grabbed a piece of granite and lifted it away.

"There's a hole."

"Look closer," he pulled her to her knees.

"There's a box in there."

"Yes, exactly. Open it."

She bent next to the stone. He placed a metal box in her hands.

"Just in case. Open it."

"My God money, so much money."

"This is my rainy day fund. Just you know. If something happens to me. You need money come here. Come alone."

"What's going to happen. Don't talk like that."

"I'm in a dangerous business. I could be killed. Papa could be killed. At best, I could go to jail for years. Better to prepare. If something happens to me, come here and get some money. Don't take much just a little at a time. Always come alone. The less who know, the better."

"You worry too much."

"No, it's better to be prepared."

"Did you put any money in the bank?" she asked.

"No, this is much safer."

"I hear people putting money in the stock market. Just a little down payment and you get big returns."

"No, none of this money leaves the cemetery unless you need something when I'm not around."

"What about Esty?"

"She is just too nervous to think straight. If something happens to me, you take the reins. And never leave those stupid cats on the boats at night."

"Why?" she laughed.

"Somebody, my business associates or the government could burn my boats. The last thing I want to regret is having those felines burn to death."

"Oh, Goldy, such a worrier. But OK. I get it. You can depend on me."

"Make sure that boy of yours doesn't get tempted with drug money. I will kill him."

"No problem, he'll behave."

When they arrived at Goldy's house, Esty and the parrot were sunning themselves.

"Papa home. Rivka here. Papa home," Polly screeched out loud.

Esty motioned to them, "Come in. We have tea."

"I got errands to run," Goldy explained.

"Always time for tea," his wife replied.

"OK," he sat next to his sister on the big swing hanging in a corner of the porch.

"Where do you have to go?" she asked as she poured the tea from the black kettle into the pretty, delicate teacups.

"I'm going to Ratner's."

"In the Lower East Side?" his surprised wife asked.

"I'm going to meet cousin Mo."

"Not a Yiddisher kop that boy. His Mama must have bounced him on his head a few times," his wife replied.

"Mo? That shmegegi?" his sister asked.

"He says he wants me to meet an Army buddy. Then I got to see Dutch."

"Oy vey iz mir, the idiot and the gangster all in one afternoon. My poor Goldy," his wife shakes her head.

"Brother, since you're going to one of my most favorite restaurants, bring back some goodies."

"Bring home pickled and cream style herring. I try and make it but they do a better job. My gefilte fish is good, but anything smoked or pickled not so good. Get lox. There's a great bialy factory, stop in there. And bagels, get those crusty bagels," his wife's list seemed endless.

"OK, get me some cooler bags for the trip home," Goldy wrote the list in his brain.

Driving the Williamsburg Bridge was one of life's great treasures. The views were magnificent, the bumpy ride kept your attention. There you were going from Williamsburg, Brooklyn across the East River. At the edge of the bridge was Delancey Street in the heart of the Lower East Side. Not far from the bridge is the famous dairy restaurant, Ratner's. It was started in 1905 by Jacob Harmatz and his brother-in-law Alex Ratner.

Goldy walked into the cavernous restaurant. Glancing in one direction and then another, he saw his Cousin Mo.

He found the table where two men were talking. One much more animated than the other. Mo's arms were flying as he spoke, the other man motionless. As Goldy approached, Mo stood up by his chair and the other man followed his lead.

"This is my cousin Goldy and Goldy this is a real Indian Chief. He is a member of the Ojibwe tribe. He lives on a reservation up north. It actually has a big river that runs along the border. Part is in America and part is in Canada. Is that amazing? He actually has Canadian and American citizenship."

Goldy shook hands with the stranger and took a seat. "First time in New York City?" he asked.

"Always wanted to visit. Then I got a letter from the U.S. Army about some war benefit. So I'm here. Tomorrow, I go to Washington, D.C."

"You served with my Cousin Mo? In the infantry? Pretty bloody, yeah?"

"A lot of guys died in battle, more were wounded and died from neglect. Trenches smelled from blood. Ever kill a man?"

"No, thankfully. I missed that war," Goldy replied.

"Mo was either very brave or completely nuts. He charged out of those trenches. He came home with metals. Did he show you?"

"No, no, Mo never talked about the war."

This guy," Mo lightly punched him on the arm, "saved my life."

"So Chief did you get a metal?"

"No injuns got metals. But I got gratitude," Chief told Goldy while slapping Mo's back.

"The Chief fought for both Canada and America. Bloody Indian right? Loves to fight," Mo excitedly explained.

"Ever eat this Jewish food, all diary, no meat but lots of smoked fish?" Goldy asked.

"We eat smoked fish. We got fishing boats like your cousin Goldy. We go on the lake catch'um and smoke the fish. Looks like this stuff," he pointed to a dish of smoked whitefish with its wrinkly skin.

"I got a little of everything for you and the Chief," Mo pointed to the assortment of smoked and pickled fish on the table.

The man looked the part of an Indian Chief. No headdress or leather hand-made moccasins, but he was tall with a reddish-brown skin tone. Goldy had never met an actual Indian. He saw a few at the movie theater. Those guys never spoke.

"You want to know why I wanted to meet you?" Chief asked.

"Yeah, exactly." Goldy answered.

"Mo and I were in the Army together as he told you."

Mo piped up, "He's like a man who fights for all countries. He was in the American and Canadian Army. He enlisted. Can you beat that."

"Nothing much happening on the reservation?"

"Starvation and cold winds, cloudless skies," Chief answers.

"Pretty dreary. Looking to vacation in New York City?"

"Mo tells me you're a bootlegger."

Goldy sent an unkind look towards his cousin. "Mo has a big mouth."

His cousin blushed and stuffed a piece of fish in his mouth.

"I think I can help you," Chief says.

"Mo can you go around the corner and get Esty some bialys. There's a factory near here. That would be swell," Goldy told him. He handed him some money.

He quickly got the message, "Sure."

When Mo was at the door on his way out Goldy faced the Indian Chief. "So how can you be helpful, a man of two worlds?"

"Indians in the north are considered their own nation. Canadian Mounted Police and US government agents don't trespass. Booze is legal in Canada. Instead of boats, I can offer a land route."

"Where's the reservation?"

"On a lake bordering New York State and Quebec Province."

"Straight north from here?"

"Right," he answered.

"Seems to me, boats would be faster."

"Maybe, but it's an alternate path. No worries about bad weather on the seas. Winter can be rough for fishermen."

"And you know about my business from Mo?"

"You're right. Mo has a big mouth."

"And your cut would be?" Goldy quickly got down to business.

"I'd let you decide how valuable we could be."

"My Canadian supplier would deliver the booze to you on

the Canadian side. You take it to the American side still on your reservation. Then I pick it up from you in a designated spot on your reservation? Right?"

"Yes, and of course we would want some extra for ourselves."

"It could be another option. Less dangerous in the wintertime than the boats. Could be?"

"You can try it. Small delivery, just as a trial run. Our tribe can be an ally. We don't like or trust the Canadian government, not the U.S. government. Prohibition is just another way to make money."

"I show you the business. You could try and deal directly with our Canadian supplier. Move around us. Take us out of the picture entirely."

"No, never, we are loyal people. Once we make a pact, smoke from the pipe, we are friends. And friends never turn on their allies."

"I'll have to talk to my boss. See if he agrees. And no Mo. He can't keep his mouth shut. You only talk to me. Got it?"

"I got it," they shook hands just as Mo was returning with a big bag of onion flavored goodies.

Goldy always viewed his relationship with Dutch as tenuous at best. He was a volatile young man younger than his nephew Moishe. He was charismatic. His fast talking ways drew dozens of other young men eager for a piece of the American pie. Goldy was guarded in his conversations with Dutch, but never subservient. He told him how he felt.

After lunching with Mo and Chief, he drove back to Brooklyn to see Dutch. His new headquarters was in a speakeasy in Coney Island. The place looked worn and shabby in the day-light. The brightly-colored balloons hung precariously from the ceiling. The place smelled of beer and sweat.

"Welcome Goldy," Dutch was sitting alone at a corner table.

"Hello," Goldy sat down facing Dutch. A man came over to the table and filled his glass with whiskey.

"L'chayim," Dutch said as the glasses clanked. "Nu, what have you to report?"

"Business, as you know is good. You get my receipts?"

"Did I make you a rich man, Goldy?"

"Not quite rich but I'm not complaining."

"You still driving that piece of shit?"

"It works so no need to be replaced."

"You're a cautious guy. Right? But I got a business proposition?"

"I'm listening."

"You should buy a speakeasy. I want to expand to the Rock-aways. With all your money you can get one. Like a restaurant chain. Yeah?"

"I'm a fisherman. I don't know anything about running a bar or a nightclub. I like to stick with what I know."

Dutch looked displeased. The broad smile faded into a frown.

"Here's what I propose, Dutch. I can be an investor. I don't believe in these stocks and bonds they're peddling. But a speakeasy, I can give you money. I'll be one of your investors." Goldy walked a delicate line. Don't get too entrenched in

21

Dutch's businesses, but keep him happy. He was a dangerous young man with a volatile temper, who liked to shoot people.

"An investor. Like Wall Street? My investor. Very clever Goldy. You are a smart guy in the best way. OK. You will be my first investor."

They reached across the table and shook hands.

"You want some money now?" Goldy asked.

"You don't believe in banks. You carry cash with you. Got it buried in the back yard?" Dutch asked with a smirk.

"I like to know where my money is at all times. Banks are only open for a few hours a day."

"Get him a steak," Dutch ordered a nearby waiter.

Goldy moved his shoulder so the just ready steak could be served. It was easy to cut a tender piece.

"Nu, what else?"

"I got a very interesting proposal earlier today. It's complicated, but the short answer is it opens up another route for our Canadian booze."

"I'm listening," Dutch cut a large piece of meat and stuffed it into his mouth.

"There's a tribe of real Indians on the Canadian border. It seems their reservation is actually on Canadian and American soil. And they have this peculiar legal standing that makes them their own nation."

"Where's this reservation?"

"Straight north on New York-Quebec Province border. Not that far from our supplier."

"What are they offering? What do they want?"

"They would initially collect our booze from Canada. It's

perfectly legal up north. The booze passes from the Canadian side of their reservation to the American side. That's where we pick it up."

"Why give a piece of the action to another party?"

"In winter, the water can be dangerous. This is simply another option to make sure the booze never stops."

"They could get greedy and take the stuff for themselves."

"I trust them. We act honorably and give them a reasonable cut. We can set the terms. And naturally they want their own firewater. They are injuns."

"Goldy, Goldy, my man Goldy. You are such an honest man. I can really trust you. Have gonifs working for me. They would see an opportunity to cut me out. Not say a word. Not you, my Goldy. The last honest man. You come to me with this proposal. I love you Goldy." He throws him a kiss.

"What do you think?" Goldy asked.

"More important, what do you think? Does it make sense? Can we trust these injuns?"

"I think it's worth a try. Once. In the winter when the seas are real rough. Me and my boy could drown. Those boats can be dangerous. The currents even just a few miles from shore can be treacherous. Boats sink in winter gales. A trial run."

"So be it." Dutch said. They shook hands. "Let's give it a trial run. See how honest they really are. If it doesn't work out I'm taking the money out of your cut."

"Let's try it," Goldy told the boss.

Goldy drove up to his house. "Papa home, Papa home," Polly screeched. He opened his brilliantly-colored feathers, which eclipsed his green face. He imagined that his new friend Chief might look nice with a few of those feathers in a headdress.

Esty was rocking herself on the porch. "Goldy sit. I go get some hot tea. Give me the pekl. It smells from heaven. I'll make you a sandwich with all these wonderful foods."

Before he could protest that he wasn't hungry, she grabbed the bags and went into the kitchen.

"Papa home, Papa home," Polly was back to his announce-ments. Goldy waved at him to stop; he just screeched louder.

"Ess," she returned to the porch.

He wasn't hungry but ate anyway. He couldn't disappoint his wife.

"Goldy, Goldy," she sighed, "who would have thought when we got married that you would become a gangster."

"Esty, I'm not a gangster."

"You carry a gun. You admit it's dangerous. That kid Dutch. What kind of name is Dutch? He is dangerous."

"Stop worrying. Nothing's going to happen. Worst case, I go to jail. Everything is under control. Stop worrying."

"Every night you go out with your Papa and I can't sleep the whole night, worrying. Will you both get home safely?"

"Prohibition will not last forever. When it's all over, we will have money. I'll go back to fishing. Meanwhile, I got dollars in my pocket. Is there something you want? Not too extravagant. I don't want the police snooping round, but something. Maybe a nice wool coat for you and the children. What do you think?"

"For winter, nice coats. A nice hat for you."

As they were eating and sipping tea Polly alerted them.

"Silvie coming, Silvie coming," he yelled.

Their oldest daughter gave the parrot a cookie. He immediately quieted.

"I got such delicacies to eat. Your father got back from the Lower East Side. I get you a nice piece of smoked whitefish and a little herring," her mother said.

"Sit down, take a load off your feet as they say," her father gave her a little poke on the arm.

"OK," the fifteen-year-old sat on the rocking chair.

"So how's school? You know you're the smartest of my five. You should go to college."

"I want to go. Right now, I want to go to Hunter High School."

"What's wrong with Far Rockaway High School where your brother goes?"

"I want to go to a better school. Hunter is an all-girls school in the city."

"Where?"

"In Manhattan on the Upper Eastside."

"How would you get there?"

"The subway," the teenager answered.

"You'd sit for hours on the subway? Every day? Yeah?"

"Yeah. It's the best."

"How much does it cost? That doesn't really matter. I got some money for you."

"It's free. It's part of the whole city system."

"Do you know someone who goes? Someone told you about it?"

Esty joins the two on the porch. Silvie rises so her mother can sit. Goldy got up and dragged another chair closer.

"Ess," she told her daughter.

"Do you know that Silvie wants to go to the city for high school? A place called Hunter High School?" Goldy asked his wife.

"Yeah, yeah, she mentioned it to me. That fat little girl, the grocer's daughter she goes. Right?"

"Right. She's very smart," Silvie told her parents.

"I'm sure," Goldy respected smart. "You would go with her on the subway to the city to school?"

"Yeah, but first I got to take an entrance exam."

"You're good with exams," her mother reassured her daughter.

"Then what? You go to college. Maybe to that Brooklyn College of Pharmacy like cousin Moishe?" her father asked.

"No, no, I don't want to be a pharmacist and make pills and syrups all day."

"Look at Cousin Moishe. Your father got him his own store. Right downtown in Far Rockaway. A regular store owner and only 22. What's wrong with that?"

"I want to be a doctor. After Hunter High School, I can go to Hunter College, then to medical school. I want to do more than count pills."

"Esty, we got such a smart kid. Yeah, wants to be a doctor. Why not? Think big. You certainly got the brains."

"Being a Jewish girl might make things difficult, but if you got your mind made up, I know you will do it. A doctor in the family?" her mother laughed with pride.

"So I can take the test. If I pass, I go with Sheila to Hunter High School?"

"You'll pass no problem. You'll go to that high school in the city. I guess you can study on the subway."

Moishe was licensed and ready to become a pharmacist. They just had to find the right place. Goldy and Rivka perused the neighborhood. Nowhere were there signs about storefronts for lease or purchase. It was Rivka who found the ideal location on a busy street right across from a bus stop. The most important feature of the building was the hatchway in the basement leading to an alleyway. An easy means of discharging the liquor loads from the alley to the basement. Izzy would construct the conveyor system.

His mother and uncle showed him the spot. They drove him in his late father's sedan. They parked in the back, in the alleyway.

"I bought the store for you and your mother. I like having the alley in the back. Makes for easy deliveries. Your mother and Izzy will be your helpers," his uncle told him.

"Look isn't this nice. Your uncle and Izzy will fix up the interior. We get a new sign over the door. Decorate a little inside, that's my job. It's clean. I got a Polish couple to thoroughly clean inside. Can't have a pharmacy that's dirty," his cheerful mother told him.

He was less than impressed with the store. It wasn't in the best part of town. "Why is the back entrance so important? You both keep pointing it out?"

"For a smart kid, I got to wonder about you," his uncle looked at his nephew.

"Moishe," his mother spoke to him in a gentle voice.

"Moishe, the bottles of booze for the cellar. Get it?"

"Booze Moishe, not drugs. Canadian whiskey the finest in the world," his uncle wrapped his arms around the stocky kid.

"OK, I got it."

"Here's the keys. Same one for back and front. Open it," his uncle said.

It smelled of fresh paint. All the walls were painted stark white. The international symbol for pharmacy was on the front counter. His license was framed and visibly hung so all the customers could read it. There were three aisles, all bare.

"You got a license number so you can order those drugs," his uncle explained.

"We can sell other things like hot water bags, canes, all kind of bandages and cough medicines," his mother was excited about opening up the store.

"One other thing," his uncle directed him back outside, "see this door? Upstairs there are two apartments. One for you to live in and the second one to rent."

"I like living with my mother and sister. I don't need an apartment." Moishe told his uncle.

"I want you to live here. I don't want the store to be left alone for so many hours. There will be very valuable merchandise inside," his uncle said.

Rivka opened the back door and joined them.

"Mama, uncle wants me to live here. I don't want to live here alone," he pleaded.

"Oh Moishe, stop being such a baby. You should be grateful to your uncle. Look what he's giving us. My name is on the ownership papers. We'll fix it up nice," his mother extolled.

"Where am I going to get my meals?" Moishe rubbed his tummy.

"Oh Moishe, I'm not abandoning you. You can walk to the house from here," his mother told him.

"Your friends will be envious. You having your own place. They living with their parents. You wait. I promise you. They will be calling you the big man in town," his uncle was enthusiastic and smiling.

"It will be real nice Moishe. We fix it up together, everything real nice. Big radio, icebox, sofa bed that opens up like you see in the magazines. Just perfect," his mother was joyful at the prospect of shopping for home furnishings.

"Don't forget what this store contains. Valuable property must be attended to. Right Moishe?" his uncle asked.

"I get it. How big is the place upstairs?" he was feeling more grateful and less resistant.

"I'll show you," his mother took him by the hand as they climbed the stairs.

"You think I can get a car?" he asked his mother as they reached the next floor.

"Moishe, open the store and start selling. First things first," his mother implored.

Goldy shouted to his sister, "I'm going home. I'll walk. You take the car."

He walked to the front. It was a nice price and a decent location. If it had been in the best neighborhood it would have cost more. This was his first real investment "Stein's Pharmacy." He whistled as he walked. Got to find places to park the cash from the bootlegging, he thought to himself. A pharmacy was perfect and one with an accessible, big basement was ideal. Moishe was a smart kid with no sense. His Silvie would make a smart, resourceful pharmacist, but she wanted to be doctor. Lots of things can change in a few years.

The ladies behind Prohibition were an honorable group. It was the next wave in a series of movements that ebbed and flowed throughout the country. The general population was thought by their elites to be a bunch of ignorant mugs, who needed to be taught how to become real Americans.

Part of the misunderstanding about drinking by the elites was how little they knew about actual hard work. While some of the black members of the Prohibition groups knew about slavery and plantation work, their white sisters were members of an emerging middle class. They knew no one who toiled in claustrophobic clothing factories in the Lower East Side. Chinese laborers on railroads in inhuman weather conditions across the West were not members. Ditch diggers' families did not flock to the meetings of Prohibitionists.

They all had God on their side. Theirs was a Protestant God that disliked Catholics and hated Jews. These immigrant malcontents were fouling the land that they loved. Their job was to take away the drink and any revolutionary thoughts.

It was an example of how a minority opinion became a national mandate. No law was going to stop people from drinking. The peculiarity of the Prohibition laws was it prohibited the sale and distribution of alcohol but not the drinking of it. The movement was doomed from the start. What it gave rise to was nation-wide bootlegging. It was a gift to the gangster class.

Goldy, the Accidental Gangster, was going to be a recipient of a misguided approach to control the working class immigrants.

At least once a week Goldy met Dutch at his speakeasy. The whole gang was present. It was payday. Some of the guys opened their envelopes and counted the cash. Not Goldy, he took the envelope and placed in his breast pocket.

"Thanks Dutch," Goldy said.

Most of the guys also thanked the boss, but it seemed more obligatory. Goldy genuinely appreciated this opportunity to screw the government and get rich. Primarily, this was a Jewish gang of knuckleheads and sociopaths. All started in the lowest step of America's ladder. But as immigrants from harsher times in Eastern Europe and some first-born Americans like Goldy, they appreciated that this was the land of opportunity.

Dutch Schultz was a young man, who had made good in a short period of time. If nothing else, Prohibition was an opportunity to get rich fast. There was nothing sophisticated or complicated about bootlegging. There was an unquenchable thirst for a familiar product. No one had to introduce the product to the general population. There was no explaining or required understanding about the nature of the product. Booze was booze in any container.

What the Jewish gangs had that gave them one step higher on the ladder was connections to legitimate booze from fellow Yids in Canada. They were not selling bathtub gin with its imperfections and potential poisoning effects. This was the real thing. Although it was true that it was all watered down a bit to preserve profits.

Goldy entered this world without any knowledge of the actual business. He was a transporter. His original role was to get the product to market as effortlessly as possible with as few bribes as hungry hands demanded. In the first years, he sat in at the meetings saying nothing. Someone might have assumed he was unable to speak.

By the third year, he had absorbed the machinations of the business from production to distribution. It remained a simple product to sell. Demand continued to grow and the local police and judges were easy to bribe. But as the profits mounted, the federal government began to become more interested in putting a lid on the distribution.

Dutch supervised a precarious empire. He had the local police with their hands out. They were easy to please with a simple request. The feds were becoming more of a danger to the business. Bribes didn't seem to satisfy most of them. These were problems that could be solved or at least managed. The greatest danger to Dutch's business was gang rivals. Satisfying them was a major problem. They were greedy. Loyalty was another problem. Dutch's gang members had a tenuous loyalty to Dutch, the man. Not Goldy.

After discussions about rival Legs Diamond, the cops and the feds, everyone left the table but Goldy.

"What do want?" Dutch asked.

"You're always asking for my advice. Usually, I don't say anything. You know this business better than me."

"Nu. What?"

"OK, I have two suggestions. You make the decisions but listen."

"I'm listening," Dutch poured a new round of drinks, "steak for my man."

"First, this is not a place for your headquarters, a speakeasy. The cops are constantly raiding speakeasies."

"Where should I go?"

"Let me find you a building, first floor your office, call it a nice social club. Put the name of the club on the front window. You look, legit."

"You going to find me a place?"

"Yeah, there's lots to choose from. You make the final choice. You like this neighborhood we'll stay here. You like better we go closer to the ocean. Smell the nice ocean breezes. Or you want to be part of the bigger action in Manhattan. I'll look."

"Next?"

"Instead of threatening and then sometimes killing Legs Diamond's guys, there's a better way."

"Yeah, like what?" his reply harsh and disbelieving.

"What do these guys really want?" Goldy waited for Dutch's answer.

"To be the boss," Dutch replied.

"No, not really. Most are too stupid to be able to manage any big operation beyond their own neighborhood. "

"What's the magic?"

"Greed. These are greedy bastards without much loyalty."

"I should bribe them?"

"No, not bribes but bigger shares in the game. Performance merits a bigger cut."

"You think any of my guys would desert me for Legs Diamond?"

"Most of them. Loyalty is a changeable thing. It can be made stronger. You can be tough but not ruthless. Fear is a good motivator, but not good for business. Too much with the gun play in the middle of the streets. A kid accidentally gets killed. Bad for business. You reward them for more distribution. You give out bonuses. Make yourself a good boss, who never cheats his guys."

"Would you desert me Goldy?"

"Never, but I'm not a greedy man. You made me richer than any dream I had. I respect you and this empire you created. You, no one else, did it. But someone will be envious of your success, but fewer will if they think they're getting a fair share."

"I knew when I first met you, I could trust you. It's not about being a member of the tribe. I got lots of Yids working for me. You are just an honest man. There are few in this business. Go find me this social club building."

The steaks were placed in front of the men.

Goldy raised his glass, "L'Chayim."

"Ess," Dutch pointed to the steak.

Rivka and Goldy started looking for real estate. The Rockaways were instantly erased from the list of potential properties. Nothing so close to them was to be considered. There were plenty of decent neighborhoods in New York City for a bootlegger's headquarters.

The essential features were similar to Moishe's drugstore. Close to a main road was required for quick getaways. Hatchway from the basement to the street was vital for the easy movement of the product. An inconspicuous appearance was necessary so as not to alert the neighbors to the nature of the business. An upstairs apartment was good for taking a nice nap in the afternoon.

"You think Williamsburg is a good neighborhood?" Rivka asked as they walked the narrow streets.

"Ideal. Close to Manhattan, just over the bridge. Delancey Street on the other side is nice wide street. Great food here and there. Now we need to find just the right property," Goldy told his sister.

What he didn't tell his sister was that every day Manhattan shined brighter in Dutch's eyes. He was a gangster looking to extend his reach as most gangsters did in those days. Territories' boundaries were an ethereal state.

Legs Diamond was constantly on Dutch's mind. How was he going to push out Legs and takeover his Manhattan territory? Brooklyn was too small for Dutch's ambitions. Problem was that Legs had close connections with Lucky Luciano from the Lower East Side. That Italian gangster had huge ambitions that went beyond the United States. They were never going to be satisfied with one territory. Nor were they ever going to be satisfied with being only bootleggers. No, for Luciano extortion was his first game. Drugs, whores and rackets figured into the big picture. It was a route that Goldy never wanted to travel.

The Jewish fisherman had one good connection to Luciano that Dutch did not have. Jew to Jew, Goldy had met Luciano's partner Meyer Lansky. And Lansky had a close connection to the biggest Jewish gangster Arnold Rothstein. He was the guy that fixed the World Series. At his core was his unquenchable addiction to gambling. That would be Rothstein's downfall.

A headquarters in Manhattan was too edgy a place for Dutch. He wasn't ready to take on the Italians. He needed more time to cultivate people in high places and accumulate more money. Destroying Legs Diamond was the recurring dream. There was still time.

Meanwhile Williamsburg had promise. It was a short drive across the bridge. They drove from Far Rockaway to the narrow streets. People were everywhere. Unlike the Rockaways, the place was crowded with determined bodies. Men and women moved in all directions without watching where they were stepping. Babies cried for milk, being wet or simply for attention as their mothers wheeled the baby carriages. Wooden carriages pulled by horses were a constant sight. More horses than cars dominated the poorly constructed streets.

"It's good I'm wearing my walking shoes," his sister said as she looked around.

They walked to the East River. "Great views." He looked over the horizon as the sun was starting to set.

Then they both spotted it. A two story building made of wood in decent condition was across from them. A new coat of paint wasn't necessary. The gutters were secured. The front steps were brick, solid material. A porch without a covering had good people-watching potential. They saw a car drive behind the house. Must be some kind of alleyway in the rear. The headlights disappeared and a tall man went down some back stairs.

"Let's go look," Goldy said.

Sure enough as they got closer," It's good." Rivka looked at the alleyway.

The streetlights were adequate. They could see the back hatchway where the man disappeared.

"Should we make an offer?" Rivka asked.

"Let's," the brother and sister went to meet the owner.

With relatively little bargaining the price was set. It was well within the price range given to him by Dutch.

"Williamsburg, I don't think I know the place?" Dutch told Goldy.

"It's nice," Goldy said. Dutch had agreed to the purchase without ever seeing the house.

"OK, let's go for a ride."

It was not too far from Dutch's speakeasy. Far enough from Rockaway for Goldy. It was plain and simple. The street was busy with some cars, a few horse-driven carts and lots of children. It was a noisy place and Goldy waited for his reaction.

"It's OK for a start. You know what I like is what Arnold Rothstein has. He's a real dapper man. Got some office in Manhattan, fancy. You don't like fancy?" Dutch's tone accusatory.

"I don't like publicity. I think it's unhealthy. Rothstein got those Tammany Hall politicians in his nice breast pocket. He sneezes and they all rush to get him a silk handkerchief. You, my friend are only one of the many who seek Rothstein's approval. I urge caution. Do what you want. You don't like this building; I'll buy it for myself."

"Alright, you win. Will settle here, at least for the moment. You find out about those Tammany politicians. I need some of them. It's all about money. Right?"

"A schmeer here and a schmeer there," Goldy's hand is in a begging position.

"You got to admit Rothstein is a smart guy. Nu?"

"Oh yeah, very smart, a man who balances numbers all the time. Invested in speakeasies and real estate. I keep suggesting more real estate for you."

"Yeah, you're right. Keep the funds in lots of pots. I got it? You don't like Rothstein?"

"I don't trust him. You got a gang, a bunch of guys loyal to you. Not Rothstein, he moves from one group to another. He's your friend today and tomorrow he's in bed with Legs Diamond your rival. Caution. You know I prefer cautious."

"Who'd think a fisherman could be so smart," Dutch taps Goldy on the side of the head.

"My life depends on being able to quickly sense what's happening. When you are out fishing in the ocean, you learn to feel the sea, the wind and the sky. You trust your gut and your instincts. This business is the same. The skies are ever-changing."

"Well, we all got an invitation to party with The Big Fixer at Lindy's. You know where that is?"

"Broadway and 49th. Do I bring Esty, my wife?"

"No, Rothstein probably has one of his whores there. I don't know your wife too well, but she looks like a nice Jewish girl."

"I'll come alone then."

"I want you to mix with the politicians and the businessmen. I want to know how indebted they are to Rothstein. Is there a place for me? Can I bribe them to do my bidding?"

"OK when?"

"Next week and get a nice suit. You got money. Don't hide it all in the mattress. You got a tailor? I got a real good one. A Jew from Germany, they do the best work," Dutch told him.

"Sure, I'll get a new suit," Goldy thought it a waste of money.

"Buy your wife a mink coat. Spend a little Goldy. Don't be afraid. Prohibition is here for many more years. We're all going to get rich like Rothstein. He has millions; we deserve millions. Right?"

"Sure," Goldy knew Prohibition wasn't going to last. And there were so many hands out demanding their piece. How was anyone, but a few like Rothstein going to get rich?

Chapter 3
1925

It was around dusk. They were exhausted from hauling the night's supply of booze. Two strong helpers designated by Dutch carried the crates of whiskey, scotch and rye from Goldy's boat to the shore. There two trucks parked on the sand were ready to start their distribution to speakeasies across the city.

Just as Zayde opened the car door in front of the house, he felt a hand on his shoulder.

His hand automatically felt for his handgun in his waistband.

"Old man, it's Bo," one of Dutch's main henchman.

"Bo what's going on?" Goldy responded.

"The feds are coming. We got word from one of the guys we pay off."

"They are coming here?" Zayde felt his face turn red and sweat appeared on his forehead.

"They heard about the boats in the Rockaways."

"Did the load from this morning get away safely?" Goldy wanted to protect his investment.

"That's OK. We heard from a guy in the Manhattan office," Bo replied.

"What should we do?" Goldy asked.

"Get the hell out and stay away for a while."

"Now?" Zayde could feel his pulse racing.

"Now, like pack a bag and leave. Goldy, you know Dutch thinks highly of you. Go visit some relative in another state."

It was clear how serious this was to all involved.

"Alright, we're going. What's going to happen to my family?"

"Don't worry Dutch will take care of them. You got to go."

As stealthily as he had driven up, Bo disappeared. The sun was rising above the tops of the fences.

"Let's go pack a bag. I'll go in the back so nobody sees me." Zayde walked to the rear of the house.

Ruby, the German shepherd, was accustomed to Goldy and Zayde's early morning arrivals. But just in case this was a stranger, she stood by the front door. Goldy heard her low growling sound.

He entered, "It's OK Ruby, it's only Daddy." She licked his hand.

Esty heard noises and walked down the steps. "What's going on? You OK?"

"I got to go," he told her.

"What you mean? You got to go. Go where?" her voice was halting.

"I got to disappear for a while," he answered.

"What's going on. Who's after you? Schultz? The police? Who?" her voice was strained as the words tumbled out of her mouth.

"It's the police. They're coming here."

"Where are you going?"

"I don't know but away from you and the house. You keep calm. Things will be OK. I promise."

"If it's the police. Get arrested. Dutch will send some lawyer. You go to jail for a few months. What's the harm," she implored?

"Let them catch me. I'm packing a bag. Zayde is coming with me."

One by one the children filed down the steps.

"Papa," Gladdy screamed.

"It's OK. I'm OK," Goldy answered.

"What's going on," Izzy asked.

"I got to leave for a short time."

"Why?" Silvie asked.

"The police want to ask too many questions," he replied.

"You're a fisherman," Gladdy told her father.

"Yes, yes I am, but it's complicated," he slipped his arms around his youngest.

"Izzy you're the man of the house. If you need anything go, see your Tanta Rivka."

"Papa you can't go," Gladdy hung tightly to her father.

Esty started crying.

"Please, please, Esty it's going to be OK," he tried to un-ravel all the arms holding tightly to him.

He untwisted tiny fingers and ran up the steps to collect a few belongings. Zayde collected his things from his first floor bedroom.

Zayde carried a small valise.

Goldy tried without success to soothe his crying wife. "Esty, it's going to be fine. Izzy you take care of things. My babies," Goldy kissed each of his four daughters.

Zayde went for the car in front of the house.

"No forget that one. Let Izzy take it. Let's go to Rivka's house."

They walked quickly to the back of Rivka's place. Rivka was up making coffee. She heard unfamiliar sounds and grabbed a wooden rolling pin.

As she was about to attack the intruder, "It's me Goldy."

"What the hell are you doing?"

"The cops are after me and Papa. We got to go."

"Go where? Where are you both going?"

"I don't know but out of town. Maybe for some time."

"A week, a month, a year. What's some time?"

"I don't know," Goldy pleaded ignorance.

"What about Esty and the children?"

"Izzy's in charge."

"Papa," she turned to Zayde, "you going with him?"

"Yes and you will help them," her father answered.

"What do you need for me to do? Tell me?"

"First, can I take your car. Second, I want you and Izzy to go out with the charter boat and take people fishing. You know where you can find money?"

"OK, money I know. I'll take out the charter boat. Should we serve booze? Go out to international waters?"

"No, no, just fishing nearby. That is of course if the feds don't confiscate the boats."

"Let me get some money for you," she went to her china chest in the dining room. She reached into a decorative box and pulled out a handful of bills.

Goldy asked his father, "You got some money from the back yard?"

He nodded his head.

Rivka returned with a thick wad of money held together with a money clip.

"I think you should have Moishe move back here for a while. Keep all the doors locked at night. And get yourself a big dog."

She kissed and hugged her brother and then her father. "Be careful." She threw him a set of keys.

As they lifted the bags into the back seat, Zayde asked, "Do you know where we're going?"

"I got a plan."

"Nu? Where? You got it figured out?"

"Jump in," Goldy said.

"Can I drive?"

"Later after we get out of the city. I'm exhausted, you must be tired. We'll drive a few hours and then rest."

They set out on their journey.

They waited listening for sirens and flashing lights. It was quiet. Polly and his cage were placed on the front porch. The children were dressed for school like any other day.

"I'm not going to school. I'm not leaving you alone," Silvie told her mother.

"OK," she told her eldest daughter, "then walk them to school."

Gladdy was crying, "Where's Papa?"

Esty kissed her youngest. "You go with sister to school."

"When is Papa coming home?" Minnie asked.

Hannah, the quietest one asked, "Where is Papa?"

No one wanted to leave the front porch. But their mother pushed them gently down the steps.

"Go, go, go," screeched Polly.

"Let's go," Silvie insisted.

"You're so bossy," Gladdy complained. The four linked arms and walked to the primary school.

Esty and her son sat on the front porch, waiting. And in fifteen minutes Silvie returned. The three sat quietly on the front porch, Polly occasionally screaming, "Where's Papa?"

Ruby sat by Silvie's side, her big snout resting on the girl's shoe.

"Should we go to Tanta Rivka's house," Izzy asked.

"No, no, we don't want to involve her," his mother replied. So they continued their vigil.

"Izzy, go to the dock and see if someone is there? Ride your bicycle," Esty said.

The teenager got off the porch and took his big bike. As he approached the dock where all the boats were moored, he knew they were there. He heard loud noises. The gulls were flying around and annoyed with these strangers. Where was the fish that they expected? So many people and no one throwing fish into the air.

He got off his bike and walked closer to his father's dock. There were some wild bushes where he hid out of sight. Men were yelling and throwing objects from the boat onto the sand or simply throwing cushions and crates into the water.

The cops left the dozen rowboats alone. They were undisturbed. Men in a variety of different types of uniforms were combing through some netting. There was not one whiskey bottle to be found. The deck was washed thoroughly by Zayde each morning when they returned from their sojourns. Not a single glass of alcohol was discovered inside or outside the fishing boat. He spied one guy in a dark uniform taking a couple of his father's fishing rods from the charter boat.

It looked like two men were heading for an unmarked car. Izzy ran for his bike and pedaled through lush grass and backyards to get home before the car arrived.

As he approached he screamed out, "They're coming."

"Go inside," Esty told her daughter.

"No chance, I'm staying," she insisted. Ruby sat up.

The big black car drove up and stopped in front of the house. Two men in suits got out. One was much taller than the other.

Polly started screaming, "Help, help, bad man, bad man."

"Get that bird to shut up," the short one shouted.

Esty got off her chair and ran her fingers slowly against the metal cage. The parrot quieted. Ruby bared her big teeth.

"You control that dog or I'll shoot him," raising a gun towards the dog.

Silvie petted the dog on the head, whispering in her ear.

The tall one approached, "Are you the wife of Goldy Goldfarb?"

Esty stood straight up like a cadet soldier on the practice field. "I am."

"Where's your husband?" he asked.

"I don't know," she calmly answered.

"We know he's been here," he continued his questioning.

"He was but now he's gone."

"Where has he gone?"

"I don't know."

"We can arrest you." The short one stepped menacingly towards Esty. Ruby got up and growled.

Polly started up, "Help, help, bad man."

A neighbor woman stepped onto her porch. "Something wrong Mrs. Goldfarb?"

Esty shook her head.

"We'll take a look inside," the taller one moved towards the front door.

Esty moved in his way. "You got a paper from a judge or a court? I got rights. I'm an American citizen. My husband is not inside. Please get off my porch."

The short one showed his gun. The neighbor woman noticed the gun.

"Esty you want me to call the police," she yelled.

Polly start up again, "Help, help, bad man."

Ruby was growling louder.

"I'll shoot that dog," the short one said.

"You want to push me around?" Esty challenged them.

The taller one placed his arm in front of the short guy. "We're going. Tell your husband we'll be back."

The men walked down the pathway. The short one turned to look back. Esty stared at him. Polly was spreading his feathers in a show of defiance.

"We should get a car here to watch the house. You want to get a court order to inspect the house?" the short one asked.

"At night, not now. If he's around, he won't show in daylight. No point in going through the house. He's not there now. We'll watch it after dark."

When they were gone, Esty walked into the house and collapsed into one of her husband's favorite chairs. She quietly sat there for a few minutes then got up. Her children followed her and the three sat around the dining room table.

"I'll make some tea," Silvie said.

"Wow, Mama that was brave. I was shaking in my boots. You standing in front of the door like that," said Izzy.

They heard a light tapping at a window. Ruby started to bark.

She walked in from the rear, "What's going on?" Rivka asked.

"You should have seen Mama standing up to that cop," Izzy whistled.

"Oh, Esty," the woman gave her sister-in-law a tight hug.

Then Esty's eyes filled with tears. "I was never so frightened for the children, for Ruby, for that crazy parrot."

"Let's have some tea and cake," Silvie suggested as she poured everyone a cup of tea.

Esty placed the small sugar cube in her mouth while the hot tea dissolved it as she drank.

"Maybe a shot of whiskey to go with that tea," Rivka suggested. She poured everyone including the children a tiny amount in their tea cups.

•••

It was a slow journey north. Father and son sharing the driving as they passed the Catskill Mountains towards the North Country. The car was not pretty, but it was dependable. It had never traveled so far. The roads were rougher than New York City streets and there were few cars. A truck here and there with agricultural products passed them by. Carts and horses and an occasional donkey pulled their loads along the route.

"What I can't understand is why he constantly lies," Zayde asked his son regarding Dutch Schultz.

"It's automatic. No thinking involved. It just comes out of his mouth."

"Why lie about his background? His family isn't from Bialystok. They're Germans. It was easy to find out the truth."

"He thought he needed that connection to bring me along. This way we're all in it together like family. It makes sense."

"I'm glad you understand. Such a liar, ligner."

"See he sent Bo to protect us," Goldy counseled his skeptical father.

"No, he sent a henchman to protect his business."

"Was I supposed to hide the boats?"

"You," the father pointed his finger at his son, "you are a keeper of secrets."

"This is our grand adventure."

"I think I know where we are heading."

"I let you guess."

"We're off to see Chief. Right?"

"We are and it's a way further so I'll let you drive."

Goldy pulled over to the side of the road. It was also an opportunity to pee in the wooded area.

"OK, we're off," Zayde happily shouted to the trees and a small congregation of deer.

The hours disappeared as the two men sang union songs celebrating the working man. It was near dusk when they arrived at a gate.

Zayde stopped the car twenty feet from the standing man. Goldy got out of the car and approached the man.

"I'd like to speak to Chief, is he available?"

The man did not respond. He walked around the car. Zayde raised his hand as if to say "How."

"You know who I am?" Goldy asked. He had made this journey several times in the winter months during the last few years. It was a different car.

"You're the Jew bootlegger. I know you. I'll get Chief. You wait here," he ordered.

Goldy returned to the car and the two men waited. And they waited. Every few minutes Goldy checked his pocket watch. After the sun had set, a lone figure appeared. He opened the gate and walked towards the car.

"Goldy, Goldy, it's springtime. What brings you here?"

Goldy got out of the car to meet the hardy voice. They embraced with big bear hugs.

"It's such a lovely time of the year. Papa and I needed to get out of the city. Breathe some nice country air."

"Who are you running from? Dutch? Or the cops?"

"The police," Goldy told the smiling man.

"Well that's good news because the law is incompetent. Now Dutch, he's a dangerous man. What can I do for you?"

"You got it. We need a place to stay for a bit preferably on the Canadian side of the reservation. We need not to be seen."

"Not a problem. Stay a week, a month, a year, for the rest of your lives. You are my guests. We are friends. Friends do favors for friends. Right?"

"That's swell. Can't tell you how much we appreciate your hospitality."

"Get in your car. You follow me. I'll show you a nice hunting cabin you can use."

Goldy drove just feet from Chief's rear bumper. Zayde sat in the back seat keeping his eyes on the car in front of them.

When they arrived, Zayde jumped out to show Chief the big surprise in the trunk.

"For you," he opened it and there were cases of rye and whiskey.

"So thoughtful," Chief opened a case and took out one bottle.

"If you need anything," Goldy offered a wad of American dollars to Chief.

"Oh no, no, the liquor is quite enough. Friends don't need payment." The men hugged again.

Neither man had planned on packing the car with booze. It appeared that Rivka always traveled with a couple of cases of whiskey. There was nothing better for a bribe. A schmeer here and a schmeer there and most problems disappeared.

They settled in their cozy cabin. It had a small fireplace and Goldy found cut firewood in the back. The weather was still nippy in the Canadian wilds.

"You intend for us to stay here how long?" Zayde asked as

they ate trayf venison a gift from their hosts.

"You think God is going to punish us for eating this non-Kosher deer?" Goldy asked his father while enjoying the meal.

"Hashem has more important things on his mind. But are we going to be living here? What's the plan? I know you son, you got a plan."

"This is just temporary. I'll talk to Chief. The less I share with you the better. Who knows maybe the Mounted Police will try and arrest us."

The next morning Chief came by to ask after his guests. He was warmly received by the Americans. In his hand, he held up a bottle of whiskey.

"A little early for me," Goldy told his host.

"Everything OK?"

"It's fabulous, the food, the cabin, no complaints from us. But, I have another favor to ask?"

"What else can I do for you? You guys took this tribe from penniless beggars to real men. You gave us all a respectable life. Ask."

"We need to get to Halifax. Can you help us?"

"You taking a boat somewhere? Across the ocean?"

"Yes, but better you know none of the details. Just in case."

"I can make arrangements to get you to the coast. I can drive you a certain distance then another tribe will take you further east. A third contact will take you both to Halifax. When do you want to go?"

"Well, we should rest up for a few days and then head to the coast."

"Do you have tickets for a specific steamer?"

"Better you know as little as possible. I will share what's necessary.," Goldy told his host. His father was learning the plan at the same moment as Chief.

"Want to go hunting with us?" the Indian asked.

"No thanks but the deer is great." Goldy responded.

"Tonight, we'll all have rabbit. You come to the communal house and join us."

"We will be there," Zayde accepted for both of them.

"I'm going to leave my car with you. I won't need it. You keep it for safekeeping. Drive it if you want," Goldy told Chief.

"I have it parked here on the Canadian side. My own car is nicer than yours. I'll put it in the barn waiting for your return."

"I don't know when I'll return. If I never return its yours."

"Goldy, so much drama," Chief laughingly said.

After several more hugs, Chief left to do whatever Indian chiefs do.

"Where are we going?" Zayde asked.

"We're taking a long boat ride. Be a test of your sea legs," Goldy laughed.

"I'm trusting you with my life."

It was arduous traveling to reach the coast. The Indian reservations where they traveled through were far from the ocean. Chief's car was new and well upholstered not so the next rides. And the roads weren't really roads. It was gravel and dirt and packed snow. Finally, they reached Halifax and the port.

They had berths in third class. Not a nice room, but livable. Zayde kept asking where they were going and Goldy told him to have patience. After several hours on the boat, it became apparent.

"Antwerp," Zayde asked in disbelief, "why Antwerp?"

"A major port city, lots of Jews and the capital of the uncut diamond market. Exactly, what we need."

"Diamonds? I got American dollar bills," he showed his son his wad of money.

"Better than currency, diamonds will take us everywhere."

"I am assuming Antwerp is not our final destination."

"We are going to Bialystok. I'm just not entirely sure how to get there. Someone in Antwerp where there are plenty of Polish Jews can direct us."

"Is the family expecting us?" Zayde was calmer knowing they intended to go back to where it all started.

"It will be like a Purim gift. You know all those little pekls for the poor."

"Who do you know in Antwerp?"

"I have a letter of introduction to a Hasid jeweler in Antwerp from the guy I bought my diamonds from in New York."

"Is that why we have a different set of clothing?"

"You look good in one of those hats. I got tefillin, tallit. We go to the shul near the Central Train Station that's the Jewish section. We get a room. I meet this jeweler. I got a plan." Goldy sat on the mattress on the bottom of the double decker beds.

The steamer across the Atlantic was relatively smooth. The Atlantic Ocean is hard to predict; its behavior beyond the reach of mankind. They had their papers identifying them as Americans. There were no monitors at the port. Someone asked who they were and they responded, "Americans." That was the extent of the government officials at the port asking any questions. It was a porous border.

Antwerp is one of the major cities in Europe. Only Brussels was as world renown. Situated on the Schelde River, 55 miles from the North Sea, it is a world-class port. Not far are the cemeteries and potted fields of death. It was the site of some of the worst trench misery of W.W. I. Located in Flemish country, most people speak that Dutch-derived language although French is also spoken.

Neither Goldy or his father spoke Flemish or French. They had to rely on the international language of the Jews, Yiddish. Luckily for them, it wasn't difficult to find the Central Train district where the Jewish jewelers carried on their trade.

On solid land after a week of travel they made their way to the Jewish Quarter. There in all its majesty was the Sephardic Synagogue.

"Put on the hat and shirt. Make yourself look like a Hasid member," Goldy told his father, as they dressed in an inconspicuous spot.

"How do I look?" he touched his new unkempt beard.

"Let's see if anyone is around to help us," Goldy said.

"They walked around the building until they found a door. It was unlocked so they just let themselves in.

"Shalom," Goldy spoke to the first man he met.

He answered, "Shalom. How can I help you?"

"We don't speak Flemish or French. Do you speak Yiddish?" Goldy asked.

"Of course," the man quickly replied in Yiddish.

So began their conversation in the Jewish mother tongue. "We just arrived from America. We were looking for a boarding house where we could stay for a few days."

"America? Are you diamond merchants?" the surprised man asked. They looked too grubby to be in the diamond trade.

"No, but I am looking to meet Herr Teitelbaum. I understand he is an important diamond merchant?"

"Yes, he is and very well respected. All of Europe knows him."

"Well, we know of him in America."

"He is not a member of this congregation. It's for the Sephardi. Are you Sephardic?"

"No, no, we are Poles, Ashkenazic."

He walked Goldy and his father out another door. It was a rear door across from a cluster of small apartment houses.

"Go there," he directed, "you will certainly find lodging off the main street in one of the narrow streets."

"Do they speak Yiddish?"

"Yes, Antwerp has many Jews and this is the quarter."

Goldy pulled out a piece of paper with an address. He showed it to the man.

"Can you also direct me to Teitelbaum's shop?"

The man stepped into the alleyway. He pointed to a series of shops. Then he took the paper with the name and used it to draw a small map.

"Thank you, you have been a mensch," Goldy offered him several American dollars.

The man pushed away the money, "Not necessary. If you must, make a contribution to the shul."

Goldy counted out one hundred American dollars in twenty–note denominations. "For the shul."

Locating a boardinghouse was easy. There were several small buildings with signs advertising rooms to let. On a quiet, narrow street, they stopped to inquire. The stout woman took their American money.

Goldy asked the landlady in Yiddish, "Are you Belgian?"

"No, Romanian. In the last five years many Jews from Eastern Europe have emigrated to Antwerp. It is a Jewish cosmopolitan center. Shuls for all types," she answered.

"We are off to find Mr. Teitelbaum the jeweler." Goldy showed her the address.

She gave him directions. "Only ten minutes away."

Wearing their Hasidic hats and loose fitting clothes, they went off to find the famous jeweler.

The door was locked when they tried to enter the shop. Goldy waved and the buzzer sounded and the door opened.

"Shalom," Goldy said to the first clerk, "Mr. Teitelbaum?"

An older man appeared with a thick beard and on his big head a purple yarmulke.

"Gentlemen, what can I do for you," he said in Flemish.

Goldy raised his arms, "You speak Yiddish?"

"Who are you?" he responded in the mother language.

"Americans. I am Avraham Goldfarb and this is my father Shlomo Goldfarb," Goldy pointed to his father and then himself.

"Are you communists?" he asked.

"No, no," Zayde answered with surprise.

"Zionists?"

"No, no we are just visitors," Goldy replied.

"But you're running away from somebody?"

"Why do you ask?" Zayde asked.

"Americans don't come to Antwerp unless they are buying and selling diamonds. You don't look like diamond merchants," he responded.

Goldy placed both hats on the counter. "We are in the diamond business. I brought uncut diamonds from a colleague of yours in New York City. He gave me this letter to give to you."

"Come in the back," Teitelbaum instructed and he said to the clerk, "prepare some tea."

They sat on metal chairs in a small back room. On one side was a giant safe and on the other a desk with magnifying equipment for examining and cutting diamonds.

He took the hats and ran his fingers around the brim, "Nicely concealed."

"We want to store some of those diamonds with you for safekeeping," Goldy explained.

"Who are you running from?"

Goldy grinned, "OK, we are bootleggers. What's wrong with having a little whiskey. Prohibition was started by anti-Semitic white women, who wanted to punish immigrants. That's what the nonsense is all about. We get first class, legal whiskey from our Jewish brethren in Canada."

"I understand," the jeweler replied, "where are you going?"

Zayde answered, "Back home to Poland."

"Perhaps we can place them in your safe," pointing to the

solid metal safe, Goldy explained.

"A few diamonds for some European cash?" Zayde asked.

"You would be better off traveling with uncut diamonds than European money. It's not America. Every country has its own currency. If you stay here for a week, I'll buy a diamond from you and give you Belgian money. As you go east my money is worthless."

"What do you suggest?" Goldy asked.

"I'll buy a couple of your diamonds. If you're going to Poland, you should take the train. Do some sightseeing. Go from here to Paris then on to Berlin and stop in Warsaw. Where in Poland are you going?"

"Bialystok is where I am from. Avraham is a real American, born in Jersey City, New Jersey," his father said.

"In Warsaw, someone will direct you how to get where you want to go," the jeweler replied.

"Should we keep the diamonds in the hat?" Zayde asked.

"No that maybe dangerous. Go to a store and buy solid, hard, workman boots and get some work clothes. Go to a millinery store and buy a material to create a heavy strap to wear around your ankles. Then come back tomorrow," he handed Goldy Belgian money.

"We don't speak Flemish or French," Goldy said.

"I'll send you to Yiddishkeit stores where language will not be a problem," he wrote names and addresses on a piece of paper and handed it to Goldy.

"We'll be back tomorrow," Goldy and his father went off to shop.

•••

They returned the next morning carrying the new boots. Teitelbaum's assistant directed them to the back room. He was waiting for them.

"Show me what you found?" the jeweler opened the bags, "good, very good."

"What are you going to do?" Zayde asked.

"Watch. I will remove the diamonds from the hats and sew them into small, hidden spaces in the boots. Then I will attach a strap to the boot, which you will always secure. OK?"

"Masterful," Goldy commented as he and his father observed the jeweler.

"You should take some for payment, for all this work," Zayde suggested with Goldy's head bobbing in approval.

"I have enough payment," the jeweler replied.

The two foreigners sat and observed as the Belgian worked his magic.

"When I finish, you will be my guests for lunch at my house. It's not far," the hospitable man told the Americans. He disappeared periodically to do other things in the front of the store. A clerk came in and offered them tea, which they accepted.

The jeweler was a busy man and they had nothing to do so they sat sipping tea.

Zayde asked his son, "How long have you had this plan? You certainly never mentioned anything to me."

"From the beginning, I knew something would cause us to flee. It was going to be Shultz or the cops. You can't possibly be in our business without something happening," Goldy explained.

"You got a plan to get Esty and the kids out?"

"I never expected them to be in any serious trouble. Rivka knows where to get money. And with money you can always escape."

"Paris and Berlin were in the plans?"

"No, but Warsaw was. That's the gateway to Bialystok. I thought that would be a safe place to hide. Who knows those shtetls but Jews like us?"

"Now we can be tourists, visit the Eifel Tower. Take a boat down the Seine River," Zayde was laughing.

"Teitelbaum will help us find our way. It's a good thing I bought those diamonds in New York."

"How much did you buy?" the father asked his son.

"Lots and just for this occasion. What is better than money. Uncut diamonds are the universal exchange."

The jeweler returned and finalized his project. "Let's essen."

As they walked together to his home, men and women acknowledged the jeweler.

They stopped in front of a modest looking house. "Inside," he told them.

His wife came to greet the visitors speaking Yiddish. "Americans, we don't see many of your kind."

The dining table was set for four. Everything on the table was elegant: the crystal goblets, the fine china, the silk tablecloth. A maid came from the kitchen laden with food.

"Where are you from in America? It's a big place," the jeweler's wife asked.

"We come from a small town called Far Rockaway. It's right on the Atlantic Ocean and you can smell the salty mist from the front porch. The sea gulls visit begging for a handout. My wife Esty has this beautiful and very talkative parrot who we call Polly. Actually, it's a he. Got a big cage where he sits on the porch screaming out warnings to the kids to get out of the street. I got five children, four girls and my boy Izzy," Goldy suddenly felt homesick. It was the first time that he talked about his family in America.

"I imagine you miss them," she said.

Both father and son nodded their heads.

"What kind of work are you in?" the wife asked.

Zayde laughed, "We're bootleggers."

"What did you do before the bootlegging. Before Prohibition in America," the jeweler was curious.

"I was a fisherman," Goldy replied.

The two Belgians looked incredulously at the Americans.

"I own a big fishing boat where I went out with my father and sometimes Izzy. And a day boat, I took people out to fish. I have a dozen row boats. People just rent my boats to go out on the ocean."

"Jewish fishermen?" the jeweler asked.

"Yeah, that was us until we got a bigger and better offer," Goldy told his surprised hosts.

"Now you decided to visit relatives in Poland, my husband told me," a most inquisitive woman.

"Yes, we needed a little break from our exploits," Zayde replied.

"We're now off to Paris, Berlin and Warsaw," Goldy explained.

"Belgium and the Netherlands are nice to visit. The Low

Countries are close to the sea. We bare many scars suffered during the last great war. The trenches filled with filth and rats. You can't believe how those men suffered. I lost a brother in the war not from a German bullet but from the infection that followed. The Belgian countryside is still full of idle trenches. The cemeteries are all over. Probably with American bodies."

"We came to save the day our Yankees," Goldy told them.

"Yes, and you did help to finally win the war. Since then and the nasty Russian Revolution many Jews from the east, Russia and Poland have arrived in Antwerp. Too much is still unsettled in this world. Uncertainty, makes people nervous about their livelihoods and the future for their children. Antwerp has long welcomed displaced people," the jeweler told his guests.

"Our family," the wife pointed to her husband, "we are part of Antwerp's long history of welcoming foreigners. My family is Sephardi. We are Portuguese, part of those crypto Jews who escaped the Inquisition. My husband his family are originally German Jews also escaping the vagaries of being a Jew in Europe."

"Come to America," Goldy quickly added.

Zayde agreed, "In the world there is always going to be people who hate Jews, the killers of Christ. But America is much better. It is the future."

"What about the Zionists. Is that not the future of the Jews?" the jeweler responded.

"That's way into the future. Now, at this moment in history, it is America. We can assist you, sponsor you and your family," Goldy offered a promise.

As they finished desert, a tall, thin young man approached his father, "This is my Yankev. He has train tickets for you. Go to Paris, see the sights. Who knows if you'll ever return."

When lunch was finished, as they were leaving, Goldy spoke to Teitelbaum, "If I don't come back. Send the rest of the diamonds to my wife in America." Goldy slipped a piece of paper with an address into the jeweler's hand.

"My Avraham, you will certainly return."

The train trip to Warsaw was uneventful. Occasionally, the police demanded papers. As Americans, the two men were never harassed. Their American citizenship offered protection from indifferent Frenchmen and bitter Germans. Paris was full of gaiety and busting with artistic creativity. Underneath Berlin's madcap Weimar days was deeply seated resentment towards the English and the French.

Poland was the home of the largest concentration of Jews in Europe. Its major cities hosted Jewish synagogues and celebrations where the people, Catholic Poles and Jews mixed. Even the shtetls permitted some integration between Jews and Poles.

The two adventurers managed to find a train from Warsaw to Bialystok. It was part of a larger system that traveled north to St. Petersburg, Russia. Bialystok was a city caught between feuding major powers. As Poland was always a bargaining chip between waring powers, so was this city. By the end of the nineteenth century, a majority of Bialystok's residents were Jews. The Russian Empire squeezed these Jews into a smaller geographic area.

Hatred of the Empire and its Czarist control contributed to Jews creating anarchist and radical labor movements in Bialystok early at the turn of the twentieth century. Political unrest resulted in retaliation by the Russian authorities with the deadly June 1906 pogrom killing and maiming more than 150 Jews.

The Great War brought German troops to the area where they stayed until after the war. The invading army caused great damage to the city. By 1921, a free Poland was established and was as anti-Semitic as the fallen Russian Empire.

To this city more than four hundred years old came the two Americans seeking a family reunion. Zayde knew where to find his sister and her family. As he walked the streets, reminders of lost family and cruel treatment by its rulers came back to haunt Zayde.

"I remember this place," Zayde pointed out a building to his son.

"Don't keel over and collapse. Your face is white," his son commented.

"Bad memories. I hated this place. We must try and get your aunt to leave."

The older man knocked. A white-haired woman opened the door. She screamed out, "Shlomo, it can't be. My baby brother. Oh my God, Hashem the merciful, has returned him. Shlomo, it's you?"

"Anat my sister. It's me and my boy Avraham."

Tears from everywhere flowed. Anat's pouring out like a waterfall. Zayde's running down his cheeks. Even Goldy was crying from watching the other two. Soon the trio were joined by other family members Goldy knew them only from faded photographs.

Kisses and hugs from many arms and hands pressed against bodies. It was a poorly choreographed ballet.

"You should have contacted us. Called or wrote, something. I have to get food for a nice dinner," she apologetically replied.

"No fuss," Zayde replied.

Her tear-streaked face turned towards her brother, "Why are you here?"

"Can't we visit?" he answered.

"No," she sat down on a nearby chair, "something is horribly wrong."

"No, not at all. We needed a vacation. I wanted to show Avraham where the family comes from."

She looked at her nephew. "What happened? The police are after you."

They were caught.

Avraham looked at his aunt, "Yes. You know we are bootleggers."

"Lots of Jews in America sell booze. Crazy to make liquor illegal. Something more terrible."

"No sister," Zayde sat next to Anat.

"I thought we should take this opportunity of running from the law to visit relatives in Europe," Goldy said.

She clutched her brother's arm, "Nothing worse?"

"No, no, it was Avraham's idea. Let's travel he suggested. Why not? It's been so many years since I left."

"Things have not gotten better," Anat told her brother.

"You must come back with us to America. We can get you

there. Bring the whole family. The worst of America is an in-convenience compared to this life."

"I can't leave. I have three daughters. One stupid son died in the war fighting for the Polish Army that hated him. I lost two to disease. We can't all pack up and leave."

"Why not? What's here? A few bodies in the cemetery," Zayde replied.

"Let's eat and then we can talk. My granddaughter Bluma," she pointed to a sweet-faced, plump girl, "will help me with the meal."

"Do people have work?" Goldy asked.

"Some went back to the textiles after the war damaged most of the buildings."

"Your grandchildren have a future here?" Zayde pressed her.

"We'll talk. I know Tzipi is gone. Nu, you live with Avraham's family? Nice?"

"Yes very nice. We have a fishing business."

"You take those boats and ship booze?" Anat wanted to learn about this bootlegging business.

"Yes, that's exactly how we got into this business with a Jew named Dutch Shultz," Goldy explained.

"Funny name," she said with a smile.

"It's not a real name. It's a gangster name."

The younger women made busy cooking and setting the large dining room table. The two Americans were their esteemed guests. Soon the male adults joined the teenagers and women. It was back to life in another era. It was Shabbos. Goldy and his father retrieved their Hasidic hats.

Old and young they peppered their guests for information about Jewish gangsters. Goldy talked about working for Dutch Shultz, drinking in speakeasies and meeting Arnold Rothstein at Lindy's in Manhattan.

"It's dangerous," Anat said.

"No, we are not the soldiers fighting in the cross hairs of the gang wars. We collect the goodies with our boats. That's our only job. We mingle with others but we keep our distance," Goldy told the hosts sitting in rapture at the stories.

"Is Arnold Rothstein as handsome as he looks in the newspaper photos?" one of the female teenagers asked.

"O, yes," Zayde stretched out the syllables.

"Do they all carry guns?" one of the boys asked.

Zayde retreated to locate his bag and returned to the table.

"See," he showed them his pistol.

"Ah, ah. Put that away," Anat reproached her brother.

"We carry guns," Goldy said with a laugh.

"In America, does everybody have a gun," another inquisitive boy asked.

"No, no," Goldy replied.

"I would like to have a gun," said a male adult, one of Anat's sons-in-law.

"Take mine," Zayde handed it to him, "keep it."

"No more guns," Anat ordered.

"Will you be staying awhile?" Bluma asked.

"If my sister allows, months to vacation here in a small city back in the old country."

"As long as you like," she answered.

•••

The days melted into weeks and then months. The Americans were perfectly happy working alongside the Polish members of the family. They did whatever was asked of them. The food was plentiful and the local produce fresh and cheap. Several young people worked in the industrial mills. The pay was poor, but there were few worthwhile available jobs.

Zayde returned to the old-fashioned religion of his youth. Even with the advent of cars and electricity, their lives revolved around rituals and rules from hundreds of years in the past. They prayed three times a day; the synagogue became the center of their lives.

And the cemetery was there. Zayde found peace when he visited. Goldy had never been to the place of his ancestors. This Jewish cemetery looked like many others. The local Jews kept it in good condition. The gravestones were standing proud and the grass was frequently mowed.

"Good thing I remembered the tallit and tefillin," Goldy told his father.

"We are living in another century. The hurly-burley is gone and that's good, but this is not the modern world. I miss what we left behind. I am overcome when I visit the cemetery or the house where I grew up as a boy. But it's old. Everything about this place is old," his father said.

"I think we got to plan on leaving. It's time to say good-bye. I got a letter from New York. We are forgotten. No police are even visiting the house. It's safe to go home. I even miss that stupid parrot."

"I must talk to my sister about us taking some of the young

people to America. I want her to go with us, but I know she won't. Our parents and grandparents are buried here. She won't leave but the young people. This is a place without a future."

"Go talk to her. I have some arrangements to make," Goldy said to his father.

Sister and brother sat together in the waning sunlight in an apple orchid not far from the center city. It was quiet except for the birds. It was a place of contemplation. Zayde had gone there many times as a boy.

"I like this orchid. I sometimes remember it when I'm just daydreaming," Zayde remarked.

"You are planning on leaving?" his sister wrapped her arms around her brother.

"We must go. Our life in America calls us back."

"I am sorry to see you leave. It was so unexpected that's what made it magical. You appeared off the train like ghosts. Mama always said you looked like her youngest brother. I pictured him when I saw you."

"I want you to come with us. Get on the boat and come to America. Bring them all. I'll sponsor you all. It will not be a problem. You leave here. We all go to Antwerp. I have a new friend, a jeweler. He will see to your comforts while I make arrangements. Leave this place. It's lovely here but it is past. America is the future."

"Don't be ridiculous, I can't leave. You want my three daughters and all their children to leave. Who will take care of the cemetery. I can't go. This is my life. I'm glad you found another."

"Ask your daughters. Maybe one will come. At least let's take your oldest grandchildren. There's Bluma and the two big boys. Let me bring them to America. They will have a future, make a living, start a family as I did. Look at my Avraham."

"He's a gangster."

"He's a rich man and Prohibition will not last. Meanwhile, he invests in stores. While we've been here he's been planning on investing in a hotel near the ocean. Maybe a small apartment house? We have a future."

"I can't make those discussions. Talk to my girls see what they say. Listen to what their husbands say."

"Will you support me?"

"Will the boys be gangsters like you and Avraham?" she laughed.

"As long as Prohibition lasts we can all make money."

"Next time you run away will they return with you?" she was amused at the prospect.

"I will talk to them all."

"Bluma is almost twenty and no marriage prospects. She will enjoy America. She loves to read about all those American gangsters. I don't know about the oldest boys. But unless you own the textile mill you are no more than a slave."

"If there's a next time you will come back with me. Promise?"

"Go talk to my daughters and sons-in-law. I can't talk for them."

"But you recognize the truth. This is the past. I offer the future."

•••

The three oldest packed small bags and with the two Americans took the train to Warsaw. There in the big city, Zayde found a guy, who knew a document forger. The three youngest were given papers to indicate they were Goldy's children. Payment was an uncut diamond.

"If someone questions you," he pointed to Bluma, and the brothers Hirsh and Zev, "indicate you can't speak. I will speak for you. You are my children. Got it?"

No one on the train ride to Antwerp questioned any of them. Goldy presented the American papers, the legitimate two and three forgeries to customs police.

The Central Station was within walking distance of the boarding house and Teitelbaum's shop. Goldy went to see the jeweler while his father took the children to the boarding house.

When he opened the shop door, he was greeted by a bear hug.

"See. I told you not to worry that you would safely return," he spoke in Yiddish.

"I have returned," Goldy turned around and around in a circle.

"Going back to America?"

"On tomorrow's steamer to Halifax."

"My son will get you two tickets."

"Actually, I need five. I picked up three young relatives. We are all going to America in better style than when we originally left."

"I'm sure America has more promise than Bialystok."

72

Goldy pointed to the door as his father and three young adults entered the shop.

Zayde got a warm embrace from the jeweler.

"Let me introduce Bluma and the brothers Hirsh and Zev," Goldy said.

The jeweler shook the hands of the two young men. He didn't touch the young woman.

"We're off to America, the land of the free and the brave."

"You'll all dine with us tonight so we can properly say our good-byes."

"We'll see you again, I'm sure of that. This is not going to be the last time," Goldy said.

"If you're on the run again, we open our arms."

With tickets in hand the five boarded the steamer to Halifax, Canada. This time they traveled in second class accommodations. Three cabins for the four men and one woman. The young people, who had never traveled beyond Bialystok, were mesmerized by everything they witnessed. If their eyeballs could have popped out of their heads, scrambling to take everything in, it wasn't enough. Here were lives spent in ways so foreign to these young travelers that words were insufficient. Oh, so many wonders.

Returning along the same paths as they originally journeyed, Chief was ready for them on arrival at the reservation. Although, he was surprised at the three additions.

"Relatives from the old country," Zayde explained.

"Welcome to America," he responded to the strangers.

They might have been mute because they had no words to

offer.

"They don't speak English," Goldy said the obvious.

Chief stood very close to the new arrivals, "Don't ever lose your original language or culture," he admonished them.

Goldy translated.

"Do you still have the car?" Zayde asked.

"This way," Chief drove them in his car.

"Tomorrow morning we leave," Goldy said.

"Hopefully, we're back in the booze business with your return," he asked.

"If the boats have been seized this is the only route," Goldy explained.

He had no contact with Dutch during the sojourn. He may have been eliminated as a partner with this long absence. In the gangster business several months could be an eternity. Goldy wasn't afraid. He had money socked away in several places. His family would survive. He could have the Irishman on the Bay side build him a new boat. Or he could buy another boat.

The little cabin provided by Chief was no worse than what the three strangers had known in the old country. It decidedly was more cramped than the steamer travel.

They rose before dawn and began the journey home. Driving along familiar roads he found himself thinking of how much he missed these places. Once they seemed like isolated hamlets along bumpy roads. Now it felt like a trip to Jerusalem.

Polly was the first to discover their presence, "Papa home, Papa home."

"Shut up," Izzy said unaware of his father's arrival.

"Papa, Papa, Papa, home," the parrot repeated.

Then Izzy spotted the five, "Papa, Papa," he ran into his father's open arms. Zayde tousled his hair with both hands.

"We're home," Goldy announced.

Then the crowd emerged. Next little Gladdy screamed, "Papa, Papa."

Hannah and Minnie appeared, "Papa, Papa," they both screamed.

"Papa home, Papa home, Don't run in street Gladdy, Papa home," Polly screeched for all the neighbors to hear.

"Goldy," Esty rushed into his arms, "you're home." The tears gushed out. "Goldy, my sweet husband. And Zayde." Ruby sniffed the strangers. They stepped back out of fear. They had never been so close to a big German Shepherd dog. Goldy rubbed the dog's neck and she responded by licking his hand.

Lots of tears and hugs followed.

"Papa, you would be so proud of Mama. When those police came, she was steely eyed. Wouldn't let them enter the house," Izzy reported.

"Your mother is a strong woman. The tears are for the safe times. When there's danger that Russian backbone comes on strong. No one is coming to hurt my family," Goldy kissed his wife.

"Did they seize the boats or worse burn them?" Zayde asked.

"No, they came looking for Papa but Mama stood her ground. Then some lawyer visited sent by Dutch. The police never returned to our front porch. They watched for weeks from their cars. But no one knocked on the front door. I check every day, the boats are fine," Izzy told his grandfather.

Then Gladdy pulled on her father's sleeve, "Who are these people?"

"Your long lost cousins from the old country. We brought them to America to start new lives," Zayde explained to them all.

Esty ran a handkerchief across her nose and looked at the three strangers. "From Bialystok?"

"Yes, these are my sister Anat's grandchildren. The boys are brothers and Bluma is the daughter of another niece. One big, happy family," Zayde explained.

"Get Tanta Rivka," Esty ordered Izzy.

"Where's Silvie?" Goldy asked.

"She's in school. It takes time on that subway," Esty answered.

Zayde looked at his daughter-in-law, "We have room for three more?"

"Of course. We have to rearrange the rooms."

Rivka arrived with Izzy to meet the new relatives. They walked through the neighbor's backyards. No one cared as they waved.

"Goldy, Papa," she embraced them both.

"Meet your Tanta Anat's grandchildren," Zayde told his daughter.

She looked over the three, "Family remembrance. I can see the similarities. No one speaks English? Not a problem. I'll refresh my Yiddish."

She hugged the three and they hugged her back. In Yiddish she spoke to them, welcoming them to America. She gently grabbed the arms of the boys.

"I got space. Miriam has her room, Moishe is living above the store so I can take these two. I like to have some strong arms around the house," she said to Esty and Goldy. She repeated herself in Yiddish for the new relatives.

"Papa, Papa," little Gladdy tugged at his sleeve, "she can share our room. I can sleep on a blanket on the floor."

"Such an angel," her father said, "I've been thinking. Izzy will help and maybe these two. We can take the biggest bedroom where the girls sleep. We put up a wall and Izzy has one side and Silvie the other. She's getting to be a young lady needs some privacy. Minnie and Hannah in one bedroom and Gladdy and Bluma in the other."

"OK that can work. Gladdy is the sweetest kid so she will be very helpful, especially since our new relative doesn't speak English," Esty said.

"I have my school books and I can teach Bluma to read and write English. I got my Dick and Jane books," Gladdy reached over and took Bluma's hand.

"We'll all learn Yiddish and we'll teach our new cousins English. We'll be a bi-lingual house. Isn't that going to be fun?" Esty said.

Everybody got something out of the new arrangements.

Chapter 4
Assassination of Arnold Rothstein

Who was George McManus? How did such an insignificant individual become a footnote in the history of Jewish gangsters during the Roaring Twenties? Men with no particular skills except ruthlessness came to rule. He was but a foot soldier in a constant war. By their very nature, gangsters were not trustworthy. There was no honor among thieves or killers. No warm blood flowed in their veins. There were millions of poor from all religions in New York City. These were immigrants from across Europe, hungry in a way not simply satisfied with money.

Although allegiances were founded, the ties were tenuous. Enemies never became friends. However, friendships were of limited durations. Out of the poverty and persecution of immigrants from the turn of the twentieth century and by immigrants who came fifty years earlier, competing gangs were established.

Jewish gangs were there in the beginning in New York City, Chicago and later Detroit. The holy land of Jewish gangsters was Bugsy Segal's dream, Las Vegas. It ended for Segal with his murder in 1947. It was not lost forever. A Jew named David Berman took over The Flamingo.

The birth of gangsterism in the New World was born of the notion of taking advantage of your immigrant brethren. The extortion game with its uncivilized beatings and violent threats started in the bowels of the Lower East Side in Manhattan. In the New Jerusalem, immigrants needed to be protected. From whom? The politicians and the police were not your servants; no, they were your enemies. The white knights were the early gangsters.

The labor movement was embraced by immigrant Jews. This was a triad, a convergence of three mighty sources, mostly Jewish. Many of the treacherous workplaces were owned by Jews. These German Jews, who called their fellow Russian and Polish Jews kikes, arrived decades before. The labor organizers, who were Socialists and Communists fought on the streets with police for the rights of workers. Into this mix were the labor racketeers another category of Jews. It was bootlegging and racketeering that were the two major sources of income for Jewish gangsters. They shared these occupations with a mix of other immigrants from Ireland, Italy and non-Jewish Slavs.

Within the sub-category of gangster included a special occupation called hitman. They came in a variety of shapes and sizes, largely male and immigrant. Every gang had its rivals and among the soldiers there was a need for these specialists. Without empathy or sympathy, murder was not even considered a crime. They were defensemen looking out for the best interests of their bosses.

Into this hierarchical order was hitman George "Hump" McManus. A man without conscience, he was paid well for his acts of savagery. He walked into the Park Central Hotel on Seventh near 55th Street. Nonchalantly, as one can be he swaggered over to his target. He took a gun from his waistband and fired several shots directly at Mr. Big. Rushed to Stuyvesant Polyclinic Hospital, he fought death for two days. Then it took him to meet his ancestors.

Arnold Rothstein, King of the Gangster Jews, had one insidious fault. He loved to gamble. Did he have restless gypsy blood? Why was he willing to flout all conventions for that next great winning poker hand? Nothing was too small that it couldn't be more enjoyable as a bet. Any bet would do. Unfortunately, he bet on his life and the result was his burial in Ridgewood's Union Field Cemetery.

How did it happen that a punk like McManus became a footnote in history? He was able to get real close to Rothstein although the bullets took a toll. He didn't die immediately. Lying in a pool of his own blood, "The Big Bankroll," another nickname of Rothstein's, was carried to a car. The mentor of Lucky Luciano, Meyer Lansky, Frank Costello and Dutch Schultz was supposedly murdered because of a bad gambling debt.

Rothstein earned so many flattering monikers because he took a small scale racket enforced by hustling and intimidation into a multimillion dollar business. The gangsters before Rothstein were half-literate immigrants preying on their fellow countrymen. He was the son of wealthy Manhattanites learning at an early age about business from his successful father. He would become far richer than his father ever dreamed. So rich was Arnold that in 1928, he was worth ten million dollars.

In 1919, he earned the nickname "The Fixer." It was the most scandalous sports event of the twentieth century. One man was able to bribe successful baseball players to throw a game. Not any game, but the World Series. He worshipped the publicity of such a slick trick. The world came to know his face on page one in every newspaper in America and across the world.

It was so easy. It fed on ordinary people's thrill of gambling on a major sporting event. It elevated them from mere listeners on a radio to active participants. For poorly paid sports heroes, it was a matter of greed. Rothstein banked on satisfying people's simple cravings – greed and excitement.

The advent of Prohibition was an invitation for smart gangsters like Rothstein to profit from other people's sins. By 1925, he was the biggest bootlegger in America. His wealth bought him houses and mistresses.

But it was gambling that consumed him. The obsession clouded his finely attuned business senses. It may have directly led to his death at age 46. The question never was who was Rothstein's killer, but who paid him to do the deed?

Goldy heard the news from a phone call from Schultz's lieutenant Abe Landau. The family was eating dinner before he made his usual run with his father and two cousins. If the load was particularly large, Izzy came along. Instructions usually came by phone call an hour before they were scheduled to leave Far Rockaway waters.

Goldy heard the ringing and answered," Yeah."

"Rothstein got shot in Manhattan," Landau reported.

"Is he alive?" Goldy asked.

"Just barely. He's in the hospital," Landau replied.

"Does Dutch want us to meet?"

"No, we got this under control. Dutch just wanted you to know before you heard it on the radio or read it in tomorrow's papers."

"Who shot him?"

"Don't know. The cops aren't saying anything."

"OK, keep me updated. Especially if he dies." He put down the receiver and walked back to the dining room.

Zayde saw Goldy's concerned face, "Nu?"

"Someone shot Rothstein."

"Is he dead?" Izzy asked.

"No, but he's in the hospital," his father said.

"Should we go to visit him?" Esty asked.

"No, we're not family or even friends," Goldy replied.

They resumed eating, but the adults were unusually quiet. The children could tell from worried-looking faces that this news was not going to be good.

"Should I clean off the table?" Minnie asked.

"No, I'll take care of things, baby," Esty kissed her daughter. As a child at age five, she cheated death from meningitis. She was a little slower than other children her age, but she was alive. She was mother's little helper.

When only the three adults were in the room, Esty asked, "This is bad?"

"I don't know. Killing Mr. Big will have repercussions, but whether it starts a gang war," Goldy allowed himself a moment of reflection. "I got you all into this life."

Esty wrapped her arms around her husband, "Don't go out tonight. Not tonight, not for a week. Maybe never. Not until you know what's going to happen. It can't be business as usual."

"I agree with Esty. It could be dangerous. We don't want to get caught up in some retaliation by Rothstein's lieutenants. Let Dutch work something out with Rothstein's men. I don't want to be out in international waters and get caught up in an unholy war," Zayde advised.

"Please let's try and be safe," Esty emphasized again.

"We got food and gasoline for the car. Money is not a problem. Let's play it safe," Zayde recommended.

"Yeah, yeah. You're both right. I certainly don't want any harm to come to you," pointing to his father, "or the boys out on the boat."

"You wouldn't want to be responsible for getting those two boys out of their homeland only to be shot by gangsters on the open sea," Zayde cautiously added.

"I get it. Keep everyone safe. Maybe get out the rifles from the basement," Goldy was considering how best to protect his family.

"I'll stay up tonight," Zayde offered, "keep watch."

"Tomorrow, I'll visit Bluma at the hotel," Goldy told them.

"She has really blossomed," Esty smiled as she thought about the twenty-year old who came to live with them. "Poor thing, her mother kept telling her she was ugly and no one would marry her."

"A nice haircut, some pretty clothes, opportunity to use her brains," Goldy recounted her virtues.

"If anyone, she needed to get away from the old country with its suffocating atmosphere. You don't have to be married with a brood of children as a measure of success. You got her involved with that dilapidated hotel you bought. Two boys helped to fix it up. She read a few magazines and got that place shining. It has so many paying visitors because of her. Am I right?" Esty asked.

"Somewhere in the family genes there's an innkeeper's genes. She got that place beaming, not a trace of dust. Lovely and reasonable new carpeting and furniture. She bargained for it all. A real entrepreneur that Bluma," Zayde smiled.

"A toast to Bluma and hope for a speedy recovery for Arnold," Esty told the men as the crystal clanked.

Goldy and Gladdy went to visit Bluma at the hotel. The ten-year old sat in the back seat.

"Onward James," she instructed her father.

"Yes Miss Gladys where are we going?" her father said.

"Take me to The Rockaway Arms," the child replied.

"Are you planning on staying. Do you have any luggage?"

"Oh Papa, can I really stay in the hotel. I know Bluma has a room there. Can I stay with her? Please Papa?"

"We have to ask the hotel manager if she's willing."

"I bet she says yes."

"We'll see."

"I brought her a book I just finished. I bet she'll like it."

"Your mother reminds me to tell you to stop with the betting."

"Oh Papa, it's only an expression."

It was a short ride to the oceanfront hotel. When Goldy purchased it he never dreamed it would become such an elegant tourist place. It was hard to believe that young Bluma, who never bought a dress in a store or ever stayed in a hotel, would have these natural talents.

Her first teacher was her original roommate little Gladdy. The child taught her to read and write from her own schoolbooks. In exchange, Bluma taught her Yiddish. Bluma's mother said the girl had a gift for numbers so Gladdy learned mathematics from her foreign cousin. Gladdy was precocious and Bluma had a child's enchantment with new things, ideas, challenges.

They were familiar guests so the doorman welcomed them, "Hello Mr. Goldfarb and Miss Gladys."

They walked to the front desk holding hands. His youngest was always going to be his favorite.

"Is the manager available?" Goldy asked.

"I bet she is Mr. Goldfarb. I'll call," the lady at the front desk said.

Gladdy tightly squeezed her father's fingers with that I told you so look.

Bluma came out to personally greet them. She was dressed for the Roaring Twenties with her flapper dress and high heel shoes. There was even a colorful scarf around her neck with a string of white pearls to accentuate the dress.

"Hello everyone," she bent down to kiss Gladdy on the cheek.

"I got a book for you. It's Tom Sawyer by Mark Twain. I bet you'll like it."

"I bet I will. Let's go into my office," she led the way to her large office off the main lobby.

Gladdy spoke up, "Can I stay with you at the hotel? Like a sleepover, here. Can I?"

"Of course, if your mother says it's OK. Yes, I would like that. You can have breakfast in bed. My bathroom has a great big tub."

"No, I don't want a bath," the child said.

"You'll like it. I promise. I have lots of things that smell wonderful."

"If you can willingly get her to take a bath, her mother would be thrilled. This can be a regular arrangement," Goldy added with a laugh.

"I don't know about the bath thing."

"How would you like to help make desserts in the kitchen?"

"Oh yes," Gladdy immediately replied.

"Good, I'll have one of the cooks take you downstairs. It will be lots of fun and you get to eat the cake first." Bluma called someone on the house phone. All the rooms had house phones. Bluma loved the modern.

Gladdy went happily with one of the cooks.

"I heard on the radio that Arnold Rothstein was shot. Is he dead?"

"I don't think so. No reports on his death. He's in the hospital in Manhattan."

"Are you going to see him?" Bluma asked.

"No, we're not that close. I'm only a minor figure in Dutch's operation," Goldy answered.

"Is Dutch going to visit Rothstein in the hospital?"

"Probably. I would if I was Dutch. If he dies, there's a huge empire at stake. Lansky, Luciano and Costello are sending flowers. They are meeting in some speakeasy planning on how to divide up the many pieces. If Dutch wants to continue or expand his bootlegging, I would be at the hospital. If he lives you want to be in the friends' column."

Bluma had no education, but she was a smart girl. Goldy saw her promise. It was much more than being good with numbers. She saw the big picture. Young, but had the right instincts.

"I got my high school diploma. Really it was little Gladdy who was my tutor. I want to go to college like Silvie."

"You want to be a doctor?"

"No, I like numbers, an accountant. I now prepare your taxes. Hopefully, the lies are realistic enough that the tax man doesn't come after you. Those G-men are barking at every bootlegger's door."

"That's wonderful. You're doing a great job for me."

"I am if I can keep you out of jail for tax evasion. Somebody in the government is chasing good publicity. You and every bootlegger is under some surveillance. This hotel is a great place to shield your money. It's nice that your setup the cousins from Poland in the service station and car repair business. That's another place to hide the money. Are you invested in the stock market? People are always trying to get me to invest."

"The only safe place for money is cash on hand. I don't believe in banks and certainly not the stock market. You might as well be gambling at one of Rothstein's games. Keep the money in the mattress. Or you invest in some real estate. I can help you find a building."

"You actually don't trust the banks or the stock market?"

"Absolutely, unreliable. You make me have a bank account for the businesses, but not for me personally. I like the idea of you going to school for accounting."

"I have many responsibilities here so I'm thinking of night school. At one of the city colleges."

"I'll pay for any expenses."

"No, you won't. You have given me the chance of a lifetime. I was nothing. My mother said I was nothing. The best she thought was marriage to some widower with a bunch of children. Now look at me. It's you and Esty and little Gladdy, you all gave me a life."

"You are smart. It's unfortunate that your parents didn't see it. What can you expect living in such a backwards place? I tell everyone come to America. I'll be your sponsor. I'm waiting for a letter from your aunts and uncles."

"They can't see the future, buried in the past. I look in the mirror. 'I say, Bluma what a life you have created for yourself' that's what I tell myself every morning. I'm going to become a citizen and change my name to Billie Goldfarb. No one can pronounce Bluma. I owe it all to your family. That was the old me. This is the new me."

"You send Gladdy home whenever she becomes a pest," Goldy rose and hugged Bluma. "From now on its Billie. I'll tell Esty, Zayde and the kids. You got a new name to go with a new life."

•••

They heard it on the radio. Arnold Rothstein was dead. The gambler who fixed the World Series was dead from gunshot wounds. It took two days, but he was gone. The Big Man was no more and just 46 years old. He left a wide-ranging empire the announcer said.

"Rothstein's dead," Bo Weinberg reported to Goldy on the phone.

"Should I call Dutch?"

"No, if he wants you, he'll call you."

"Is it appropriate for me and my family to go to the funeral?"

"I'll ask Dutch and get back to you," the call was finished.

"He's dead?" Esty asked.

Goldy nodded his head in the affirmative. Esty, Zayde and Goldy sat at the dining room table. The faces were glum. It was the uncertainty. Only Goldy had met Rothstein regularly. Zayde was excluded from the bigwig conversations. Goldy was a minor player usually sitting in an inconspicuous spot in the room. Esty had attended a few parties. Once they all ate in Lindy's restaurant.

"What next?" Zayde asked.

"Only God knows," Goldy told them.

The phone call broke their heavy breathing and sighing.

It was Bo, "You can go to the cemetery and bring the wife and your father."

After the call, Goldy returned to the dining room, "Esty, find a black dress to wear. You got a black suit Papa? We're all going to the cemetery to pay our respects."

•••

Jews bury their dead quickly so the funeral was the next day. A swarm of reporters from newspapers from all over the world were cramming to take photographs of the mourners. Close by the assembled were a bunch of G-men also with cameras. It was part circus and only a small measure of a funeral.

The three addressed the widow with their condolences. Then they retreated into the massive crowd. Goldy thought he saw one of the mistresses in the shadows. The famous bad boys were all there. Lansky wasn't wearing a dark suit, but Lucky Luciano was appropriately dressed. Frank Costello hung around in the Italian corner. Dutch was dressed for the occasion except for the bright flower in his lapel.

The service was short. The rabbi seemed to know Arnold Rothstein or at least his father. He was remembered for his philanthropy. The manner of his death was not even whispered. Everyone knew. Only his wife seemed completely surprised. The end for bootleggers and narcotics peddlers was often violent. Rothstein had been at the game for a decade. In crime annals that was probably the equivalent of a lifetime. Just as Prohibition was a business of the moment, all criminal activities had a beginning and an end.

As Goldy and duo were leaving the cemetery, he felt a hand on his shoulder. He turned to see Dutch.

"I got a favor to ask."

Goldy walked with Dutch to a quieter area surrounded by the dead.

"How can I help?"

"Goldy, you're an honest man. Probably the only one in my crew who isn't terribly greedy and shows some respect."

Goldy had heard this before, "Happy to be of assistance."

"I want you to snoop around. Find out what you can about Rothstein's death. Who shot him? This McManus the police want. Who is he? Keep it quiet. I want you to share this information only with me. OK?"

"Sure. I got some cop associates. I can check it out."

"Start with the hotel where he was shot. Supposedly, the hotel doctor was one of the first to see him. Also the hotel has some house detective. He might know something. I'll get you some money for the schemer here and a schemer there. Money in the pocket opens lips."

"I can afford some bribes. I'll let you know what I find."

"Remember not a word."

They separated. Dutch went to his chauffeured-driven car and Goldy met his companions in front of the family sedan.

"Dare I guess what he wants?" Esty asked.

"He wants me to snoop around and find out about Rothstein's murder."

"Why you?" Zayde asked.

"He always says I am one of the only honest men he knows."

"Not sure this compliment is going to be a good thing," Esty loudly sighed.

Goldy immediately got to his task. Rothstein was shot in Room 349 at the Park Central Hotel on Seventh Avenue and 55th Street. The hotel lobby was quiet. No one was asking for assistance from the front desk clerk.

Goldy stepped to the front of the desk. The clerk smiled at

Goldy, who returned the friendly gesture, sliding a folded twenty-dollar bill in front of him.

"The night Arnold Rothstein was shot; he was attended by a hotel doctor. Is that guy here today?" Goldy asked.

The man nodded his head slipping the twenty into his pocket.

"Where can I find him?"

"Dr. Kenneth Hoffman. He's your guy. Keep walking towards the kitchen. You'll see his office."

"Thanks," Goldy slid another twenty towards the clerk, "you never saw me."

"Never," putting the additional twenty in his pocket.

Goldy walked down a crowded corridor with people in crisp white uniforms moving up and down. Some carried trays of food and others empty dishes. He kept walking. There he found a white door with a metal name plate, "Dr. Kenneth Hoffman."

Tapping on the door, Goldy waited for a few seconds and then entered.

"Are you sick?" the doctor asked.

Goldy sat across from the doctor away from the examining table. "No."

"So how can I help you?"

Goldy slipped a hundred-dollar bill onto the doctor's desk. "I'm looking for information."

"You're not a cop?"

"No, I'm just a private citizen looking for answers. Great admirer of Arnold Rothstein."

"What kind of questions?"

"I read the papers, but what happened that night? From your vantage point. You being the first doctor to see poor Arnold."

The doctor pocketed the hundred-dollar bill. "He was shot."

"I know that. What can you tell me that I can't read in the papers?"

"Stand up," the doctor ordered.

Goldy was afraid he was going to be ushered out of the room. It was going to take more than a hundred dollars.

The doctor stood up, "Come closer to me."

Goldy obeyed.

Then the doctor put his arm around Goldy's waist.

"See," the doctor said, "it seems like the guy who shot Mr. Rothstein had his arm around his waist. So I got one arm there and one arm is up probably with a gun in that other hand. See?"

Goldy nodded, "You think it was maybe an accident or two guys fooling around?"

"No, Mr. Rothstein wasn't laughing it off as a joke gone bad. No, the guy was threatening him with a gun. It went off sideways hitting Mr. Rothstein in the intestines and bladder. He wasn't shot either directly in the front or in the back, but this convoluted angle."

"Did he say anything about who the killer might be?"

"No. No, not to me. But you should talk to Joe Fallon. I think he was a cop. He's the hotel's house detective. He actually found Mr. Rothstein on the third floor walking in the hallway. Blood was dripping out. Really not too much blood with that kind of injury."

"Where can I find Mr. Fallon?"

"He's got a real nice office upstairs on the second floor."

Goldy put a second hundred-dollar bill on the doctor's desk, "You never saw me."

There was a staircase, which Goldy followed to the second floor. The door opened and women in neat, white uniforms were rolling big carts filled with clean sheets and towels. There were also little bottles filled with some kind of booze.

No one stopped him as he studied the doors. In the corner was a door with a metal nameplate, Joseph Fallon. Goldy knocked, waited a few seconds and walked in.

"Who are you?"

"Just a guy, who was a big fan of Arnold Rothstein."

"You're not a cop? You don't look like a menacing gangster. Are you?"

"Not me, just a regular guy."

"You're a reporter looking for a scoop."

"Well sorta of," Goldy answered. He liked the idea.

"What do you want to know?"

"Who came after him. Who wanted him dead?"

"Plenty of people wanted him dead like that George Mc-Manus, who was owed big money. You can't welch on a poker game. That's what this is all about. Rothstein, Mr. Fixer, was supposedly cheated at a poker game set-up by McManus. Over three days Rothstein lost $350,000 to McManus and refused to pay. You don't do that and get away it. No way. Despite the nice clothes and the fancy girls, Rothstein was a gangster."

"Is it possible that McManus went up to see Rothstein and

threatened him. Had no intention of killing him and things got out of hand," Goldy suggested.

"It's possible. Why do you say that? What do you know?"

"Think I read that Mr. Rothstein was shot in the intestines and bladder. Those are organs of the body found on the sides like you have two kidneys on both sides. Not like a heart or a brain. Funny places to be shot."

"I don't know anything about that. The room wasn't torn apart like if there was a big struggle. No furniture broken. The door wasn't jimmied. Guy just walked in," Fallon added.

"Couldn't it still be a surprise. So many people have keys to these rooms. Anyone could have quietly opened the door."

"My guess is he knew the guy and let him in. It could be the intention wasn't to kill him. But McManus is the key. He wanted his money. That's my opinion," Fallon finished.

"Thanks for everything," Goldy got up and was heading out the door without offering a bribe. Fallon was the kind of guy who lived off of people's indiscretions. Married men were caught with prostitutes. Sweet-looking ladies left syringes behind. Men playing with men got caught in the shower.

"Don't forget to make sure you spell my name correctly in the papers," he yelled out.

Goldy found a back route out of the hotel. In the alleyway, he saw a young colored boy helping with the garbage. The boy was struggling with the heavy load so Goldy lent a hand.

"Tell me, were you here when the shooting took place couple of days ago?"

"I was here. I'm always here," he said.

"Did you hear anything?" Goldy slipped a folded ten-dollar

bill into the boy's hand.

He unfolded it and lovingly stared at the money, "Yes sir."

"Tell me, there's more where that came from." Goldy waved another bill in front of the boy's eyes.

"I tell you sir. I was standing over there," he pointed to the opening of the alleyway.

Goldy moved in the direction of the pointed finger, "Here?"

"Yes sir."

"Then what?"

"I hear glass breaking. I look up and something's thrown out the window. The glass all broken and in middle I see a broken pistol. Like two pieces in the glass. I pick up one bullet," he showed it to Goldy.

"Wow, what a find. One you got. Do you know how to count?"

"Yes sir," he answered holding dearly to that bullet.

"How many bullets were there on the ground with all that glass?"

"I got one and the police picked up the gun in two pieces and there were four bullets."

"That's mighty smart. Can I hold the bullet?" He gave the second ten-dollar bill to the boy.

"Yes sir," begrudgingly, he gently placed the bullet into Goldy's palm.

Goldy stared at it, rolled it in his palm, "That's a .38 caliber bullet. Probably from a Colt."

He grabbed it out of Goldy's hand, "It's mine."

"Yes it is. Thank you for letting me see it and hold it."

"OK," placing the bullet back in his pocket.

"Tell me my friend," Goldy squatted down to his knees to be even with the boy.

"Yes sir."

"Do you know the housekeeping staff? Like the ladies who change the sheets and clean the rooms."

"Yes sir."

"Can you show me where I can find the lady who cleaned the room where Mr. Rothstein was shot? It was Room 349."

"Yes sir, follow me to the cleaning ladies."

Goldy followed him to the laundry room. It was a huge, sweaty place filled with young women in white uniforms pouring hot water into vast tubs. The sheets were pulled through levers. That squeezed out the water.

"Those women," he pointed to an older pair, "they work third floor."

Goldy handed him a third ten-dollar bill.

Goldy was ignored by the female workers. Their eyes were focused on the job of cleaning small mountains of white sheets and pillow cases. He heard Polish.

He walked towards the older pair. In Polish, he asked, "Anyone know who cleaned room 349 after the shooting?"

The taller Polish woman looked at him, "Who are you?"

"An interested party," Goldy answered, waving a twenty-dollar bill.

"Not police?" the shorter one asked.

"No, just a concerned citizen," he answered.

She stared a full minute, "What do you want to know?"

"Was the room messed up, glass thrown around, broken furniture. Lots of blood."

"No, no, no, and no. The room was neat. Little blood. Glasses on the table."

"How many glasses? You remember?"

"Three glasses. I was in room with police. They had a funny-looking brush. As if painting the glasses."

"They were fingerprinting the glasses. Did the cops take the glasses?"

"No, they left them behind."

"You have been very helpful." He gave each of the two Polish ladies a twenty-dollar bill. He handed out five-dollar bills to the others. They were all crying out "Thank you" as Goldy left.

Goldy's next stop was Stuyvesant Polyclinic Hospital where Rothstein died. It was not the closest hospital, but that's where he was taken by ambulance. Located on Second Avenue in the East Village, it was more than a mile away from the shooting. Dr. Kellogg was already a minor celebrity having been photographed in all the New York City newspapers. He was labeled the guy who tried to save Mr. Big, the notorious gangster. Rothstein was never the guy who actually got his hands dirty. He had plenty of associates who took care of the murdering and thieving.

Goldy asked at the front desk of the hospital, "Do you know where I can find Dr. Kellogg?"

"You and everyone else," she bitterly remarked.

Goldy took one of his folded bills and placed it in front of her, "Does this help?"

"Another newspaper guy looking for the big story?"

"Just a concerned citizen looking for justice," Goldy replied.

She quietly stuffed the bill in the sleeve of her blouse, "Ambulance Entrance."

He followed the outline of her pointing finger. Then he saw the sign painted on the hospital wall, "Ambulance."

Goldy waited for Dr. Kellogg to finish his conversation with other doctors. They were swarming around the new celebrity. Goldy had enormous patience as he lingered in the shadows of the busy area. Eventually, the men in white dispersed. Duty was calling many of them. Dr. Kellogg was suddenly alone. With no one to listen to his exploits, he wandered into an office with his name hand-painted on the glass door. Goldy stayed a few more minutes and then knocked on the marked door. He didn't wait to be invited inside.

"Hi, Dr. Kellogg, I presume," Goldy was smiling.

"Who are you?"

"Just a concerned citizen wondering about the shooting of poor Mr. Rothstein. Such a shame."

"Another newspaper flake?"

"No sir, just an interested citizen."

"You don't look like a gangster?"

"I'm not," Goldy never considered himself to be a gangster. Bootlegging, while illegal wasn't really a crime.

"What do you want?"

"I was curious about poor Mr. Rothstein's wounds. As a physician who studied his wounds. Do you think he was shot accidentally?"

"How would I know?"

"The wounds, not as a result of a gun being fired directly into his chest or in his back?" Goldy matter-of-factly asked.

"Rothstein could have moved slightly, the bullet meant for his heart."

"It was only one shot?"

"Only one. I couldn't get it out. So Rothstein actually died from an infection."

"Of course, he never said who shot him. No indication of the identity of the shooter?"

"Who the hell are you?"

"Actually, Dr. Kellogg I'm from the insurance company. Mr. Rothstein held many life insurance policies."

"So what does it matter?"

"Accident looks nicer for our records."

"In my professional opinion, whoever shot him meant to kill him. Put that in your records."

"Thanks so much for your trouble," Goldy stood up to walk out.

"Which insurance company is this?"

Goldy ignored the doctor's question. He left the hospital to drive north. In the local newspaper a name of a police detective was given. He was on his way to try and locate the man. The G-men were threatening because they were not on the take. The local police were easily bribed. The local politicians in the Tammany Hall machine were all accepting bribes to keep the speakeasies open and thriving. Law and order had fallen away in an era of loose booze and open hands.

Goldy walked into the police station. No one blinked an eye. He stood in front of the desk sergeant's desk.

"I'm looking for Detective Patrick Flood," Goldy asked.

"Across the street at Jack's," he answered without looking

too closely at Goldy.

Jack's was a favorite speakeasy in the mid-Manhattan area. It was frequented by many in Rothstein's circle being close to The Fixer's informal headquarters at Lindy's. It was typical of its kind, dark and smelling of beer and whiskey.

Goldy refocused his eyes as he entered the darkened place with only a few streaks of sunlight penetrating the dirty windows.

He approached the bartender, "Detective Flood?"

He pointed a finger at a solitary figure sitting in a booth.

Goldy stopped in front of the sitting man, "Detective Flood can I join you?" He didn't wait for any approval to sit. He signaled to the man at the bar to bring some whiskey.

"Who the hell are you?"

"Just someone who wants to commiserate with you over The Uptown Man's untimely death."

The bar man brought a second glass.

"Leave the bottle," Goldy requested and handed the man a twenty-dollar bill.

Detective Flood asked, "Who are you?"

"Just another guy paying tribute to a great man, Mr. Rothstein," he lifted his glass and took a small sip while Flood quickly finished the contents of the glass. Goldy poured him some more.

"You're not a cop. You some kind of newspaper man?"

"No, I'm in insurance. Checking on the cause of death for Mr. Rothstein's policies. We like to have as much information as possible when any person dies," Goldy thought that lie was effective.

"Poor bastard, Rothstein, got it in the intestines and bladder. Crummy death."

"Can you tell me what happened?" Goldy refilled Flood's glass.

"Mr. Big was sitting in his usual spot at Lindy's. Like a king holding court. The men, the dames, the booze. He was like invincible. Then whack," he slammed his hands together. Goldy lifted from his seat.

"So he was eating and drinking with friends."

"Bus boy comes to the table and tells Rothstein he has a phone call. He gets up, presumably listened to the caller. Quickly leaves."

"Do you know who called him?"

"Never said. No one ever said who the caller was," Flood continued drinking.

"He leaves for the Park Central Hotel."

"Yeah, Room 349."

"He's alone?" Goldy asked.

"He goes there by himself and we're not certain who was in that room," Flood said.

"Someone in that room shot him. Right?"

"Yes, but we're not certain exactly who that was. We traced the call to a phone box near Rothstein's office on West 57th Street. We found three glasses of whiskey in the hotel room so we can assume there were three people in that room. We got this new stuff. Dust for fingerprints. One person in that room was George McManus. We know that."

"How can you be so sure?"

"His fingerprints and in a rush he left behind his overcoat."

"How do you know it's McManus' coat?"

"Because it had initials GM on the lapel."

"You arrested him?"

"Yeah, but we can't hold him; we haven't enough evidence," Flood was getting tired. His eyelids kept closing.

"Rothstein supposedly owed McManus a lot of money from a poker game months before. Motive. Maybe he wanted to scare him and not kill him," asked Goldy.

"No, he would have wanted him dead as a lesson to anyone else who tried to welch on a game. Mr. Rothstein, himself, told me, 'I'm not going to give them a damned cent and that goes for the gorillas and gamblers. I can be found any night at Lindy's if they are looking for me.' That's what he said. Others heard the same story."

"So McManus did it as a lesson. You got to pay your gambling debts," Goldy said.

"Rothstein thought that poker game with McManus was rigged."

"Isn't that ironic that a gambler who fixed the World Series would accuse others of cheating," Goldy laughed.

"Ain't life a bitch."

"Were you questioning him at the hospital?"

"Yeah, but he was mum on the name of his killer. He knew him for sure. What does he tell me? 'You know me better than that Paddy,' that was his final words."

"So McManus shot him."

"You know how McManus got his nickname, "The Hump?"

"Can't tell from the picture in the papers, but does he look like the guy in the silent movie, Lon Chaney?"

"Sorta. He's this big guy, broad-shouldered, who walks in a hunched-up position as if he's that hunchback in the movie."

"You got the killer but not enough evidence," Goldy added.

"I'm not so certain."

"Well, who else is a suspect in your mind?"

"I know that Rothstein was threatened about this gambling debt. At least twice before shots were fired in the street. But I'm not convinced it was McManus who shot Rothstein."

"Who else?"

"Dutch Schultz. Nothing to do with the gambling debt. Schultz had it in for Rothstein since his associate Legs Diamond shot and killed Joey Noe. They were very tight. Schultz's killing Rothstein was opportunistic. People all talking about the gambling debt. A chance to kill Mr. Big and make it look like someone else."

"But McManus was there in the room."

"McManus is a low-life gambler. He could have arranged the meeting to erase some gambling debt he had with Schultz or just for the money. We lost a real gentleman," Flood put his head on the table and seemed to fall asleep.

Goldy passed a folded hundred-dollar bill to the barman, "I was never here."

He nodded his head and continued to wipe the glasses with a dirty rag.

Goldy heard enough. Off he went for home to mull over the evidence. Everything had to be hush, hush. Schultz told him to keep all his findings to himself. Only Ruby was up when he arrived home. He quietly led her onto the porch. They both watched the cloudless sky. The best part of living in Far Rockaway, away from the lights and excitement of the city, were these kind of nights. The stars shown so brightly.

"Ruby, Ruby," he scratched the top of the dog's head, "what am I to do?"

She nuzzled her long snout into his hand.

"Dutch Schultz asks me to investigate a murder that he committed. Look for any loose ends. Very clever man. He doesn't look it, but it's more than pure ruthlessness that guides his decisions."

Both gazed at the universe of stars and planets, "Time to go inside. Big doings tomorrow."

She followed him inside and up the stairs to the master bedroom.

The next day, Goldy left before he could answer any questions. Esty and Zayde stood on the porch shouting at him.

He arrived at Schultz's social club when few were around. Bernard Rosencrantz, Dutch's bodyguard and chauffeur, was munching on a bagel.

"Is Dutch around?" he asked Rosencrantz.

"He's gone to his favorite breakfast joint. Check down the street," he pointed with a clean finger. The rest of his hand was sticky with cream cheese.

Goldy walked to the place and saw Dutch eating alone. Then he saw Bo Weinberg and his brother nearby.

"So Goldy, who killed Rothstein?" Bo asked.

"It was a hush, hush, snooping," Goldy placed a finger on

his lips.

"Dutch doesn't know from keeping a secret," Bo gently slapped him on the back.

Dutch saw Goldy at the front door and signaled for him to come to him.

"Sit down. What do you want for breakfast?"

The waitress edged closer, "What can I get you?"

"Eggs and a bagel with cream cheese," Goldy told her.

"So what did you find out? Who killed Rothstein?"

"I thought you said this was hush, hush. Bo asks me the same questions."

"Did you tell him anything?"

"No, of course not."

"Good man, who killed him?"

"McManus, the gambler is the prime suspect. Cops don't have enough evidence to arrest him. They know he was there. He has a real motive. There was a huge gambling debt. Enough to feed a hundred families for life."

"I heard something like $350,000. No other people suspected?" Dutch asked.

"There were three whiskey glasses in the room. Cops using some fancy tools. Dusting for fingerprints. I guess they got Mc-Manus. And his overcoat he forgot in the room."

"Cops closing the case?"

"I guess. Cops seemed to like Rothstein, but he's gone and others will follow in his footsteps. The bribes continue."

"A whole bunch of guys want a piece of Rothstein's pie."

"That's what I want to talk to you about. Rothstein owned two freighters that were capable of crossing the Atlantic. Not ocean liners or those steamers that brought our relatives to America. More like big yachts. Fast. We should have one. If they're dividing up his goodies, we need one of those."

"You know how to operate one of them?"

"No, we need the crew. Keep his old crew. But my boys will take care of the booze. We can easily get to Canada. No more middle man. We directly pick up the product. Rothstein boasted that one ship went to Scotland and got the booze from the distillers. We can do that."

"It's big so where does it dock?"

"Rothstein's got his on the Westside docks in Manhattan. I got a more secure place for it."

"In the Rockaways?"

"Exactly, nice quiet place. And instead of me and those two little boats going out five evenings a week. We get this big mother and we're talking once a week. Great investment for you. Rothstein can't use them anymore."

"It sounds good. I'll have to meet with Lansky and Luciano. Make some kind of deal. Yeah, you done good Goldy. Real good. Go see Abbadabba and find out how much extra cash we have floating around."

"Thanks boss," Goldy walked back to the social club to see Dutch's financial guy Otto 'Abbadabba' Berman.

Goldy told him about his freighter request.

"I get it. Cut out the middleman. More control, bigger loads. Sounds good Goldy. We took a hit a few weeks ago, five figures. But I think we can manage. We're not actually going to buy it are we? We're going to make a deal to get it. Dutch will negotiate, right?"

"Yeah but there may be some money involved. It's going to be a big revenue booster. I'm going to the Westside to check out the two freighters. See if I can meet the crew. I think the boats are similar, but I'll go see for myself," Goldy reported.

"Yeah, Goldy can you do me a favor?"

"Sure. What needs to be done?"

"You heard what happened to Joey Noe? Got himself killed. Him and Dutch were close since they were kids. He gives the widow some money. Usually, I got Bernard to bring it to her. Dutch has him doing all kinds of other errands today. I would have to do it. But since you're headed to Manhattan. Can you drop off the money?"

"Sure, sure, no problem. Write down the address."

"Thanks Goldy, you're a pal."

He took the envelope with the money. The address was neatly handwritten in Otto's precise writing. Goldy drove right onto the Williamsburg Bridge to the Lower East Side. Since he was near his favorite restaurants and bakeries, he would bring home lots of goodies for the family.

Most of the housing off Delancey Street was a massive clump of poorly maintained buildings in the Lower East Side. Mainly, two and three story apartment buildings from a hundred years ago. Not fit to raise rats and certainly not children.

He was surprised to find Noe's house. It was detached, small, but well maintained. He knocked on the front door and a small child opened it.

"Is your Mommy here?" Goldy asked.

A lovely-looking woman came to the door. She was barefooted with the smallest of feet.

"I'm taking Bernard's place today."

"Who are you?"

"I'm Mr. Mensch."

"That's a Jew word. Right? Mr. Nice Guy is that you?" she asked.

"That's right. Just call me Mr. Mensch or Nice Guy," he laughed and she mimicked him.

"You sent by Dutch?"

"Bernard had a few errands to run today. This is from Dutch," he handed her an envelope.

"Thanks," she took the envelope, but didn't open it. She assumed its contents held the appropriate amount.

"I'm sorry about your husband."

"Did you know my Joey?"

"We met a few times."

"My Joey and Dutch they grew up together. It was tough in those days. Real hard. Nobody had any money. Know what I mean?"

"Yes, I do. My family didn't have much."

"If it wasn't for Prohibition, pretty much we would have nothing. Who ever thought it was going to cut down on crime. Bunch of fools. The beer was good. But Joey and Dutch had bigger ideas."

"Crime pays," Goldy added.

"Before that when they were kids doing burglary jobs. And robbing crap games. Pretty petty stuff although Dutch did get pinched and spent time on Blackwell's Island. It was the beer that saved us. Then it was liquor. I don't remember seeing much of you Mr. Mensch."

"Me and Dutch got together with the whiskey. Wanted something more expensive for the customers uptown."

"That bastard Legs Diamond killed my Joey. He shot him right outside Chateau Madrid. You know the joint on 54th Street. Shot him down like a dog. And what happens?" she started to cry.

Goldy handed her his handkerchief.

"The bullets," she began to sob, "he lay here in this house for a month before he passed."

"I'm so sorry," Goldy touched her shoulder.

"You married Mr. Mensch, got any kids?"

"My wife is Esty, Esther. I got five kids."

"That's a nice Biblical name. You know you don't look like a Yid."

"It's my blond curly hair and blue eyes," Goldy said with a smile.

"Yeah," she sniffled and blew her nose into Goldy's linen handkerchief.

"Why did Diamond shoot your husband?"

"To get back at Dutch. They were carving out a piece of the action in Manhattan. Show Dutch not to mess. Now Diamond's boss man Rothstein is dead. Good. He started as Rothstein's bodyguard. Kissed his ass enough that he got to share in the profits. It's a nasty business this Prohibition."

"We all take risks for our piece of the action. You, unfortunately, paid the biggest price," Goldy said as he rose from the chair.

"You take care Mr. Mensch and stay away from that Legs Diamond. Although if you could kill him, I would gladly give you every penny I had."

"People have tried. He's been a lucky son-of-a-bitch. You take care Mrs. Noe. It was a pleasure to meet you."

Goldy left for the Westside to the piers to look over those two freighters. In times of flux, it was best to find the most promising deals. This acquisition would change their bootlegging operation. No longer would it be required to go out five times a week. With this new capacity, they would sail the oceans, but once a week. It was such a step-up. Rothstein was dead. He wasn't going to miss it. Legs Diamond was out of his league.

Chapter 5
Dutch and Meyer

Dutch Schultz and Meyer Lansky were never friends, but they were business associates. If the suave Mr. Rothstein was Lansky's mentor, the rougher-edged Mr. Schultz was a reliable business partner. There was so much money to be made during the thirteen years of Prohibition that many hands shared in the profits. Some gangsters were too greedy and paid the price. The smarter ones, those who kept a lower profile lived to enjoy their profits. The in-your-face type of guys paid dearly for all the flattering newspaper and radio stories.

Goldy had no interest in being on Page 1 of the New York Daily News. If his face was unknown that was exactly what he wanted. He was not a greedy man. He watched as men who antagonized Dutch became front page stories. Their bodies riddled with bullet wounds, blood on the street. They made it to Page 1, but their widows and children were left to pick up the pieces.

The new freighter that was Goldy's prize. It was not for him to own, no never. He would guide its path and ensure the delivery of prime whiskey and scotch. He was fearful of it achieving any notoriety. He wasn't going to dock it before hundreds of people. He was going to hide his new charge.

He went with Zayde to find the right location away from any prying eyes. On the banks of the mild waters of Jamaica Bay were a few repair shops. The most important of these was a boat repair shop owned by two Irish brothers. For several generations the family was part of the shipbuilding reputation of those from Belfast, Northern Ireland. Nearby were docked coal barges.

The father and son drove up in the sedan.

"Hello," Goldy had spoken to the older brother on the phone.

"You got a big boat you want docked here?"

"Yes, it's a freighter. The size of a big yacht not an ocean liner. It has to be deep enough," Goldy reiterated.

"We helped build boats for the Royal Navy during the Great War. We know what's needed. We can design you a lift to keep the freighter out of water and then lower it for you to take out to sea. We will dredge that part of the bay for you. No damage ever."

"That's great. I got a few photos and specs from the captain. You can read the information," Goldy handed him a roll of foot-long papers.

"Come inside. We'll have some tea," the younger one walked with the visitors to a small building with the older brother following.

The older one rolled out the freighter specifications on a long table. During the next hour the deal was concluded. Goldy handed the younger one a thick envelope.

"It won't take long. We'll go see the freighter for ourselves.

We're experts don't imagine any problems."

Handshakes sealed the deal.

Goldy was surprised to get the phone call.

"Goldy, it's Meyer, join me for lunch?"

Although they were not blood brothers, the name Meyer was instantly recognizable. He wrote the address on his hand and proceeded to Manhattan.

It was the perfect opportunity to stop into the dairy restaurant for smoked fish and crusty bagels. Esty loved the smelliest, onion-scented bialys. The bakery was nearby.

"Meyer, nice to see you," Goldy shook the man's hand as he seated himself.

"I understand from Dutch, it's you who wanted one of the freighters. Going to bring the real scotch from Scotland?"

"Well, most trips will only be to Canada. I know Arnold liked to bring home the real scotch from the distilleries. Whiskey from Ireland. I assume someone is keeping that other boat."

"Only interested in one boat?"

"I can only handle one. I'm sure you have people who can use it."

"Arnold's not cold in his grave and people are carving up his empire."

"I guess that's what happens in our line of business," Goldy said. He was handed a warm bagel and a cup of black coffee.

"Arnold was a man who changed everything. He had new ideas. None of this Wild West shit. Keep the shooting to a minimum. Minimize the rivalries. Divide things up so everyone is rewarded. When guys wanted to go to war against each other, he stepped up and mediated. Treated this all as a business. Men talking around the table like gentlemen."

"He was your mentor. I understand. And he found ways to make money no one had dreamed of before he did. He got paid to negotiate for others."

"Before Arnold, bootlegging was a nasty business. Too much shooting each other. Bad press is always bad for business. No one understood that as well as Arnold. He was a master."

"And now he's dead at 46. I'm almost that age. I sure as hell don't want my wife to be a young widow. So Meyer, what can I do for you. Busy guy that you are."

"I like you Goldy. You run from the press. I think you help to calm your boss. Dutch can be a wild man. He still has that Wild West mentality. Arnold used to remind him it's better to talk than to shoot."

"I'm only a bootlegger. I'm not interested in other activities."

"No narcotics, no whores, no speakeasies. What do you do with your money?"

"I like to race greyhounds," Goldy told a white lie.

"Anything else interesting?"

"Arnold had that casino he managed with the roulette and crap games. That's the future of gambling not these high-priced poker games. Get more people in and lots of ordinary people. Everyone loves to gamble. It can be fixed and only a certain elite would care."

"What happened to Arnold was most unfortunate. Who killed The Fixer?" Lansky asked.

"McManus. As a gambler, Arnold should have known you got to pay your debts. Isn't that what the police are saying. You think different?"

"McManus was there at the Park Central Hotel. He called Arnold at Lindy's that night. He was overheard talking to Mc-Manus. But who pulled the trigger?"

"Some goon for McManus," Goldy replied.

"There's other talk that your boss paid McManus to pull the trigger," Meyer announced.

"Dutch, no. Why, when things are going so well?"

"Revenge, Dutch is a hot-head. Retaliation for the murder of his pal Joey Noe by Legs Diamond."

"So he jumps to the conclusion because Noe is killed by Diamond then he must kill Diamond's mentor Arnold Rothstein. Makes no sense."

"You know Joey Noe? They were buddies since they were robbing people on the street. A hoodlum. No loss to society. But that's your boss's problem. He makes giant leaps. No concern for the consequences. He starts wars, the opposite of Arnold. He's a thug."

"You are much too harsh on Dutch. Bootlegging is a tough business. Sometimes you got to show others who's the boss."

"Goldy, you keep to that boat and stay away from more lucrative ventures. Just keep that beer and booze flowing from Canada."

"I heard from Dutch that everybody who owed a gambling debt to Arnold invaded his apartment looking for documents. Arnold had people sign I-owe-you's."

"It was all part of doing business. The cops are going to

raid lots of places. Keep your boat out of the public eye for a while. Wait until things settle down. And they will because a bunch of those marks were signed by politicians and high ranking cops. It's those G-men who make me nervous."

"I pay my taxes," Goldy proudly told him.

"You keep paying those taxes. And keep skimming off the top of all your other businesses if you want to keep away from that J. Edgar Hoover."

"You think there will ever be another to replace Arnold Rothstein?"

"Your boss thinks he's the one. We'll see. If we learned anything from Arnold, it's better we all sit down together and work things out. Last thing business needs is blood in the streets. Don't want some poor innocent kid shot and his bloodied face on Page 1."

"It's always good to have a chat now and then. We Jew boys have to stick together," Goldy smiled as Meyer got up to leave.

Goldy didn't mention that Lansky's best buddy was a thug he grew up with named Lucky Luciano. Bootlegging brought so many different people together from across the big cities' immigrant class. Meyer Lansky was born in Russia and Luciano in Sicily, Italy. They all suffered from a feeling of not really belonging.

Schultz and Goldy were both born in America, real American citizens from birth. They were different than many of the other bootleggers. But they were from poor families. Not like Rothstein who had wealthy parents. It wasn't desperation or few options that brought Rothstein into illegal activities. His Achilles' heel was the gambling.

There was a certain camaraderie among these gangsters about being Jews. If none were religious, they all expected a proper Jewish funeral. It was these ancestral ties. Still, Lansky was closer to Luciano than Rothstein, and Schultz emotionally linked to his boyhood friend Joey Noe.

Two years passed and it was as if Rothstein's death was part of some urban legend. Miraculously, the city didn't turn into a blood bath. His empire was peacefully divided among his associates. The loser in all this was Rothstein's wife. His wealthy parents had more than enough assets. Arnold Rothstein and his wife Carolyn Greene never had children. There were none to avenge their father's untimely death.

Goldy got a call to meet Schultz in one of his speakeasy joints across the Williamsburg Bridge. As he hung up, his father watched as he took a hand gun from a cabinet drawer.

"Where're you going?" his father asked.

"To meet Schultz at one of his speakeasy's downtown."

"You need a gun? I should come," Zayde demanded.

"No, no, not necessary. He asked for me, not you and me."

Esty heard a loud conversation, "Where're you going?"

"Into the city to meet Schultz."

"At this time of night," she also saw the gun.

"I should go with him," Zayde added.

"These are dangerous men. I go when I am requested to appear. We got involved with these people and guess what? There are consequences. I couldn't get out of bootlegging if I wanted. And truth be told, it's been good to us. Everyone likes to drink and gamble."

"Prohibition isn't going to last forever. Then we get out. They won't need us," Zayde said.

"I hope it's true. Once this craziness is finished, we can resume our old lives," Esty finished with a deep sigh.

"I'll go with you. You shouldn't go alone," Zayde insisted.

"No," he told his father, "you stay and mind the house."

"I'll be OK. At this time of night, there'll be no cars," Goldy headed out the front door.

Goldy drove alone and was met at the entrance of the speakeasy by Dutch's bodyguard Bernard. He pointed to a side door. Goldy entered the joint, which was still filled with people. You heard loud voices and live music.

One of Schultz's lieutenants Abe Landau was standing near Dutch. The boss motioned for Goldy to get closer pointing to an empty seat.

Goldy sat down. A waiter offered him a glass of whiskey, which he accepted.

"Things going good. Right?" Schultz asked.

"Everything's fine," Goldy said as he saw the steak coming. It was an odd time to eat, but he picked up the knife and fork.

"We're still settling on Rothstein's properties. That second boat. You remember," Dutch reminded him.

"Sure," he answered and put a piece of steak in his mouth. Then he washed it all down with a swig of whiskey.

"Lansky is coming here to discuss that second boat. Can we use it?"

"Isn't it docked on the Great Lakes, bringing Canadian whiskey to Chicago and Detroit?"

"Yeah, we could add a route."

"No, I don't think so. I don't like the things going on in Chicago. Didn't Ike Bloom just get whacked. He had the nightspots. What was it? Midnight Frolics and Kreiberg's. No, not for us. No messing with the things going on in Chicago."

"Lansky's coming to get us to start thinking big."

As Goldy was taking his second piece of steak, Lansky walked in. Unlike his pal, Luciano, Meyer brought no entourage only a single bodyguard.

"Sit, sit Meyer. I got Goldy here to talk about things."

They all shook hands and Meyer sat between Schultz and Goldy. He was uncertain whether their earlier meeting should be acknowledged. Goldy searched Lansky's face for clues.

"Ess, I'll have one of those," Lansky asked pointing to the steak. His was a poker face, no signs of emotion.

Goldy stared into Lansky's eyes. He saw a slight turn of his head. He felt it was a sign. Goldy had no intention of making Dutch aware he had met with Lansky.

"I've been talking to Goldy about the second boat," Dutch said.

"It's amazing that after two years it's as if Rothstein never existed. Public remembers the World Series Fix, but all these other businesses. The man was a genius," Goldy said.

Lansky smiled, but not Dutch. He was solemn, never uttered a word. If looks killed the two other men at the table would be dead.

"You're doing such a great job with that freighter. Up and down the coast. You've taken it to Miami. I bet you could take it to Jamaica and pick up rum. Couldn't you?" Lansky asked.

"Sure I can and we travel close to the coast, never too far from the international line. Don't want to press our luck with Mother Nature. She's far more dangerous than the G-men," Goldy replied.

"How about taking control of the other freighter? The one on Great Lakes," Dutch asked.

"No, no, too much risk. Mother Nature can be cruel on those Great Lakes. And I don't want to start messing around with the Chicago and Detroit gangs," Goldy repeated his hesitation. Dutch had also heard his warnings at prior meetings. This time the two of them were going to gang up on Goldy and his caution.

"We can make arrangements," Lansky insisted.

"Find someone else. You know that we shake hands tomorrow with these guys in Chicago and the day after they'll be coming after the boat. And me and you," he pointed to both men. "No thanks. I can offer advice on how to avoid detection. But I have no interest in that part of the country," Goldy was firm.

"OK, I can respect that. You have always been honest and not always against thinking bigger," Lansky said without malice.

"You know Prohibition is not going to last. Those boats will need to find another purpose," Goldy added.

"Like transporting heroin," Lansky offered.

"Hell no. Why would you risk seizure by the G-men when all you need is a valise to take the drugs from Europe to here."

The two men looked at Goldy and both grinned. What Goldy never liked about Lansky was his approval of Luciano's

Sicilian involvement with heroin. Booze was fine, but not the drug trade.

"What's a better use?" Lansky asked.

"Turn the boats into floating casinos and park them just beyond the international line. They can be moored anywhere outside of law enforcement's reach. The freighter has speed. I've got my shipbuilders to modify the engines so Dutch's boat is faster than whatever the G-Men have in their boatyard." Goldy wanted to make certain that everyone understood that the boat belonged to Dutch. He was merely the operator.

Lansky put his hand on Goldy's shoulder, "That's why I like this guy. Using his noggin."

"Smart fellow, Goldy," Schultz added his voice.

"I'll tell Luciano that we had this chat. Floating casinos!"

"I got that idea from Rothstein. He understood the value of casinos. Bring the people together not just for cards. Get the ordinary Joe's to spend money," Goldy suggested. Never a gambler himself, he saw the power of this lust for gambling, an obsession. If McManus had not personally killed Rothstein over a gambling debt, it was tied to his death.

Schultz was unusually fidgety when Goldy arrived for his regular meeting with the boss so soon after their meeting with Lansky. Goldy always felt that there was unease when he met with Lansky. It was a silly school-boy type of jealousy by Dutch. All these gangsters wanted to be loved. Lansky preferred the shadows, but not Dutch or Luciano. They clambered for the spotlight. If Goldy had his preference, they would meet in the Lower East Side rather than Harlem. He was never asked for his opinion.

"Trouble getting here?" Dutch's hand was on his pocket watch.

"Traffic gets thicker. More cars than ever even during these tough times," Goldy sat across from his boss.

Dutch moved closer to Goldy as if to whisper in his ear, "I need a favor, a big favor."

"Anything boss."

"I know how nice Lansky always is when we all meet together. Seems so reasonable. Right?"

Goldy was dreading the favor, "He's all about business."

"You don't think he harbors at least mistrust towards me because of Rothstein. He still thinks I killed Rothstein. You know it's a lie. But he still thinks that."

Goldy could smell Dutch's breath they were so close. He tried to stay calm. "Rumors, just idle gossip."

"They're up to something with that son-of-a-bitch Legs Diamond. I know it. A little bird told me Diamond is off to Europe. Expanding business or something like that. I think he's going for Luciano or could be also Lansky. It's about expanding the heroin trade. Maybe going to Sicily to make deals with those WOPs."

"Lansky and Luciano know we are not interested in heroin."

"They may drag us into their business. Money is there."

"What do you want me to do?"

"I had Abe buy you a ticket. Diamond is going to Europe sailing on the ocean liner on SS Burgenland. It's going to Antwerp. I know you have contacts in that city. I want you to follow Diamond."

"You want me to follow Diamond to Europe? Really?" Goldy's mouth was ajar.

"Yeah, you're the only one I trust. You take that ship that Diamond is booked on. Abe got you a first-class ticket. Not like in steerage. Let's you get real close. You're on the same deck."

"When is this ship leaving?"

"Boat leaves on August 30."

"And you want me to follow him through Europe?"

"Right. I'll give you money. You may need bribes. And I got something for you." Dutch pointed to a box in the corner.

Abe brought over the huge package.

"This is a camera. You know how to take pictures? I want you to take pictures of the men Diamond meets. You pretended you were a newspaper guy before with the Rothstein investigation so here's the proof."

"I might need an extra hand to work this thing," Goldy touched the wooden tripod.

"OK. Take your boy. Abe will get you another ticket. You share the room."

"My wife will be wondering where I'm going."

"You can tell her you're on a job for me. Spare the details about Diamond. And don't go to Sicily. I don't want you killed."

"You are not expecting me to set-up Diamond to kill him in Europe?"

"No, no," Dutch poked his arm, "you're not a hitman Goldy," Dutch laughed.

"How long will I be gone?"

"I don't think more than a couple of weeks. If he's going to make contacts, he will do it quickly. I got to believe the police in Europe will be watching him."

Goldy went home to tell his wife to pack his bags. At first she was alarmed about another peculiar assignment by his volatile boss. Then she thought it seemed harmless. But who was going to be his traveling companion?

"You're not taking Izzy. I won't let you," Esty told her husband.

"I never was thinking of him. I wanted a big guy to schlep this damn camera. I'll ask Hirsh. Big and broad and strong. I'm sure he will agree."

Hirsh was delighted to be invited as Goldy's guest. He knew nothing about cameras, but he could take a car completely apart and put it back together. He figured how difficult would it be to take pictures with the bulky camera. He spent the few days before embarking studying the camera. He found magazines about photography. It actually looked like fun. He was eager to go along and visit Europe again.

The two men boarded the SS Belgenland as just another couple of guests bound for Antwerp. He had sent a letter to the jeweler Teitelbaum informing him of his arrival.

Legs Diamond was followed by a slew of reporters and cameramen even before he boarded. They surrounded him. Then there were his wildly enthusiastic fans.

One reporter shouted out, "Why are you going to Europe?"

Diamond replied, "For my health. I'm bound for Vichy, France to take those mineral waters."

The gangster failed to mention that his occasional breathing problems were from his limited days as a soldier in the U.S. Army during W.W.I. It was a dangerous place being a soldier in those trenches. However, Diamond deserted and then was imprisoned by the authorities. That messy part of his earlier life he never discussed with the press or with his groupies. How would it look to be a deserter, a traitor? But he never regretted his decision. After all, he was alive and many other soldier buddies died during the Great War.

The evenings crossing the Atlantic were filled with celebration. There was Legs surrounded by adoring women as he played cards with the other guests. He ordered champagne for everyone. He was the party man's partyer.

Hirsh and Goldy watched from afar. The card table where Legs played was completely surrounded by other guests. Goldy studied the crowd to determine if any of these adoring fans were actual contacts. Most on board appeared to be Americans or from America. Goldy was watching for Italians. He even studied the ship's staff to observe any drug dealing. If he was on this ship to create a drug network, the most likely couriers were going to be younger, more poorly paid staff.

They left the bulky camera in their room. It was completely impractical to haul the object around. Instead, the smart-thinking Hirsh brought along a less cumbersome camera he found in a Far Rockaway pawn shop. If he wore a big raincoat, he could hide the camera from its target.

Goldy and Hirsh walked far behind the adoring crowds surrounding Diamond. It was too far away for Hirsh to get a good camera angle. Hirsh like Goldy had patience. He followed the celebrity and patiently waited for just the right opportunity to catch his image on camera.

"Look how much they love him," Hirsh was star struck like the others.

"He's a murdering gangster. These fools have no idea."

"When I tell people my cousin runs with Dutch Schultz, suddenly I get this respect. People love gangsters," Hirsh put his large arm across Goldy's narrower shoulder.

"They have no idea how mean and ruthless these guys are. Keep your eyes on any men who are physically close to Diamond. We are looking for potential contacts. It could be crew members."

Hirsh managed to take dozens of photographs but none of the people seemed like couriers or business contacts. Most of the time the men were playing poker. The women liked to touch his hair, sometimes his face. A few daring ones kissed Diamond.

Once Hirsh followed the gangster for hours. He saw the man head for his suite with a couple of beautiful young women. He observed the suite door closed. After hours of stationing by himself near the doorway, he returned to his room without any important news.

They found nothing unusual during the voyage. Everywhere Diamond walked on the ship, he was followed by blushing women and fashionably dressed men. All the men and a few of the women wanted to play poker with him.

Goldy was given enough money by Dutch that they lived well on the ocean liner. There was no prohibition against alcohol on the open seas. Whiskey was available and the English drank gin. Hirsh liked the German beer.

The master investigator got close to the white-uniformed waiters who constantly refilled his glass. They were happy to receive money for some bits of information. In particular, Goldy wanted to know who was playing cards with Diamond. Was it the same crowd? Did anyone speak Italian?

The waiters' lips were flapping. The information was just dull. None of the waiters understood Italian. For their twenty-dollar tips, he learned nothing interesting. He waited to disembark and continued following his target.

"Why is Dutch so focused on Diamond?" Hirsh asked as they strolled the deck.

"Because Diamond has no manners. He's always stalking someone else's territory. An undependable partner. Here he seems so charming. He's a killer with no regard for existing agreements."

"Diamond is not alone in grabbing more territory. Isn't that the way Dutch operates?"

"With Schultz, it's an old wound that still festers. Can't get rid of it."

"It's all about Rothstein?"

"Less you know the better. Keep your ears open to Italian."

The Captain announced that the ship was ready to dock. People crowded the outside decks and watched as the sailors worked to get the ship next to the dock. Antwerp, Belgium was a major international port with ocean liners and cargo vessels from across the world. Disembarkation would begin. Since Dutch made arrangements for first class accommodations, the duo would leave at the same time as Diamond. It was easy to keep track of him with so many adoring fans circling. Goldy and Hirsh followed the whirling circle.

Guests literally walked the plank. Meeting the ship was a cavalcade of police cars. The sirens were silent, but a wave of uniforms greeted the arriving guests. Goldy and Hirsh watched in amazement.

"What is going on?" Hirsh asked an equally perplexed Goldy.

"No idea."

Then it became obvious. A man in a suit stepped forward. He grabbed Legs Diamond's arm and shoved him into a waiting marked police car.

"Wow," Hirsh said.

"Yeah, what's going on. Looks like the police are arresting him."

Goldy and Hirsh finally noticed the men who had come to greet them. There was Teitelbaum and one of his sons. They were easy to locate dressed in their black coats and hats among an ocean of colorfully clothed greeters.

The men embraced. Several times, Teitelbaum shook the arm of Hirsh. He spoke in Yiddish, "You look wonderful. My have you grown. Last time, I saw you here in Antwerp you were a shy foreigner, afraid of the big city. Now, I see a gentleman."

"I told you America is a great place. Really, the land of opportunity," Goldy said.

"I see some American being arrested by the police," Teitelbaum replied.

"Is that the local police?" Goldy wanted to know.

"No, actually. It's a different uniform. I think they were sent by the national government. Looks like federal police from Brussels. Not police from here in Antwerp."

"Do you know who that man is?" Hirsh was interested in how big the circle of celebrity reached.

"A gangster. You know that man?" the jeweler asked.

"I do. I'm actually here to follow him, at a distance. What happens to him is important to me. Where are they taking him?" Goldy's eyes returned to the commotion.

"I know the Antwerp police station is not far. Brussels is a train ride away. How's your Flemish?" Teitelbaum knew the answer.

"As poor as before. He's no better," Goldy pointed to Hirsh.

"Take my son Shmuel with you. He knows how to get to the police station and can translate for you."

"That's very nice, quite generous. He's of course in no danger if we're going to visit the police."

"Who are you going to say you are?"

"Newspaper reporter. They all follow Legs Diamond."

"Go with my son. Hirsh is not as useful. He will return home with me. We will wait for you. My wife made up a bedroom for you both. A nice dinner awaits you. Go. Do what you are here to do."

And that's when the two went off to the police station. A few people's eyes glanced at the Hasidic outfit, no one said anything. In springtime, black seemed inappropriate, stand-offish, but not uncommon in the streets of Antwerp.

From across the street, Goldy and Shmuel observed. The well-dressed American was escorted into the police station.

The hands were not rough as they directed Diamond to an inside room. Goldy and Shmuel stood outside with their backs against a building, waiting. The police, batons in hand, pushed away men with cameras. A single line of police encircled the station as if they were expecting a riot.

An hour passed and Legs was still inside the station. A man in a fine suit was allowed to enter the station. Goldy guessed it must be the Belgian equivalent of a lawyer. The imagined riot never appeared and slowly the line of police dissipated. Goldy saw one officer standing alone nearby. He took a few steps and ventured to the man's side.

Goldy offered the officer a cigarette, "Smoke?"

The man in uniform took a cigarette from the pack. In halting English, he said, "American, nice. Hard to find here."

"Lots of excitement," Goldy looked at his face to see if he understood.

Shmuel walked over and translated into Flemish.

"Who is in the station house?" Goldy asked.

"American gangster. Americans love their Gangsters."

After the translation, Goldy laughed, "What are they going to do with him?"

"He says he's only visiting going to Vichy, France to drink the mineral waters."

"The police don't believe that?"

"We found documents. He's actually heading for Germany."

"Germany? Why Germany?"

"Prohibition in America. Wants to buy rye whiskey to import to America. We can't have someone like that here."

"What are you going to do with him?"

"Send him to Germany. Arrangements are being made to put him on a train for Eifel. Possibly tomorrow."

"Is Eifel far from here?"

"No, it's in western Germany near Belgium."

Goldy slipped the pack of cigarettes into the officer's hand, "Thanks."

The next day Goldy and Hirsh watched as Legs with a full police escort boarded a train for Eifel. They sat in another train carriage. Passengers on the train were stopped by armed police guards from getting too close to the prisoner. He was being treated as a prisoner. The investigative duo heard Diamond singing. That sound alternated with his cursing out the officers. If any spoke English, they were unmoved by either the singing or the screaming.

When the train stopped, Diamond was removed by the police guards and handed over to another set of police. This time the German secret service took control. Handcuffed in irons, the prisoner was escorted to his new prison cell. The Belgians had been polite. The Germans roughly threw the prisoner into a police car. Kept in solitary confinement, Diamond entertained the rest of the prison population with Irish drinking songs.

The American found an English-language newspaper. Legs Diamond was a prisoner and being held without the possibility of bail. The German authorities in Berlin considered him a menace. He was deemed a dangerous threat to the German people, labeled an enemy of the state.

Goldy and Hirsh took turns watching the prison where Diamond was being held. The newspapers never mentioned what was to become of their prisoner. No stranger to jail cells, Diamond seemed unconcerned about his future.

The investigative duo was unable to get anywhere near where Diamond was being held. The entire area was surrounded by unsmiling police officers. None seemed approachable. So they waited without having any idea what was going to happen.

Then on the radio, Goldy thought he understood the German-language announcement of Diamond being deported. After a week in prison, Legs was being moved. Hirsh overheard one officer saying something about Hamburg. That made sense to Goldy; it was an important destination. Steamers and freighters often called at this North Sea port.

There was another surprise. He was not going to be transported by train. The two observed Diamond being picked up at the prison and thrown into the back of a black sedan. A marked police car was in front of the unmarked car while a third car was behind the prisoner. The police drove in the opposite direction of the train station.

Goldy and Hirsh couldn't follow the police cars on foot. Unable to have a conversation in German about where to obtain a car, they headed to the train station. Unless he managed to escape, the duo would arrive in Hamburg before the police cars.

At the train station in Hamburg, Hirsh and Goldy overheard someone talking in English about Diamond's deportation. Crowds were forming at the dock, kept away by a stream of police officers with batons in hand. The German officer in charge removed Diamond's metal handcuffs. He walked up the plank waving to an adoring crowd although much smaller than the group in Antwerp.

Hirsh asked Goldy, "Should we get a ticket for that freighter."

"No, we have remained invisible until now. It's clear he's headed back to America. I saw something about the destination of the freighter is Philadelphia. That's where he will disembark."

"Nu, now what?"

"We're going to Poland to see the relatives. We can get on a train and be in Warsaw shortly. Then we take another train to Bialystok. I was hoping to get you home so you could see your mother and father. Short visit. I need to report to Dutch. He might have already heard stuff so I'll send a telegraph."

Goldy was experienced at traveling from Germany to Poland. Hirsh spoke fluent Polish although with the relatives he continued to speak Yiddish. Bialystok looked even less appealing after a five-year absence. The streets needed paving, the houses fresh paint and the people new clothes. Poland always seemed backwards. In Germany, cars dominated the streets and new trams run by electric power. In this land where so many Jews called home, the kindest description of the place was shabby or neglected.

The entire extended family converged on Tanta Anat's house when they heard of the return of the two adventurers. Hirsh's mother never stopped crying, his new shirt was soaked in her tears. His younger brothers touched his new shoes as if they were made of gold. The grungy kid who left five years ago had returned as an emperor. Relatives' jaws dropped when they met the new Hirsh. It was not only the material possessions; it was the confidence. He was becoming a real American. Hope was the elixir. The New World was above all else the land of great expectations.

Tanta Anat cried, "Why didn't you tell us you were coming."

"I hoped to come here, but I actually was in Europe for a reason. I didn't want to promise I would come with Hirsh until we were actually here," Goldy explained.

"He looks very good. Bluma and Zev write. Now that I see Hirsh, I wish you could have brought the others. They couldn't come?"

"No, I couldn't bring too many people. But you see Hirsh, how well he looks. A new man your grandson. Which proves my original proposition to you when Papa and I came five years ago. The entire family must leave Poland. Please come with me to America," Goldy pleaded.

"He is a young man with few responsibilities. We are old. Our family has lived here for generations."

"And look around you. What do you see? Poor people without any future. America means a future."

"I read the papers. America has troubles too. Businesses fail, people are hungry. That Dust Bowl with so much drought. America is not perfect. Here we have lived with the good times and the bad times," she refused to accept any different future.

"If you can't persuade your daughters to leave how about your grandchildren. Look what has happened to Hirsh. Bluma and Zev have also done well. Please, let me take someone back to America. More teenagers."

"Can it be so easy?"

"I bet that forger in Warsaw is still in business. We'll get papers for them, as many as your daughters will let go. You talk to them. I want them to be eager to leave just like the three who did."

"Hirsh will talk to his cousins. I'm sure someone will return with you. I never met your Esty, but she must be a good woman to take in these strange children. My Rivka always had a big heart. You too Avraham. Even if you're a gangster."

"It's only alcohol. Everyone likes to drink," Goldy explained without shame or remorse.

"I also see that Hirsh has lost much of what made him a Jew. Hashem is certainly not a major part of his life."

"Hashem, Tanta Anat, is not enough. There is so much more."

"Avraham, Hashem is life."

Goldy hoped to bring three more to America. None of the boys wanted to leave. Hirsh spoke to every boy except the married ones. He was living proof that America was certainly the land of opportunity. The trouble was their minds were blocked to any concept of life, liberty and happiness. Their small, confining world provided more comfort than any dreams of great expectations. It was beyond their comprehension.

Just two sisters, both teenagers, agreed to leave the only life they knew. They looked at their surroundings and saw drudgery. Married at seventeen or eighteen, life was babies and crowded living, nagging mothers-in-law. Dreams died in Bia-lystok.

On this journey to America, the four left from Gdansk, Poland. The entire boat trip the sisters cried themselves to sleep. Nosy women in an adjoining cabin began to ask questions. They watched Goldy and Hirsh, looked for bruised hands on the part of the men. Strangers were concerned the girls were being mistreated or stolen away from their families. Their modest dresses covered up much of their anatomy. One spoke Polish and tried to engage the girls in conversation. The girls kept their mouths shut around these people during the week journey.

Goldy was so pleased to be back in America. Too much time was spent with teenage girls. In the best of circumstances, he barely understood them. Only with Gladdy was he comfortable talking about anything important. In this situation, these homesick girls were emotional wrecks. Hirsh was better with them. He explained about all those peculiar things he had to learn when living in America.

What they enjoyed the most was his descriptions of cars. Women drove cars in America. When he told them, they refused to believe him. He sketched with a pencil, pictures of the many cars he had worked on in his shop. He wasn't' a peddler, but a real store owner. He and his brother were paid for fixing other people's cars.

Once they arrived in New York, Goldy was relieved. His responsibilities changed from impatient guardian to just a relative. Their daily lives would be in the hands of women. There was Esty's motherly intuition. Rivka would assist. Although he was the father of four daughters, his wife was a mother with lots more hands-on experiences. There were so many bodily changes that required a woman's touch.

On arrival, he then discovered that Bluma had been writing to these girls. Goldy knew she wrote to her mother, but these other relatives. They had been corresponding for a couple of years. It seemed that Bluma had offered to sponsor their immigration. She had filled them up with hope. Unlike the other family members in Poland, they saw a future. It was uncertain, but it existed.

Bluma asked if she could accompany Esty and Izzy to pick up the voyagers. Bluma was an excellent Manhattan driver making many trips to Harlem for her evening entertainment. Reluctantly, Izzy allowed her to chauffeur the Buick to the docks.

The dock was crowded with those awaiting the arrival of friends and family. Others had the same idea as the Goldfarbs, bring those foreign relatives to the safety of the New World. Men in uniforms offered to help with the luggage. Between the four of them, there were three valises. They had sufficient hands to move the girls' lifetime possessions to a waiting car.

It was Bluma who first spotted the four in the crowd as they were disembarking. She raised her arm pointing to the quartet. Esty waved to her husband. He waved back pointing to the girls. Hirsh screamed out his hellos. Izzy, caught up in the excitement, screamed out their names.

The girls collapsed into the open arms of Bluma. The girl they knew from Bialystok had been transformed into an American. Immediately, they changed personas from frightened outsiders to hopeful immigrants. The two calmed down, tears forgotten. Hirsh without long hair, stubby beard and payos was not as much as a transformation as the chubby, timid Bluma in her fashionable clothing and bobbed hair.

Esty looked at the two teenagers. She expected more. Obviously, despite his charming ways, her husband only convinced two to leave Poland. Hirsh helped them into the Buick's backseat. They fondled the leather as if it was made of golden strands.

Goldy and Esty spent a few minutes apart from the others. He told her that he wasn't immediately returning to Far Rockaway. He had an important assignment to complete.

"Go home," he told Esty, "I got to see Dutch."

"How will you get home?" she asked.

"I'll take the subway like most New Yorkers," he replied.

He kissed them good-bye and hailed a cab at the docks for the trip north to Harlem.

It was a short ride. His face pressed against the taxi's window, Manhattan was always a delight for a boy from Far Rockaway. At the door of the speakeasy, hands waved at his appearance. Goldy found Dutch at his favorite table in the rear where he viewed all visitors.

"I just arrived in New York. I thought it was important to see you," he sat down.

"Get the man a steak and a glass of whiskey," the boss yelled.

"Diamond was never after heroin. You got my telegrams."

"When he arrived in Philadelphia on that freighter the cops there picked him up. The ultimatum was to leave town that day or go to jail."

"Where is he now?" Goldy asked.

"I hear that he got himself a place near Albany. He's chased out of New York City. Bastard is not going to find any comfort here," Dutch reported.

"Good. He finally got it through his thick Irish head that he was unwelcome."

"Without Rothstein, he has no protector. Now's the time to hunt him down and whack him."

"No Dutch. Why get the police all worked up? Forget about him. He's no longer any threat to you and your businesses."

"You keep an eye on him for me. I'm sure he's not going to be satisfied living in the boonies. He loves being in the newspapers. Got to have a dozen dames fawning over him."

"OK. I'll find out what's going on. Remember the G-men are after him. The smartest move is to let the feds arrest and put him in jail for years. Let the law take responsibility. They'll get rid of him for years."

"Where's the camera I gave you?"

"I left it in Europe. Too bulky to move around with that thing. I can pay you for its value," Goldy reached into his pants pocket for his roll of bills.

The waiter put down the steak and a glass was filled to the brim with whiskey.

"Forget about it. Tell me, you think we should be looking into German whiskey? Who knew Germans like whiskey. Beer, everyone knows Germans like beer."

"Periodically, I take the freighter to Scotland to bring back here good Scotch. Germany, I don't know. Lots of ugly noise coming out of Germany. I don't think it's a good place for Jews to be involved with booze. And you said it. Who knew Germans made good whiskey?"

As Goldy finished his steak, Dutch spoke about what was next for his underling.

"You keep that freighter going. And keep tabs on Diamond. That's your orders. Now go see your family."

When he returned home, Ruby was the happiest to see him. She put forward her greatest energy to greet him with barking and licks of love. He sat on the porch while the dog nuzzled his hand.

Polly watched in his cage, "Papa home, Papa home," the parrot screamed out to the neighborhood.

Soon the others emerged including his sister Rivka and her two children.

"It's good you go to see the family. And ever so thankful you're living in America and not Poland," his sister said.

"We got everything arranged. The two new girls Sisel and Tzipi will share Gladdy's room. Everything else remains the same," Esty reported the plans.

"I offered a room in my house. Moishe doesn't live at home. Miriam is barely there going to college. But your wife insisted. Gladdy was so good with Bluma, she has the next set of relatives to Americanize."

"Tzipi is most impressed with the piano. Gladdy is going to talk to Mrs. Levine about giving her lessons."

Esty kissed Goldy on the top of his head, "You're a mensch Avraham Goldfarb. Hashem smiles on you."

•••

Goldy was at home relaxing. He had just returned from his European excursion. He realized more than ever that the new freighter netted more bottles of Canadian whiskey on one trip than a dozen the old way. This seemed like a relatively easy way to make a buck. He had an experienced crew and he only supervised the loading and unloading of the product. His take was substantial, although the G-men were constantly in the newspapers confiscating illegal booze.

He was on the front porch. Polly was singing some bird song while Ruby was sleeping dreaming of those lost puppy days. Her large legs running on some imaginary race.

"Papa, I got some great news?" Izzy told him.

"What?"

"I'm going to get married."

"Wonderful news," he gave his son a big hug, "your mother knows?"

"Yes and Zayde too," he told him.

"I'm the last to know," he laughed, knowing he had not been home.

"Esty, come to the front porch," he cried out through the open front door.

"Esty, Esty, Esty come out to play. Esty," Polly screamed.

"How long do parrots live?" Goldy pointed his finger at the bird.

Esty walked onto the porch, "Fifty years."

"It's a good thing he makes you happy."

"Papa's here, Papa's here," the bird continued.

"Our boy is getting married. Who's the lucky girl?"

"Sarah, the jeweler's daughter. Family shop on Central Avenue," Izzy replied.

"Well, they must have a few bucks. Where did you meet her? Can't be at the docks where you work?"

"No, actually I know her from shul. I saw her last year at High Holidays. We got talking. We were in the same class in school. Kinda re-connected," he answered.

"That's nice and romantic," father told his son.

"Yeah, she works in her father's store. She waits on customers."

"You got a ring for her?" Esty asked.

"Papa, I know you got friends in the diamond business in the city. Should I buy a ring from her father?"

"I can get you a better deal. I own some beautiful uncut diamonds, but let's make nice. Sure get it from her father's store. She can pick it out. Buy her the very best. We can afford it. Make a good impression. Nothing cheap about the Goldfarbs. Right Esty?"

"When are you thinking about getting married? And where?" Esty asked.

"Soon while the weather is nice. There's always the hotel. Bluma would make it beautiful."

Esty linked her arm around Izzy's arm, "What do they think your father does for a living?"

"He owns a cargo shipping business. Takes a big boat down the coast delivering merchandise," Izzy explained.

"What kind of merchandise? Do they have any idea?" Goldy laughed and poked his son in the ribs.

"Nobody asked too many questions," Izzy said.

"Maybe they're afraid to ask questions," Esty chuckled to herself.

"Laugh Esty, laugh, Esty," Polly screamed.

"Izzy, what do they think you do for a living?" his mother asked.

"I tell them the truth. I work with Tanta Rivka taking out fishing parties. I help run the party boat business. I get paid to take rich people fishing in the Atlantic Ocean."

"Goldy, is that an occupation for a married man. Hopefully, they have a family? What kind of money can he make? Your sister is not doing this for money. We know you operate this business as a front to keep the taxman away."

"Izzy my boy, what do you want to do for a living?" his father asked.

"I want to own a movie house," he answered.

His stunned parents looked at their eldest child.

"A movie house?" his mother asked.

"There's one on Central Avenue. I spoke with the owner. He's tired of the business. Gonna be too expensive going from the silent to talkies. It's a great location right in the middle of Far Rockaway, close by the jewelry store."

"Besides liking to go to the movies. Do you know anything about running a movie house?" his father asked.

"No, but Murray, that's the owner's name. Murray Kaufman, he will show me how things work. We could open the latest, most modern movie house in all of the Rockaways. Wouldn't that be the greatest?"

"I could go with you and sit down and talk to Murray," Goldy offered.

"I think talking movies are going to be the biggest hit. Entertainment for the family," Esty said.

"I know nothing about movie houses. But there are different parts of the business. Right? You need a projector and a projectionist, a screen to show it. To get the movies since you're not making them, you need a distributor. Comfortable seats would be nice. Great sound system so you can hear the talking," Goldy summarized.

"And food," Izzy said, "candy and soda and lots of snacks. That's where you can make money."

"There we go. You already know something."

"Isn't your sister Chayna's husband in the movie business. He writes screenplays. He could be a helpful contact," Esty suggested.

"Yeah, Irving. I can call him. We all can take a train ride to Los Angeles. Lots of Jews in the movie business."

"Now, we got you a respectable business to run," Esty said.

"Is Sarah thinking about a big wedding?" Goldy asked.

"I don't know. You both need to sit down with her parents," Izzy told them.

"Will we have to invite Dutch Schultz?" Esty frowned.

"If we have thirty people, no. If we have more than fifty people, yes," Goldy replied.

"What about the others like all of Dutch's henchmen. The bodyguard and the accountant, the Weinberg brothers," Esty sarcastically added.

"How about Meyer?" Izzy excitedly asked.

Goldy laughed, "Whole mishpachah."

"You think nice people want to sit down in shul with a

bunch of gangsters?" his mother skeptically asked.

"Oh yes," Izzy answered, "ordinary people think gangsters are romantic figures."

"They should ask Ike Bloom's widow or Joey Noe's," Goldy responded.

"OK, my son. It looks like you and your father will discuss with Mr. Kaufman your future. I will invite Sarah's family for dinner. Do you think we can have just thirty people?" Esty liked that number.

"No, although jewelers are probably feeling the effects of this financial crisis. Hope, he didn't have too much invested in this rigged stock market. I always said, cash is king. It doesn't belong invested in some worthless stock certificate. Or those banks. Cash, on hand that you can count. My philosophy. Izzy my boy, you are growing up. Your mother will have you deliver an invitation to dinner. You and I will go tomorrow to see the movie house guy."

With his shipping routes and new freighter, Goldy found himself much more of a presence in his children's lives. Esty asked him to do the ordinary around the house.

"Goldy can you take Gladdy to her music lesson?" his wife asked.

"Why not. Get your music Gladdy," he screamed in the doorway.

"Gladdy get music, get music. Gladdy don't run in the road. Get music," Polly pronounced.

"Do you know where Mrs. Levine lives?" he asked his daughter.

"Yes Papa. It's closer to the ocean. She has a beautiful house and a Steinway piano. You'll love the piano."

He drove her to the music teacher's house. It had a spectacular view of the Atlantic Ocean. During stormy nights the place probably shook when those gale winds came through. Goldy paid the music lesson bills, but never met the piano teacher.

"This is my Papa," Gladdy told Mrs. Levine.

"Hello Mrs. Levine," he found an empty chair, the sunlight poured into the high, front glass windows.

"Gladys tells me that you are a piano player. Is that right?" the teacher asked.

"Oh, I just fool around," he modestly answered.

"Papa is a great piano player. Play for Mrs. Levine. Please Papa play a song," Gladdy begged.

"I don't want to disturb your lesson. I'll just sit here and listen."

Gladdy could be very persistent, "Papa just one song."

"Go ahead Mr. Goldfarb. Play us one song," Mrs. Levine asked.

"Well, here's something new. I heard an incredible young singer named Billie Holiday play it in a Harlem nightclub. Here goes," Goldy played from memory. He just had to listen a few times to correctly get the arrangement.

Mrs. Levine clapped loudly, "That was amazing Mr. Goldfarb. Gladys says you have no formal musical training. You play by ear. Is that right?"

"Thank you, you're most kind. Gladys is trying to teach me to read music. She's a good teacher."

"Gladys is a fine student. I'll be happy to teach you myself. Do you visit many nightspots in Harlem?" the teacher asked.

"Yes, I like to go there. There's some fabulous talent. When Gladys gets a little older, I'll take her with me. Now Gladdy show us what you learned."

He listened while the teacher occasionally corrected Gladdy. His youngest child was an obedient music student. Her ear for sound wasn't quit developed, but she was a child with so much to learn.

"Mr. Goldfarb, Gladys has this wonderful advantage in playing the piano. She has these long fingers. It will aid her greatly as she plays more demanding pieces."

"Papa, we're going to have a little recital. Me and Mrs. Levine's other students. I told her that it would be great to have it in the side lobby of your hotel."

"Oh, that's a great idea. I would love to host a recital at the hotel. I know the spot Gladdy is talking about. It's off the main lobby. Big windows. There is a piano there, not a Steinway, but it plays nice. I sometimes play there to keep the guests entertained."

"Cousin Bluma could serve milk and cookies," Gladdy excitedly explained.

"Sure, Mrs. Levine. We can host a recital and provide refreshments at The Paradise in Rockaway. That's the hotel's name. You know it?"

"I do and that's a lovely invitation," Mrs. Levine stood up and she shook Goldy's hand.

"Great. Then we just need to know when." He reached into his pocket to pay the teacher.

"The parents and grandparents come to listen at the recital. Your hotel has a wonderful reputation sitting by the ocean. I especially like that grand front porch. Every chair has a view of the ocean. If you can't sleep you can always just sit and watch the waves. It hosts lots of parties and weddings. My friend had a wedding there for her daughter."

"We aim to serve. Reasonable prices and top notch rooms. Everything elegant. My cousin runs it and she does a perfect job."

"I'm certainly so happy you came to Gladys's lesson. I hope you join us again."

"I will try and attend more lessons."

Gladdy and her father drove home together. She ran up the steps to make the announcement to her mother. "We're going to have a recital at the hotel for me and Mrs. Levine's other students. Isn't that grand?"

"I guess Papa and Mrs. Levine got along?" Esty laughed. "Go finish your other schoolwork." Gladdy went inside the house. The two adults sat on the front porch.

"Papa's home. Papa's home," Polly screamed out.

"Did you call Izzy's future in-laws?"

"I did and they're coming over for Shabbos dinner. I don't know how religious they are, but I keep a kosher home."

"I know that jewelry shop. He's no Hasid although he must know them. I bet he gets some of his uncut jewels from those guys in Manhattan."

"It's the bride's call about the wedding."

"But it's the groom's call about the service. I'll go see the

149

rabbi at The White Shul. We can have the ceremony there.
We're members. Should be orthodox enough."

"I doubt they want a small wedding. The hotel still could
work. Then of course you have to invite your gangster boss, his
whole group of followers. If it's going to be really big I guess
you need to invite Meyer Lansky and that Italian hoodlum
Lucky Luciano."

"So approving," he kissed her on the cheek, "we got all this.
Dutch didn't make me rich, but we are all comfortable because
of him. Try and show a tiny bit of gratitude."

"What happens when Prohibition ends? What will he want
from you?"

"It will all work out. Don't fret. Izzy will have a glorious
wedding. I suggested to Rivka that she rent him an apartment
in that apartment house she owns. First place, small, but clean,
nicely maintained with the flowers and shrubs. Good start."

"We'll talk about this at dinner. God knows what they really
think you do for a living."

The boss called. Goldy liked to go to Harlem and hear the jazz
players. As a piano player, he respected those musicians. The
Roaring Twenties was good for Harlem. Booze, music and
dancing they seemed perfectly fitted for each other. There were
the famous clubs and the 500 speakeasies. Dutch had his hand
in several as did most of the gangsters.

Goldy arrived on time and was directed to Dutch's table.
Good booze from Canada, the kind Goldy was responsible for
importing was on the table.

Dutch poured him a few ounces, "Good to see you."

"Who's playing?" Goldy asked. His eyes wandered to a nearby table where Landau and Bernard were sitting.

"Who knows some schvartzes?"

"Is there a reason you wanted to see me at 2 am?"

"Meyer is coming. He likes you. He tolerates me."

"We all here for a nightcap?"

"No, he has a business proposition."

"You know what kind?"

"I'm not sure. Meyer asked for you."

"I guess that's good news," Goldy said, always instinctively cautious when dealing with notorious gangsters.

"I would like to get closer to Luciano. He has influence across the country."

"You interested in heroin? Since when?" Goldy asked.

"No, gambling. Why doesn't Luciano like me?"

"He thinks you killed Rothstein."

"It's two years. You think I killed Rothstein?"

"No, McManus killed Rothstein," Goldy publicly came to Dutch's defense. But he knew that either he paid McManus to kill Rothstein or he did the deed himself.

"Luciano doesn't trust me. I trust him."

"Well, you need to explain things to him. Your innocence. And business is business," Goldy said as he saw Lansky enter the speakeasy.

Meyer shook hands with Goldy and his boss, and sat down close to Dutch.

"So Meyer, what brings you out tonight?" Goldy asked.

"I liked your idea of a floating casino. I like it very much."

"Prohibition is going to end and other sources of revenue

need to be found," Goldy explained.

"I know you dislike the heroin business. It is very lucrative," Lansky said.

"Not to my taste. I like gambling. It makes more sense. It's something people naturally like. You don't have to get them addicted. Casual gamblers can make us money as well as big time guys. You don't import anything," Goldy told Lansky while Dutch silently observed.

"Let's not get too goody, goody. Gambling is illegal," Lansky said.

"Yeah, you're right, but again it comes naturally. People will always drink. You can't stop them. But it's not an addiction."

"Dutch and I have been talking about the idea of floating casinos. Boats outside the three-mile international zone. I still got one of Rothstein's freighters. You're right about Prohibition. It's not going to last forever. Got to find lucrative substitutes."

"You're thinking of gambling on the Great Lakes where that boat is now?"

"No, bring it outside New York. You got some boat builders that you work with. I 'd like to have that freighter refigured to become a floating casino. What do you think?"

"I know two brothers who work with me. I can ask," Goldy replied.

"You think that's a good idea?"

"I don't know. It might be a big deal to bring that freighter to the East Coast. Might be simpler to just build a new boat. I'll ask my Irish brothers what they think."

"You get back to Dutch and he'll get back to me," Lansky

signaled to the waiter and pointed to his mouth.

"You like the music?" Goldy asked.

"I hear you're a piano player. When Prohibition ends you can get a job in a place like this?" Lansky laughed and lightly touched Goldy's shoulder.

"I might have to," Goldy laughed.

"My pal Goldy has lots of good ideas. Yeah? We can make good money. You and me and Luciano. Everybody gets a fair share. Right Meyer?"

"Right Dutch. Money for everybody including our friend here Goldy Goldfarb," Lansky said.

"Us Yids need to stay together. Protect each other," Dutch added.

"Except for Arnold Rothstein. Somehow we didn't stand up for him," Lansky's bitterness never dissipated.

"Meyer, Rothstein was a compulsive gambler. He cheated a guy out of $350,000. How could we protect him?" Dutch realized the depth of the chasm.

"Well fellas, it was fun as always. But I got to get home. I live in the boonies in Far Rockaway. I'll talk to the boat builders tomorrow. It's been nice," Goldy stood up.

As he walked out of the speakeasy, he noticed her. He looked and then took a second look. She was with a few young women. They all wore those fashionable flapper dresses. She was smiling and laughing, but more importantly she was holding another woman's hand. That followed with a kiss.

When she noticed him, her heart must have stopped. Their eyes locked. Never too fearful, she dropped the woman's hand and approached him. Playing dumb was not a good strategy.

She had to directly confront him.

"Cousin Goldy," she nervously said. They stood less than a foot apart. The street was noisy so it was necessary to stand in close proximity.

"Bluma. Who expected to see you here?" Goldy cast glances at the woman who held Bluma's hand while he spoke to his cousin.

"I know you can't understand, but I hope we can keep this meeting unspoken," she anxiously told him. She followed his eyes to the dark-haired woman waiting.

Goldy had become a man of the world. Gangsters like Lucky Luciano earned vast amounts of money operating speakeasies for certain specific types of clientele: men who preferred men, women who loved other women, racially mixed couples. The gin was three times the cost of any other speakeasy. Then there was the threat of exposure. He was known to call the police on his own speakeasy to create that scary atmosphere. For many, it was the reason they were attracted to these places.

"Bluma your life belongs to you. I don't have to understand. Right? In America, you can be whoever you want to be," he told her.

She sighed with relief. The waiting lady watched from a distance.

"But, don't bring any of your lady friends back to the hotel. OK?" He was not threatening; however, it was a warning.

"Oh, Cousin Goldy, I appreciate your discretion. I'm not sure anyone else shares your openness."

"It's not my life. I would not want it for any of my daughters. You came from nothing and now everything is so exciting and new. Maybe, this is you trying something new. It's not for me to judge. But others will. I have a hotel to maintain. You understand?"

She reached over and kissed him on the cheek, "I do understand. I will never bring home any friends of mine. I promise. I owe you everything Cousin Goldy. My life in Poland was so suffocating. Freedom is a little frightening. But I understand. My personal life will never cross our business arrangements or hint at any other life style. Please, I have one favor. Stop Esty from forcing me to meet young men. You can see I'm not interested."

"I will try; she is determined to find you a husband and the boys wives. It's her motherly nature. To her it means you're settled."

"I will continue to offer excuses," Bluma looked at her friend now standing within a circle of women.

"Be careful. These speakeasies are all owned by gangsters. That one," he pointed to the one she had just left," is known by its clientele. It gets raided. Cops have to show their not utterly owned by crooks. I don't want to get you out of jail one evening."

"Thanks for the warning. You're the best."

Izzy's bride-to-be came from a family of enterprising new Americans. Sarah was American-born but not her parents. At the Shabbos dinner Esty prepared, they were more accommodating about the forthcoming wedding plans than Goldy had feared. They had relatives and a few friends that must be invited, but their list of guests was less than fifty. If there was a demand, it was that they wanted to plan the event. The goal was not for extravagance but distinctiveness.

Goldy and Esty spent the next days determining what their role was going to be at this wedding. They pledged to Izzy's in-laws to cover half the costs. Everyone agreed to The White Shul for the actual wedding ceremony and the hotel for the reception.

It was only Goldy and Esty on the front porch discussing plans. "Why is it so important that the wedding be different than most weddings? Is this Passover?" Goldy laughed at his joke about how the Jewish holiday of Passover differentiated between the ordinary day and one of the holiday's eight days. During Passover Jews ate only unleavened food, matzo instead of bread.

"I know how we can be different than any of the neighbors. Let's invite Dutch and one of his whores. Then there's Lansky. Does he have a wife or mistress? And for good measure, Lucky Luciano to add an Italian flare. Let's not forget the Weinberg brothers. Oh, how about the bodyguard Bernard. There's Abe Landau," Esty sarcastically said, listing the gangsters in Goldy's circle of workplace colleagues.

"I got to invite Dutch. I'll tell him to bring his wife. He will be flattered that we invite him. And insulted if he wasn't. So we have to sit him at a table with Rivka. They get on well enough. He knows her as the party boat lady. I'm sure he knows she's my sister."

"Go see the new rabbi at The White Shul and make arrangements. Her family are a bunch of those reform Jews.

But everyone knows The White Shul. Your mother would want her grandchildren married among the orthodox. Go see him. Today's a good day. Let's get as much done as possible."

"I don't like Sarah's parents buying them one of those new bungalows by the water on Beach 26th Street. They should spend a few years renting. Taking a one-bedroom apartment in Rivka's building. It's near the beach."

"That's not the point. They want them to own a home. You and I didn't have that kind of money. But it's OK. Let them buy the new couple a home."

"They should struggle a little. It builds character," he sulked in the front porch rocking chair.

Polly looked at him, "Papa mad. Papa mad. Bring Papa his paper. Bring Papa food," the bird screamed.

"I can't stand that bird. Is it really true parrots live fifty years? I don't know. Too scrawny as dinner."

"Polly loves you," Esty scratched the parrot under his chin.

"I'm leaving," he told the bird.

"Papa going. Love Papa," the bird bid farewell.

Goldy walked the half-mile distance to the corner of Dinsmore Avenue and Nameoke Street to where the synagogue stood. He rang the side door bell. A man in a full gray beard answered the door.

"Hello Rabbi. I'm Avraham Goldfarb. I live nearby. My family are members."

"Yes, yes, come in. I remember you from High Holidays. I don't see much of you at morning services. What can I do for you?"

"It's a mitzvah. My eldest and only son Israel is getting married to the daughter of the jeweler in downtown Far Rockaway, the Silversteins."

"Mazel Tov," he slapped Goldy's shoulder, "let's sit. Freidel bring us some tea and a bite to eat."

"I'm a lucky man, Rabbi. The banks are sinking and the stock market tanked. Never kept my money in either one. I can smile because of this simcha."

"Very nice news. And this is a beautiful synagogue, built only a few years ago. I can see with my own eyes how much the local Jews respect the Torah."

"How do you like it here?" Goldy asked.

"I was puzzled at first. I come to The White Shul. It opened as a reform shul eight years ago. Now this year, it's magic and it's orthodox. So I'm here. It's not as if the shul was here for a hundred years like Europe, but overnight everything changes. I don't understand. There's a lot about America I don't understand."

His wife the Rebbetzin entered with a tray of home-made cookies and a pot of steaming tea. On one side of the silver tray was a small glass bowl of sugar cubes.

The Rebbetzin poured out the tea into two china cups. Goldy placed the small sugar cube onto his tongue and let the hot tea dissolve the sugar.

"So tell me Avraham where is your family from?" the rabbi asked as he blew the steam from the tea cup.

"I'm a real American, a Yankee Doodle Dandy. But, I wasn't born on the fourth of July."

The perplexed rabbi asked, "What does that mean?"

"It's a funny American song about being patriotic, that's all.

Americans like to have fun."

"Too much fun and not enough Torah study," the rabbi frowned.

Goldy thought to himself. No wonder young men don't want to just study the Torah. Way too serious.

"Where are you from rabbi?"

"My family is from Breslau. But we are actually Poles. I was born in Germany and my family had permanent resident status. But in current times not being a real German has its disadvantages."

"How did you come here to Far Rockaway?"

"A rabbi friend from Germany is involved with Congregation Shaarey Tefilla here in Far Rockaway."

"The one on Central Avenue near Neilson Avenue?"

"I'm new to the community so I guess you're right. I don't know street addresses."

"All you need to know is where is the ocean. We love the beach. It's what brings most people to Rockaway. You wake up and can smell the salt air. Live close enough and the seagulls are in your backyard. We are a pretty insulated community. We live here to escape the whirlwind city life. It's about big front porches and small bungalows all leading to the ocean."

"Modesty does not permit me to accept women and men wearing those little things at the beach. Men and women cannot swim together. It is not allowed."

Goldy realized that the rabbi was living in the wrong place. It was going to be a slow education before he appreciated Hashem's bounties in the Rockaways. Goldy was not going to be his teacher.

He changed the subject, "I have relatives in Poland. My father is from Bialystok."

"Have you recently been there?" the rabbi asked.

"A few years back. I was able to convince my aunt to allow me to bring some younger members of the family to America. These young folks, they love America. At first, they were frightened. This is not anything like Europe. But they got comfortable. When the time is long enough, they will apply for citizenship."

"This is not like Europe," he added sorrowfully.

"They hate Jews everywhere, Christ-killers. But in America you are safe. Not like Poland where the government sends in the Cossacks. They force the women and children into the synagogue, lock the doors and burn it down. The smell of human flesh burning doesn't disappear."

"I'm afraid you're right. Still, America's mores are too flamboyant, not enough modesty and adherence to religious laws. Life is too loose. Too much freedom."

"My wife is from outside Minsk and my mother from Hungary. They love it in America. Not once did my mother, God rest her soul, want to return to Europe. Nor my wife. This is the safest place in the world for Jews."

"Unless they lose all that made them Jews."

"Wait. I think the longer you stay here; you will come to love life here."

The rabbi managed a smile, "Let's discuss what you need from me."

"My only boy Israel is getting married. We would like you to officiate and have the service in the synagogue. Is that possible?"

"In Europe, we don't perform weddings inside the synagogue. Of course, no funerals. Dead bodies are prohibited. You are not the first to ask about weddings."

"In America, it's not an unreasonable request," Goldy insisted.

"Rabbis perform weddings in the courtyard of the synagogue. This is a beautiful building but there's no adequate outside courtyard."

"I have a solution. There is a kosher hotel not far. It has a beautiful courtyard. That might satisfy your requirements. What do you think?"

"Show me the place," the rabbi said.

The wedding took place in the hotel's courtyard. Bluma organized everything with her helpers, Goldy's younger daughters Hannah and Minnie. The flower arrangements were described by several guests as "simply gorgeous." The fragrances permeated every corner of the courtyard.

The men were separated from the women as was the rules for orthodox services. Sarah's parents had to be persuaded it was only going to last for the service itself. The rabbi was dubious about the hotel kitchen's adherence to kosher dietary laws. He planned on performing his duties and then leaving. Once the rabbi completed his religious duties he left. As his silhouette exited the building, several men appeared and all the tables and chairs were rearranged.

Some people never followed rules. Dutch arrived with his wife Frances. They managed two chairs in a corner far away from the rabbi's disapproving eyes. Goldy saw them and placed his hand to his heart as a gesture of respect. Farthest away from the ceremony sat Meyer Lansky sitting alone in the men's corner. He displayed his knowledge of Hebrew by appropriately responding to the relatively short service. The audience knew it was over once the groom shattered the glass wrapped in a linen napkin.

Meyer waited for some of the crowd to enter the ballroom for the dancing and dinner. He found Goldy bracing his back against a wall as many hands embraced his.

"Nice ceremony, Goldy, it was nice of you to invite me. I got to get back to the city," he handed Goldy a thick envelope. Then nodded his head.

"Izzy thanks you. I'm glad you could join us."

He walked away. At least one person recognized his face. That guest turned completely around and watched as the so-called "Accountant" left the party.

Esty spent time talking to Frances, who with her husband was seated with several relatives. It was the most time the women had ever spent together. If anyone recognized Dutch, they were discrete. In the public's perception of gangsters, Dutch was in the dangerous category while Meyer seemed benign. The wedding guests had no idea what actually went on during the Roaring Twenties. Most of Goldy and Esty's relatives knew about his bootlegging. The new machatunim, in-laws, might have guessed but never asked questions.

Chapter 6

Legs Gets His

A real American, he was a son of the city of Brotherly Love. The grainy black and white photos in the newspaper made him look twenty years older than he was. Dead at 34, just when most men were starting their careers. Jack Legs Diamond seemed invincible. So many had attempted to kill him, Dutch said: "Ain't there anybody that can shoot this guy so he doesn't bounce back." Gentleman Jack erroneously thought he was immune from fatal attacks.

Within an 18-month period, three assassination attempts were made on his life. It was more likely he would land up in jail and not in a cemetery. The brazen attacks accelerated by the end of 1930. He was relaxing at The Hotel Monticello in Manhattan's Westside when gunmen entered the premises and popped five shots into his chest. Miraculously he survived, more arrogant and more convinced of his immortality.

Why was he a target so often? What made the public fall in love with his charms while his fellow gangsters kept conceiving plans to eliminate him? He started as a petty crook just like many others, Dutch, Meyer, Lucky. They rose together in pursuit of easy money. Prohibition was every gangster's invitation to earn fast bucks.

Jack was not a Yankee Doodle Dandy, but a W.W. I deserter. He wasn't going to die for Wilson's War. Fresh from jail, courtesy of the U.S. Army, he went to work for Arnold Rothstein as his bodyguard. Of course, he tragically failed as a protector of The Fixer since Rothstein was unceremoniously shot in a hotel in 1928. Diamond's enemies included many Jewish gangsters. His Irish charm failed to appease them. His mortal sin was greed.

Goldy got a call from his boss to meet. Tensions were high in Manhattan because the bootleggers couldn't sit down together and come up with an agreement. If only Rothstein had lived to mediate. Schultz refused to listen to anyone and opened his second office in Harlem.

Before Goldy was seated, Dutch started with a tantrum. It wasn't because of his drinking too much. Dutch was in one of his famous bad moods.

"That Irish dog, why can't someone kill him already. He wants what belongs to me."

Goldy tried to sound reasonable, "There's room for both of you."

"Yeah, if only he would stay in his place. We got the best booze of anyone. All because of you and that freighter. I bet we could increase our territory if we could get our hands on Rothstein's other boat."

"I'm not taking over that freighter in the Great Lakes. Let's keep control in New York. I'm not putting the boat or me or you in danger by pushing ourselves on the Chicago and Detroit gangs. Simply suicidal. OK? Have we had this conversation too many times?" Goldy was tired of repeating himself.

Dutch finished his glass of whiskey, "OK."

"I know you harbor bad feelings about Joey Noe's death. I know. I respect that. Friends are all we have. Right?" Goldy's tone was soft and calming.

"I get it. But Diamond, he wants our territory, slimy dog. Gentleman Jack, what horseshit."

"My police informants tell me that Diamond is being investigated by G-men. Have patience and let the police lock him up."

"Goldy, I'm sure we're all being investigated."

"No, this is more concrete. They are watching him. He has gotten under the skin of not only you, but the government. They hate how the newspapers make him out to be a Prince Charming. They want him. Let them do their work. If he's in jail, then you have a better opportunity to take over his territory."

"Always trying to be sensible. That's you Goldy. That's how you make friends with our competitors. And you have patience. I don't have any."

"I'm an older guy. I have lived longer than you. If you want to obtain old age have patience."

"Can you picture me with white hair stumbling down the street?"

"Gang war is bad for business. That makes the G-men crazy seeing blood in the streets. Some poor innocent mother walking her baby carriage in the street. They both get shot and killed, accidentally. The police are hearing from the politicians, the religious leaders. Get those criminals. Then business suffers. You always have to consider the consequences."

"Meyer wants to talk about something. He asked that you be present. What does he want?"

"I don't know. Got something for me to eat?" Goldy smiled at his boss.

Dutch sat back in his chair. "Give the man a steak and where's the best whiskey?"

While the men were eating, Meyer walked into the place. Abe Landau got him a chair. They all shook hands.

"Essen fellows. What I have to say can wait," Meyer said.

A waiter brought Meyer a steak and a glass of whiskey. He placed the bottle on the table.

"I have news that will interest you Goldy, and you Dutch," he slowly sipped his whiskey.

"What's going on?" Dutch asked.

"Have you ever heard of Las Vegas?" Meyer posed the question.

"What is it?" Dutch shook his head.

"You heard of Nevada?" Meyer kept raising questions enjoying this playful banter.

Dutch was a man of limited patience, "Get to the point. Enough of these games."

"Nevada in the middle of God's tuchus, desert, dry place. Las Vegas is some town not too far from Los Angeles. The state legislature legalized gambling. The state is broke so they're looking for revenue. Legal gambling."

"That's interesting," Goldy said as he paused to finish his whiskey.

"Better than boats," Dutch replied.

"Safer, not having to navigate more than three miles out to sea. Build casinos in the desert. How will we get people to come," Goldy asked them?

"We need to check it out. You're the one," Meyer pointed to Goldy, "who's always talking about after Prohibition. This is it."

"Maybe," Goldy was nodding his head.

"What's wrong with the numbers rackets we already got going? Why start something new in a place I never heard of. Some desert." Dutch needed convincing.

Meyer looked at Goldy, "I know you see possibilities."

"Maybe. This is certainly an interesting development. Might make other states consider it since they all have no money," Goldy continued shaking his head.

"My guy Ben sees all kinds of possibilities in this desert. Lucky also likes the idea. Why fight cops and G-men, open seas and endless bribes. More money for us. No need to pay off the politicians. The state of Nevada did it all for us."

"You think people will travel by car into the desert to gamble?" Goldy was interested if not convinced.

"Benny thinks they will. He's even talking about putting in a small airport. Can you imagine an airport in the middle of the desert? Like from the Bible. The Jews wandering in the desert for forty years."

"And instead of the Ten Commandments they get a poker game," Goldy laughed with Meyer and even Dutch joined the laughter.

"So what are you waiting for?" Dutch asked.

"If it's going to be legal it takes time to prepare legislation and get regulations. The Nevada government sees this as an investment in its future so they're inclined to act carefully," Meyer replied.

"What does the Nevada government expect?"

"Benny says we need glamour. A bright, beautiful hotel with swimming pools and gorgeous women. Dancing and dining. It's got to be worth the car trip from Los Angeles. It needs movie stars," Meyer's arms were moving excitedly.

"I see it. Yes, I do, something really different in a place where you can buy land for pennies," Goldy offered his enthusiasm.

"We got numbers right here in Harlem. Why the hell build some eyesore in the middle of the desert," Dutch needed more convincing.

It was news on the radio. Again, an attempt was made. They heard it together and she was distraught. Not for one moment had she any sympathies for his life, but he was a household name. Jack Legs Diamond was shot three times while a guest at the Aratoga Inn near Cairo, New York.

"Listen, it's Diamond again," Esty told her husband, "again."

"He doesn't die," Goldy laughed while scratching the top of Ruby's head. The good girl was slowing down, almost thirteen years old. She pressed her graying snout into his open hand.

"He's evil that's why he doesn't die. Pure evil is that Diamond."

"No, no, not so harsh. He's part of a competitive system. They all have to carve out their territories like wolves."

"No comparison, wolves are much better animals. Diamond is just dangerous. He's going to retaliate against someone. I worry it's Dutch and by extension you. I'm too young to be a widow."

"You worry too much. Diamond doesn't know who I am."

"You don't know that, but it could be that you're in the same room as Dutch. Boom, boom, boom, gunfire everywhere. You're dead."

"I never have been around Diamond. We have never actually been introduced. Hirsh and I tracked him on that streamliner to Europe. If he saw me, he saw lots of people. You worry for nothing. I got my territory with the freighter. No one is going to highjack me on the ocean."

"Someone should finish him off already. He's not worthy to be an American. A first-rate traitor to this country. Wouldn't even serve in the Army during the Great War. Who deserts? Cowards. That's the best description of his soul."

"He's a handsome brute with more lives than any of our cats."

No one was around the house. Silvie was in Baltimore waiting to study medicine at Johns Hopkins Medical School. It was one of the first to admit women and a pioneer in taking medicine into the scientific rigors of the twentieth century. Izzy and his new bride were at the movie house transforming it from a silent movie theater into the modern age of talkies. Hannah and Minnie had jobs at the hotel. Minnie worked in the kitchen under the strict hand of chief cook Mrs. O'Brien. Hannah helped in housekeeping. Gladdy was in school. Her mother hoped that she would go to college like her older sister and cousin Miriam, Rivka's daughter. Little Gladdy told everyone that she wanted to be a piano player like her Papa. Her mother was steering her into a career as a music teacher.

The phone rang and Goldy went to answer with Ruby following closely behind.

"It's Dutch. I need you. How fast can you get here?"

"Are you in Harlem at your favorite spot?"

"I am. Get here as quickly as possible," the phone went dead.

"What?" Esty asked with that wrinkly worried face.

"I'm going to Harlem to see Dutch."

"You be careful because that's how things end. You go to that miserable speakeasy and Diamond's guys drive by with machine guns and kill you all."

"Don't be so dramatic. I'll be back soon," he kissed his wife on the forehead. "Keep dinner for me."

Goldy's Buick got him from Far Rockaway as fast as any car on the road. More stylish than the Fords of the day. In those early days of the Great Depression, times were brutal for car manufacturers. In 1931, Goldy bought the car for a great price. It was such a great deal that he bought one for Izzy.

Waiting for him at the table was Dutch and two of his most loyal henchmen, the Weinberg Brothers.

"Sit," Dutch ordered, "get the man a steak and some whiskey."

"You heard about Diamond that son-of-bitch seems again to outfox the gravediggers," Dutch said while shaking his head.

"Well, he's a man with nine lives," Goldy said.

He pointed to the brothers, "Leave us alone."

Goldy and Dutch were alone at the table. Most of the men were at the bar drinking.

"I want you to go to upstate and find out what happened to Legs. He couldn't have survived that attack. I want you to find out more. It's springtime up there. Should be very pleasant. Take the wife. I want you to look like some ordinary guests."

"You still have me chasing Diamond?"

"Yeah, exactly. How is it they missed again another escape from the undertaker. Who helped him?"

"You should leave it all alone. He was arrested by the police days before he was shot. If he recovers he will face a trial. Let the cops do the dirty work."

"I don't trust cops. They're all crooks. Easy to bribe. No guarantee he 'll go to jail."

"He was arrested for kidnapping and assaulting that truck driver. People saw it. There are witnesses," Goldy stressed the simplicity of the case.

"They released him the next day from the county jail. He paid a $25,000 bond. He's got lawyers. Find out whatever you can. Go to this Cairo. Go and investigate. This could be your new business."

"You mean after Prohibition."

"It's that or casinos in the ocean. Maybe casinos in the desert. Find out for me who was responsible for shooting him."

"OK, it's the end of April. I could take my wife for a vacation. She likes the mountains. I love the ocean. We could just behave like vacationers."

"You might find a nice house there."

"I'm gathering information for you. You can't expect me to kill him or set him up."

"Of course not, Goldy you're not a killer. You're the only honest man I know. I trust you to find out information. No one has to know what you're doing for me. You see I leave the Weinberg Brothers over there. This is between you and me. Just us two."

"As I recall, several people knew I was asking questions about Rothstein's death."

"This is going to be more hush, hush. This bastard is after my business. You know that. No matter what the papers say, he is no good. And he keeps getting shot and yet he lives."

"Off I go to Cairo."

"I don't know where that is somewhere in the Catskills. He was taken to a hospital in Albany. Check that out. Stay as long as it takes on my dime. Who tried to kill him and who saved him? Why is he still alive? Talk to the doctors and the hotel staff. I trust you to do a good job."

"OK, I'll leave tomorrow. The freighter is in good hands with my Irish guys. The whiskey is always first-rate."

"The state police picked up Diamond for beating the shit out of that trucker last year. But he might never see the inside of a jail. If you hear anything about that let me know. There are telephones somewhere up there. Keep in touch."

"I'll see what I can find," Goldy stuck his fork into the steak and cut himself a fine slice.

"I'm depending on you," Dutch swallowed the entire contents of his glass in one gulp.

•••

It was a holiday for two, Goldy and Esty in the Catskills. A map provided the route and the Buick the transportation to find out what happened to Legs Diamond. The Irishman's problem was that he was going into businesses where other men had already established their territory. He and his brother Eddie were interlopers. It started with Rothstein and the heroin. Narcotics was lucrative, but it was not good enough. It was the 1920's and Prohibition was the law of the land. So Diamond had to find a way into the bootlegging business. Already the territories were staked out. Dutch Schultz was not a tolerant man.

From the start, the man made bad decisions. Dollar signs filled his eyes and somehow his brain failed to function. His brilliant idea was to hijack trucks belonging to other bootleggers and attempt to sell back the product for a profit. It was a messy and bloody example of extortion. His marks were two Irishmen, Owen "The Killer" Madden and Big Bill Dwyer. The plans disintegrated when Diamond realized these two rivals were supported by a much bigger syndicate run by Schultz, Lansky and Luciano.

Diamond found security and acceptance by becoming a bodyguard. It started with the Jewish gangster Augie Orgen (Orenstein). He gave Diamond formal entrance into the bootlegging game. Diamond graduated to become Arnold Rothstein's bodyguard and this allowed his rising importance in bootlegging. That put him directly challenging Dutch Shultz, a man who never forgave even the slightest insult. The best that happened to Diamond was the murder of Orgen in 1925. They were walking together along a street in the Lower East

Side when Orgen was fatally shot in the head. Diamond was shot twice in the right side. He not only recovered but took over Orgen's bootlegging operations.

Goldy told his wife to pack for a vacation. It was a holiday just for the two of them. Bluma and Rivka agreed to take care of the girls. Esty was hard to convince that the trip to Greene County, New York was a vacation. She was suspicious from the start.

"Be honest, Mr. Mensch, tell me why we're going. No lies," she blinked her eyes several times in an awkward display of co-quettishness.

"Diamond is in the hospital after someone shot him and Governor Roosevelt has declared war on bootleggers. Dutch wants as much information as possible about what's going to happen to his arch enemy."

"I don't know why women find that Legs Diamond so at-tractive. He's got a receding hairline. He's short and skinny. Looks like he had a mother that never fed him."

"Ah, my dear. You have led a settled life. He wears expen-sive suits and spends money as if it would go on forever. He peels off the bills, one by one, from a thick wad in his pocket. You look too critically."

"Are we going to look for a place in the country for us and the children?" she asked.

"Yes, there's actually a property available that I want us to look at. It's a bungalow colony. There are eight little cabins all consisting of one room and a bathroom. A main house is nearby where we can serve meals and party. It's in Sullivan

County not Greene."

"OK, are we going to the Aratoga Inn?"

"No, it's like a road house. We deserve something nicer. I found a cute inn. I'll drop you off. I'm heading to Albany to the hospital to find out about Diamond's condition. I'm also going to check out the County Courthouse. Diamond was arrested for beating up a guy, Grover Parks, days before he was shot."

"Don't get killed. Don't forget you're Mr. Mensch," Esty told him as the bellhop took their bags from the car's trunk.

Goldy decided it would preserve time if he went to the Court House before the hospital. The place was packed with criminals and lawyers, plus a few judges. Ordinarily, these were cheap people to pay off. Just a few hundred dollars satisfied their dreams of wealth.

He found what appeared to be an official clerk of some kind. He wore a pin with his name on it.

"Hey," Goldy approached him. He had folded several twenty-dollar bills in his coat pocket.

"Yes," the man's spectacles balanced precariously on his nose. A big sneeze and they might shatter on the marble floor.

"I hear big news here in Cairo. Big time gangster comes to town. Flashing some big bucks. What are people saying," he slid a folded twenty-dollar bill towards the man.

The clerk looked at the single note and wrinkled his nose. Goldy took out two more twenties and the man's eyebrows relaxed.

"You mean Legs Diamond?" he asked.

"That's the crook."

"You a newspaper guy or what?"

"I'm a free-lancer. Could be the story of my life. Get me a by-line. I'm happy to share my happiness," he offered the clerk a fifty-dollar bill.

"That poor guy Parks just a trucker doing his business hauling hard cider. That Diamond fellow, nasty piece of work, beats the living daylights out of him. Lucky, he's still alive."

"Is he going to testify against Diamond?"

"He's not afraid. But with money you can buy anything. Diamond got himself the best lawyers around. If anyone can get him free it will be these guys. Oh yes. I wouldn't bet money on Diamond ever seeing the inside of a jail cell. Oh, no. These lawyers are slick."

"You think the attempted murder of Diamond is related to Parks?" Goldy playing newsman asked.

"No, but Diamond is a marked man. I know the stories how he's survived a dozen attacks. Someone will get lucky. It probably won't be the state troopers who get him, but one of his own kind, gangsters. Just because they throw a little money around doesn't mean these guys are Robin Hoods."

"When will the trial resume?"

"Can't happen until he's better. I hear he bought a house in Cairo. Throwing his money around. Got the ladies practically dying to see him. Shopkeepers love him. Like your type, reporters and all kinds of others in town. This was a dead place until Diamond came to town. Lots of people grateful."

"Not you. You see things differently."

"No matter how much you dress him up. That Mick is a dangerous guy. You should be careful."

"I thank you my friend. You know the address of his place here in Cairo?"

The man wrote an address on a piece of paper.

•••

Goldy drove to the capital of New York where Governor Roosevelt called home, Albany. The hospital was buzzing with excitement. The most entertaining events ever seen in this provincial capital were happening. He overheard a hospital employee mention where Diamond was resting after the attack. The front entrance was filled with speculators. Goldy found a side door and walked up the empty stairs to the second floor. He was out on bail, but state troopers surrounded the room.

He found a lounge and recognized Diamond's wife sitting with a few other people. He walked in the opposite direction. A nurse was just lighting up her cigarette. Goldy lit the match and she breathed in the tobacco.

"Exciting. Right?" he asked her.

"You can't imagine. Here in Albany Hospital a real live gangster. I mean Legs Diamond. My mother wants his autograph."

"He seems like a very lucky guy. Turn around and someone's trying to kill him. They don't miss, but he's still alive. Amazing," Goldy told her.

"What are you? A reporter?"

"Just call me Mr. Mensch."

"That a Jew name? You don't look like a Yid."

"It's the blue eyes," Goldy pointed to his eyes.

"I guess," she inhaled and let the smoke slowly escape.

"Did you hear what happened?" Goldy asked.

"Crazy some guys shot him right outside where he was staying."

"Aratoga Inn, kind of a dump in Cairo?"

"Yeah, so they say. He was shot three times as he was walking out the front door," she cracked a loud noise imitating the sound of gunfire.

"How did he get here?"

"A local guy just saw him lying in blood. Put bandages on the wounds and drove him here. It's a ride to here. He must be made of metal cause he lost quite a bit of blood."

"Just can't die. It's going to be his epithet."

"Yeah," she spoke as the smoke rings circled her oval face.

"Going back on trial once he recovers."

"I don't know. I hope I can get his autograph," she snuffed out the cigarette in a nearby ashtray. Then she walked towards Diamond's door.

Goldy drove back to Cairo where he had left Esty. On a hunch, he decided to stop by Diamond's house. From the distance, he saw state troopers hauling boxes from the house. Might they be doing something similar at that road house. Goldy turned the car around and headed for the Inn. Again, the state police cars surrounded the Inn. A group of them were removing boxes from the Inn. The objects looked heavy.

Without fear, Goldy walked closer to the Inn.

"I was going to stay here," Goldy pointed to the front door.

"Can't," said an officer with a couple of stripes on his sleeve.

"What's happening?" Goldy played innocent, turning his body in a half-circle to observe a group of officers.

"Jack Legs Diamond was shot right there," he pointed to a bloody spot in front of the Inn.

"Is he dead?"

"No, bastard's still breathing."

"Are you guys looking for something?" he displayed his most angelic look.

"We found lots of money and barrels of booze. Governor Roosevelt will not be intimidated. Can't have these gangsters destroying our communities," he indignantly responded.

"Yes, I agree get rid of the booze," Goldy smilingly returned to his car. Along the way back to Esty, he found a phone to call Dutch.

"Unbelievable," Dutch's first words after he heard the news.

"I'll return in two days. I'm still on vacation. Remember?"

"OK, take your time," the boss replied.

"I'll keep looking around in case there's something interesting to report. He's not dead yet. Maybe someone will get a better shot at him."

"While you're up there see if he gets discharged from the hospital."

The impossible actually happened. Diamond was dead. Goldy didn't have to call Dutch the news was on the radio. Finally, the last of his nine lives came up empty. So who killed Jack Diamond? His enemy lists were long in length with some people holding grudges for years. He was born John Moron, and died on December 18, 1931. His actual death was less dramatic than some of the attempts on his life.

There were two competing theories about the gangster's demise. Many felt that Dutch had finally brought down his adversary. This was a man, who irritated him for years. Clearly, Dutch benefited from the murder. Now that bootleg business belonged to him without any competitors. And Dutch, a man with a long memory, still pined for Joey Noes.

The majority opinion was that Albany politicians, aided by local police, had ordered his murder. They, unlike many residents, were opposed to Diamond's expansion. The local political boss, Dan O'Connell wanted to put an end to the New York City gangster crowd meddling with local bootleggers. They had a business to preserve.

Jack Legs Diamond had just been acquitted of serious crimes of bootlegging and kidnapping on December 17 in a Troy, New York courthouse. Try as hard as they could, the authorities never convinced a jury of his peers that he was guilty of kidnapping and bootlegging. He was starting to really irritate the locals. That very evening, after the acquittal, Jack was partying with friends until the wee hours of the morning. He left his mistress, Marion "Kiki" Roberts, at 4:30 am. So drunk, he found it difficult to find his own room. But he managed to pass out on his bed at the Kenmore Hotel. Sometime before morning, two gunmen found him loudly snoring. They pumped three bullets into the back of his head.

The news spread rapidly across the country. Distraught politicians breathed easily, agreeing this was the best possible conclusion to Diamond's business activities. Lansky had no words. He remained neutral. Dutch ordered up a party with champagne from France.

The magical spell was over. Diamond was dead.

Chapter 7
Election of 1932

Two men could not be more different. Both were desirous of one of the greatest treasures on earth. New Yorkers, they were in these most incredibly difficult times. Men from the opposite ends of the railroad tracks. They promised to change the lives of ordinary people although neither one was in the least bit ordinary.

Frank Delano Roosevelt and Alfred Smith became political rivals. Once allies, they hungered for the presidency of the United States. Smith was crushed by his run in 1928 by Herbert Hoover. Being a Catholic was one disadvantage he was never able to shake. The spring months brought Democratic primaries across the country. The Convention was held in the summer in Chicago, a hotspot of the bootlegging business.

Neither Smith nor Roosevelt favored Prohibition. The bootleggers were sensing the end of a dynasty and a significant source of revenue. The world was about to change in many ways. Most saw the end was in sight. The moralists were giving way to the practical politicians. Prohibition had not changed people's ways. No one gave up the drink. What was lost was government revenues and jobs.

Roosevelt and Smith promised the end of Prohibition. They

campaigned on that promise. In 1932, the fear of more job losses and declining revenues to support broad government policies fed the rising support to end Prohibition.

The year 1932 was well remembered by the Goldfarb family. Not only were both of the major presidential candidates declaring an end to Prohibition, Silvie was off to medical school in Baltimore. She wanted to go to Johns Hopkins because it was renowned for its scientific approach to medicine, and more importantly, it was one of the few to admit women.

Esty took it as a sign from God that Johns Hopkins Medical School was in Baltimore. Extremely anxious about allowing any of her children to leave and relocate to another city, Esty was comforted by the fact that Goldy's family had strong roots in Baltimore.

Silvie was not going to live in some strange dormitory but with relatives. His cousins Blanche and Ike would give her their spare bedroom. They didn't need it any longer because the last of their children had married and moved out. No one left Baltimore. It was viewed as a good place to live as a Jew.

The history of Johns Hopkins Medical School and women intrigued Silvie. It was truly fascinating and like much of the ways of the world was dictated by money. It was founded at the turn of the last century in 1893. And it started with admitting women. Why was that when almost all others were strictly limited to men only?

It began with a group of wealthy men who meant to leave a legacy behind. In Europe, especially in Germany, medical schools became citadels of knowledge and research. These

Americans wanted to import that educational orientation to America. Their new medical school would be just like the Europeans. But along the way, the money was never realized. It was bad investments and poor financial management. So they had an idea for a medical school but no money.

Along comes a group of wealthy women. They offer to raise $500,000 to open Johns Hopkins. The proviso was that the medical school admit women. So the first class admitted three women. This then began the tradition of admitting women when most medical schools refused.

Silvie loved that story. Esty and Goldy loved the fact that it was located in Baltimore. Goldy's family was pleased to have Silvie in their household. It was nice to have another girl. After all, Goldy had gotten Ike his job at the docks.

For bootleggers, 1932 was the kiss of death for an industry that had supported thousands of workers and made some of them wealthy Americans. What were bootleggers going to do? Being engaged in local politics was one avenue. Dutch's operation always included more than bootlegging. There was the gambling, another sin that was not going to disappear because the cops declared it illegal. Dutch called a meeting to discuss the future.

Goldy drove to Manhattan to meet Dutch and associates. The deepening financial crisis gripping across the nation had little impact on bootlegging, gambling or prostitution. Men always found money for life's sins.

"Goldy, you know your local politicians, the guys in Rockaway?" Dutch asked.

"I do. I pay my dues to the politicians. And they greedily

take my dollars."

"We got to do something. G-men and government commissions. It's people who hate immigrants that's what these investigations are all about. They're picking on us. Jews and Italians, the Irish. It's us they're after. Those Bible-thumpers in the boonies what do they know about the good life."

"There are no good options. It's the end of Tammany Hall. These reformers are not going to be bribed."

"We got to try and protect Tammany Hall. The cops and the judges are in our back pockets. We lose them, the guys on the bottom will be arrested. Too many arrests and business suffers. It's not only the booze. We got judges and prosecutors all on the take. The prostitution game is very lucrative if not for you and me then Luciano."

"I understand, but I'm not sure we can do anything about it," Goldy tried to explain.

"Roosevelt is a dangerous guy. He's after all of us."

"Al Smith is not going to be our champion. We got to look beyond Prohibition and let Tammany Hall sink of its own greed."

"I'll go see the guys I know on the take. I'll let you know what I find," Goldy took his marching orders.

The local Democratic Club was located on a side street off the main drag in Far Rockaway. Someone was always there listening to complaints. It was the place for local businesses to leave off their contributions to Tammany Hall's well-being.

"Benny," Goldy announced himself.

"Sit, sit, my friend," the man offered an uncomfortable

metal chair.

Goldy sat down and put an envelope in front of the man.

"A drink Goldy?" a quiet man in the corner brought over two glasses and a bottle of whiskey. It was Goldy's product.

"What is happening with the big guys in the city. Papers say it's the end for Tammany Hall. What do you know?"

"It's that Seabury Commission. You read about it. That bastard is after us. Governor Roosevelt, rich son-of-a-bitch, what does he know about us poor schnooks."

"The number of friends is fast disappearing. Al Smith is no friend. We got these elections coming up. Where's our protection? We've been good to you."

"I know, I know," he gently tapped Goldy's arm.

"There's pressure on Mayor Walker. That little Italian La-Guardia he's trouble."

"It's Roosevelt and that Commission," Benny had his own enemies list.

"That was a whole different racket that wasn't part of anything I did."

"Well it started with the murder of that Vivian Gordon. She was killed and somehow that started the investigation," Benny explained.

"We talking about the "frame-ups" with unlucky girls who went to hotel rooms. They were innocent not knowing anything. Cops raid the rooms. Accuse them of prostitution and extort money to not make the arrest? Is that not a piss poor way to make money? Taking advantage of innocent women. You guys never had any shame."

"Don't be such a moralizer Goldy. Money is money. Well

that's where it started, but Seabury wasn't satisfied. No, no, he wanted guys higher up the economic ladder. He wanted the Judges and even the District Attorney's office. It's a mess."

"If you lose the judges and the prosecutors, what good are you guys. We've been paying for years. Now what?" Goldy demanded an answer.

"We're up shit's creek. Prohibition is gone for sure. The extortion rackets are gone. It's a new world my friend," Benny said.

"This is the last of my envelopes. Tammany Hall is dead. We're all on our own."

"Now Goldy, don't say that. We've been friends for years. Remember there's also speeding along permits and squashing tickets of all kinds. We're still here," he pleaded.

"No Benny, it's all coming tumbling down."

"Goldy, you still need our protection. It's not all gone. Even if Prohibition ends, you guys are in all kinds of businesses. You still need us."

"You guys had a good run. Nothing happened without a schmeer here and a schmeer there. Eventually, everything ends."

"You stay in New York; you'll still need us. We'll be here forever. Nothing gets done in this city without Tammany Hall."

"Bye Benny. I know where to vote."

Not that it was a carefully developed business plan, but Izzy's movie house was a huge hit. It made more money for the family than any other venture. It was the times. If people needed escape from life's miseries what better entertainment than a movie.

Goldy's sister Chayna 's husband Irving was a screen writer. He wasn't famous, just had a contract with a major studio. He churned out "B" movies by the dozens. Once Izzy had embarked on his new business, he kept in regular contact with his Uncle Irving.

Goldy and Esty took all the teenagers to the movies. Izzy was the manager and supervisor. His wife Sarah worked the concession stand. Every day the place was packed. Goldy was so proud of his son. Although he enjoyed a good movie now and then, he went to admire his son's business acumen.

"Papa," Izzy said, "I spoke to Uncle Irving. He wants us to go to Los Angeles."

"I think that's a great idea."

"There's a new movie coming out. I'm getting first crack at a screening. Uncle Irving has been speaking to the studio. And we're not only getting to show it first. But. And this is the best part. The stars of the movie are going to come to our movie house."

"Wow. That's wonderful. What's the movie?"

"It's *Scarface; The Shame of the Nation*, Papa."

Silence prevailed.

"Is that OK?" Izzy asked unsure of his father's reaction.

"Well," Goldy finally said without a smile.

"Uncle Irving knows you're a bootlegger. And of course he saw Dutch Schultz and Meyer Lansky at my wedding."

"Who's the stars?"

"The movie stars Paul Muni, Ann Dvorak and George Raft. Raft's got that great gangster look. Uncle Irving says he can get at least one or two to come to Far Rockaway to our movie house. Can you imagine? We can have our own parade on Central Avenue."

"We can put them up in our hotel. Got a great view of the ocean and with the new Boardwalk the city's building. Nice attraction."

"So it's OK with you?"

"Do I look like a gangster?" the father asked the son.

"No, Papa you look like a regular guy. You don't even wear a fedora."

"You done real good, my boy. I am very proud of you. This will last long after the illegal booze is just a memory."

"I'm not a fool Papa. If not for your bootlegging none of this would be possible."

"Think of it as your stepping stone. We always knew Prohibition wasn't going to last forever. I'm surprised it lasted this long. I'm just pleased I was able to take the money and put it to good use."

"And you helped out other relatives. We all got these businesses. Booze made it happen. We are all grateful to you Papa. You didn't waste the money. Didn't gamble it away. Always thinking of the family."

"You can put that on my grave stone," Goldy laughed.

"You're going to be an old man when you die with lots of grandchildren."

"Izzy my boy, from your lips to God's ear."

People were fearful. Bank panics had happened in the past. This was much more frightening. It seemed as if the world was coming apart by the seams. It was the whole world. There was no place to escape. Among the regular working folks, job losses were understandable, but not to these extremes. The American Dream built on hope was fading. Not yet dead.

Politicians intended to take advantage of the fear. President Herbert Hoover had no clue about the depth of the despair. War veterans from the Great War were homeless and hungry. They camped in front of the White House and demanded their Bonuses.

The American heartland was suffering. Farms were taken over by heartless bankers. Babies were starving. Breadlines were common. Who was going to save the people?

The summer of 1932, the national political parties held their conventions. Hoover was virtually unchallenged for the Republican nomination. Al Smith and Franklin Roosevelt had to wait in Chicago over the course of four ballots before a winner was declared. Democrats across the country rallied around Roosevelt.

Other politicians were seeking the trust of the American people. Foremost among the outsiders was Norman Thomas, the Socialist. Political philosophies on the left and the right hoped to gain popularity. The Communist William Foster garnered hundreds of thousands of votes. Less than Thomas or any of the major candidates. Fringe candidates included men running on the Prohibition Party, Liberty Party and Socialist Labor Party.

Only Hoover and the Republicans thought nothing was about to change. Although Al Capone was locked up in Atlanta on federal tax evasion charges, gangsters were still contributing to the General National Product. But their lives were caught in a national realignment. Booze was gone. What was going to replace it?

Goldy intently listened to the radio as the announcers were discussing the balloting at the Democratic National Convention. It was in his best interest to support President Hoover. He was the only candidate in favor of keeping Prohibition. However, Goldy was a patriot. Roosevelt or Smith were the only two candidates capable of leading the country out of this economic disaster.

Esty joined him on the front porch. Polly announced her arrival.

"Mama here, Mama here. Bad dog. Bad dog." The parrot screeched. Ruby Two was not as forgiving as her predecessor. The big German Shepherd growled at the bird.

She sat down next to her husband while the dog stretched out across their feet.

"I'm certainly glad you never invested in the Stock Market or put our money in banks," she said.

"Things will change. Roosevelt is bad for my business but not for the country."

"If Smith or Roosevelt win and Prohibition is gone what will Dutch have you do?"

"I don't know. He knows nothing about legitimate business. His whole life is about illegal activities."

"But you. Will he free you from his gang? What else do you know except smuggling booze?"

"There are certainly many more illegal activities that Dutch can pursue."

"I'm worried about you. I know he's involved with the numbers racket. I can't understand anyone wanting to put money down on just numbers. I can see betting on horses or playing poker. Numbers, pick a number. Silly."

"I don't see a role for me in the numbers game. But, I'm not sure how I can free myself from him and his other activities."

Daughter Hannah joined them. She was returning from her part-time job at the hotel.

"What's going on my little Hannah?" her father teased.

"Oh Papa, I'm not little anymore."

Esty kissed her on the cheek, "No my Hannah you are getting bigger. Finishing high school, what's next?"

"I want to go to beauty school. I want to cut hair."

"Oh, that's a nice job. Who told you about it?" her father asked.

"Billie, that's what we call her. She doesn't like Bluma. Too old-fashioned sounding. I like the name Billie."

"I like it. Where is beauty school?"

"There's one nearby. I have to take the subway to Brooklyn. I don't go every day."

"Nice, very nice. What do you think Esty? Our daughter a hairdresser, nice."

"Billie said that when I finish, she's going to make a space for me in the hotel. Lady guests after the beach visit the beauty shop. I can wash ladies' hair and cut it. Style it. What do you think?"

"Another business in the hotel. Yes, I like it. Your own business, a beauty shop. What do you think Mama? Good idea?"

"Sounds very good. It was Bluma's idea?"

"Yes. Since I always liked to play with hair, cut it and wash it. I use my left hand as well as my right hand. She said I had the best hands. I can use scissors with either hand."

"Perfect, Hannah my lovely, you can be a hairdresser. I'll talk to Billie," he laughed at the name.

"When does beauty school start?" Esty asked.

"In two weeks."

"Are you enrolled?" her mother inquired.

"No, I wanted your approval. I have money from working at the hotel. I can actually pay for it myself."

"No, no. I will give you the money. Save your money. Buy new clothes," her father told her.

Polly saw her first, "Tanta Rivka coming. Hello, hello Tanta Rivka," the bird screamed out her name.

"How's my favorite bird? "she nuzzled the parrot. Nose to nose they were. Out of her pocket, Rivka gave Polly a cracker.

"He's greedy," Goldy warned.

"Good girl," Rivka gave the parrot a second cracker.

"You know that the parrot is a boy," Goldy told his sister.

"I know but Polly is the name. Nu, what's going on with you folks?"

"I'm going to beauty school," Hannah announced.

"That's wonderful," she tapped the teenager on the shoulder.

"I got to go," Hannah saw a friend.

"Hannah go, Hannah go, don't play in the street," Polly told everyone.

"Listening to the convention? No matter which of these guys wins you are out of bootlegging. What's a fellow to do?" Rivka teased her brother.

"I need a new occupation," he suggested.

"I know just the one," his sister told them.

"Nu, what should I do?"

"Become a Private Investigator, a PI, just like in the movies, Goldy Goldfarb. He can get results. Didn't you always do the snooping for Dutch?"

"I like that," Esty smiled at her husband.

"I'll have to change my name. Wouldn't want too many of my old pals to know I'm in the investigating game. I'm sure they might find that suspicious."

"What's going to be your new name?" Rivka asked.

"Gilbert, Avraham Gilbert," he said.

"Why Gilbert?" Esty asked.

"I love Gilbert and Sullivan operas."

"Great. I could be Sullivan. Rebecca Sullivan. I got a spare studio apartment in my building. It can be your new office. I'll get a guy to paint the name on the door," she smiled.

They all laughed. Goldy looked at his sister, "You're not kidding?"

"No, I can't be schlepping the fishing equipment forever. And you do know how to get information. I can take the photographs. I know how to use a camera."

As they were chatting, Polly saw a visitor, "Moishe here, Moishe here. Polly want a cracker Moishe."

Rivka's son the pharmacist arrived. He always carried at least two crackers for Polly.

"Sweet Polly," he gave the parrot one cracker, which was consumed quickly.

"Give her the other," his mother said.

He obeyed, "Here Polly." He rubbed the top of the bird's head.

"I was listening to the convention. What am I going to do with all the booze in the basement? Prohibition is dead," Moishe said.

"We could have a fire sale," Goldy offered the suggestion with a smirk of a smile.

"I'm serious. You know if Smith or Roosevelt are the nominees, Prohibition is gone. Do we have to depend on Do-Nothing Herbert Hoover to save us?"

"So nu, what's your idea?"

"I know you don't like this," Moishe was starting to speak when Goldy put up his hand.

"Nothing doing. I know what you're going to say. No way." Goldy stomped his foot on the wooden plank.

"I sell morphine, legally. How much of a stretch?"

"No drugs. Luciano, he's big in this narcotics trade with his Sicilian brethren. Not us. You only dispense what's legal. I hear you're selling drugs illegally Moishe, I burn down the store. And I'm not kidding."

"OK, just thinking of you and the family. I'm sure Dutch has ideas. He must have other businesses," Moishe and Polly went nose-to-nose.

"Your uncle and I were talking about what's next," his mother said.

"What's next?"

"We're going into the PI business. Gilbert and Sullivan, Private Investigators."

"You're kidding? Right?"

"Who knows. Your uncle would like to get away from his overseer."

"What are you going to do?" the nephew was concerned.

"Well, Dutch has two other businesses, which I don't like. Numbers rackets isn't my kind of game. Then there's extorting money from restaurant owners for protection and workers for protection. Times are tough. Every restaurant needs money to keep afloat."

"You think Dutch is just going to let you go? Return to fishing? The two big boats are still in the marina with the dozen small rowboats. That's what you think you'll go back to?"

"I don't know. What I am interested in is casinos. Nevada last year legalized gambling. Lansky is big on gambling in Miami and New Orleans with his Italian buddies. They're building a Boardwalk here in Rockaway. Got plans for ten miles of wooden Boardwalk. I got a hotel on the beach in Far Rockaway. This might be the future."

"You and Lansky in business? Think Dutch is going to like that?" Moishe skeptically asked.

"Money is money. If I convince him about the beauty of casinos maybe, he'll let me be his middle man. I don't know. I have not flushed out all the details. Loyalty and greed. I have to work those ingredients into our new formula for success."

"These are all dangerous men, Schultz, Lansky and Luciano. I wish Goldy, if you could just walk away. We have money. We're not rich, but we have everything we need. I'd rather you and your sister went into the PI business chasing unfaithful husbands and wives. That's safer than working for those guys," Esty said.

When the Democratic Convention concluded on July 2, 1932, Franklin Roosevelt emerged the nominee. It took four secret ballots to achieve the nomination. Many of those in attendance as well as New Yorkers had a love affair with his opponent Al Smith. They loved him, but they saw him as a loser. He had been the 1928 Presidential nominee. The election results were disastrous. The Democratic Party lost everything.

Now Hoover was president and he was a disaster for the country. The Dow Jones hit a chasm that fortunately was never reached again. On July 4, 1932 that economic indicator registered 41. World War I veterans started their campaign against the federal government in late May. They created campgrounds near the White House to demand cash benefits. Eventually, Hoover ordered the U.S. Army to forcibly evict the men. Other politicians, the press and the public were outraged.

Who was going to save the country? Al Smith was labeled a loser. No Catholic nor a Jew was acceptable to the nation as a President. The ethnics of New York City and Tammany Hall mourned that reality. Although not always expressed, the old-time politicians of Tammany Hall felt that the earth was turning. Since 1930, Roosevelt as Governor of New York had Tammany Hall under investigation. Their days of control after more than a hundred years was under threat with this election. Roosevelt was after corruption and the influence of the gangsters. Their constant hold on the finances of the city was lost money to the coffers of New York State.

Ultimately, the decision was based on electability. The Catholic Smith had limited appeal. People were desperate for a new beginning. The patrician Roosevelt was someone with a national appeal. Southern Democrats liked Roosevelt, he often visited Arkansas. He was favored by rural farmers losing their properties to bankers. Interestingly, American intellectuals found Roosevelt to their liking.

Goldy got the call to meet Dutch in his favorite speakeasy. What were they going to call these places after Prohibition? On the car ride to meet Dutch, Goldy kept thinking about new names. They weren't pubs or taverns. No restaurant would accept the decor. Why not Dutch, Dutch I, Dutch II, Goldy mused to himself. Despite the economic downturn, cars were everywhere and he had time to consider the best name.

When Goldy entered, he noticed a man with Dutch. His presence made him uneasy. He recognized him and hoped the man did not recognize him.

"Sit down Goldy. You know Lepke?" Dutch asked.

"I don't think we've met," Goldy answered.

Louis "Lepke" Buchalter stared at Goldy, "No, we've never met."

Goldy knew the face of the man who headed Murder, Inc. The group was more affectionately known as the Brownsville Boys because they were all from Brownsville, Brooklyn.

"Lepke and me are finishing our business," Dutch said.

That meant Dutch ordered the murder of someone. It was reported that Buchalter and his partner Vincent Mangano, and their dozens of soldiers had murdered between 400-1,000 people. The original partner Albert "The Mad Hatter" Anastasia was murdered.

If you wanted someone snubbed out just call on Lepke. His Army of Italian and Jewish gangsters was legendary. They were the muscle behind Luciano and Lansky. Bugsy Siegel helped to form Murder, Inc. for the purpose of keeping informers and witnesses silent.

Among a stable of ruthless killers, most notorious was Harry "Pittsburgh Phil" Strauss. They all called home at Rosie "Midnight Rose" Gold's candy store on the corner of Saratoga and Livonia Avenue. Goldy hoped to never be on their list and his face to become invisible.

Both men watched as Lepke left the speakeasy. You could almost hear the collective sigh of relief from all the patrons.

"You know why I contacted Lepke?" Dutch started to speak.

Goldy put up his hand, "I don't want to know."

"It's all about what's next. Prohibition is unlikely to last. Roosevelt and Smith they hate us. Hoover can't find his own dick. We got to think about the future."

"Yes, I agree. What are you thinking?"

"Stiff-arming labor, that racket. You know that other Brownsville group headed up by Martin Goldstein and Abe Reles. I like Reles' nickname "Kid Twist" ain't that a swell name?"

"I know them by reputation. I've never personally understood the attraction of labor racketeering. Poor fools have to pay to work. Seems pretty unfair. Things are rotten as it is."

"That's always going to be your problem Goldy. You're too much of an honest guy. That's the point. If jobs are scarce why not tack on a premium."

"I'm thinking what are we going to do with the freighter?"

"Casino gambling that's what you like. Use the boat to take out players into international waters."

"Exactly, people love to drink and people love to gamble. I can have the freighter refitted to be a floating casino."

"How much is that going to be?"

"I'll talk to my Irish boat builders. I think we could come up with a reasonable price."

"You going to get high rollers?"

"Not necessary. In fact, the city is building a beautiful Boardwalk across the Rockaway shoreline. Talking about eight maybe ten miles. Hotels will spring up just like in the best times during the 1880's. No lack of potential gamblers. And for special occasions people can rent out the boat. Then we get high rollers. It's a clean business. No knocking heads and threatening people."

"Casinos seem like a huge overhead. I'm not sure."

"Think about it," Goldy asked.

"Bugsy Siegel is thinking casinos. I want you to go to Miami and meet with Lansky and his boy Bugsy. They got big operations in Miami and New Orleans. No floating casinos as far as I know. Take the wife on vacation to Miami."

Desperate people needed a hero. Although he was crippled and seemed unhealthy, Roosevelt was the people's champion. His decisive victory sealed the end of Prohibition. Interestingly,

Herbert Hoover's public service did not end at his defeat.

On November 8, 1932, millions of Americans went to vote. The electoral college results were resounding and not surprising given the necessity of hope. The human spirit can only survive and prosper in an atmosphere of hope. Roosevelt won 472 electoral votes versus poor Hoover's mere 59. To make the radical changes possible, people voted for a new Congress that was overwhelmingly Democratic in the US Senate and US House of Representatives. The party swept all elections across the country.

Goldy and family were happy for the nation. His future was very much in doubt. But an optimistic man by temperament, they celebrated the start of a new nation. They were one of the first to attend the opening of Radio City Music Hall on December 27.

Chapter 8
Death of Prohibition

It was cold and snowy during the winter of 1933. Goldy followed the urging of Dutch and took Esty to Miami for the winter. The train ride was fun gazing out of the big train windows at the American Southland. The country looked so vast. Here were the bankrupt farmers trying to hold on to their dignity. Starvation in winter was possible.

Goldy and Esty were guests of Goldy's recently widowed sister Laila. She lived in a small house near the tip of Miami Beach. Her husband was in the tobacco business. Mendel's business tentacles reached out across the Northern Hemisphere. One business imported Cuban cigars. He also had contracts with farmers from the islands of Jamaica and Dominican Republic. He went where the cigar tobacco grew best. One source of leafy cigar wrapping was in Windsor, Connecticut.

When they arrived in Miami, they saw the local newspaper headlines of January 25, 1933. "'Schultz indicted in New York State for tax evasion." Thus began a two-year odyssey for Schultz. The first part was hiding from the New York State troopers.

"Now what?" Esty asked as she handed the newspaper to her husband.

"No idea. I better find me a new protector or maybe some way out of this entanglement. I'm glad we're here and he's somewhere else."

It was a short taxi ride to his waiting sister.

"Welcome my big brother Abe. So nice to see you. And Esther you both look wonderful," Laila kissed each cheek.

"Nice to be here in winter," Esty sat on the biggest chair on the front porch.

"Here take some iced tea," they both took the tall glasses.

There were home-made cookies on a small round table. She was the best baker of his four sisters.

"How was the trip?" his sister asked.

"No problems. It was fun just to watch the scenery go by," Goldy said.

"Really, this is the only place to live, here in Miami. The goyim hate you in the rest of Florida. Those fields you saw out of the train window, right out of some antebellum novel. You wouldn't know the blacks in the fields weren't slaves. But here. This is our little Jerusalem."

"It's been a long time since I was in Miami. Got a little business to conduct down here. Plenty of time for the beach. We got that beach bum blood. Can't be too far from the ocean. Somehow we just can't function without sand in our toes."

"My gangster brother. I read today's headlines. Schultz headed for jail? What are you going to do?" she hugged him so tightly.

"I'm the Accidental Gangster. I wasn't born to break the law. It just happened. Now my boss is looking at prison just like Capone. I pay taxes," he explained.

"When I told people here that Dutch Schultz and Meyer Lansky were at your son's wedding, jaws dropped. I went from tobacco widow to new status. I'm a local celebrity," Laila exclaimed.

"Your brother is in a very dangerous job. At any time either a rival gang kills him or the police. He carries a gun. At first, I thought it was only going to last a few years. But Prohibition is over and Dutch is still having him do jobs."

"And Papa, you made Papa a gangster."

"He loves it. He carries a gun," Goldy laughed.

They both hugged, "Who would have thought my father, who never owned a business that prospered and my sweet brother running around with the most notorious people on earth. Who would have thought? Amazing," she laughed so hard that she started hiccupping.

"Do I look like a gangster?"

"No, the face is too sweet. But the ambition. You take after Mama. If she wasn't pushing Papa, we would never have enough to eat. Our Hungarian mother, Hashem, may she rest in peace. She was a fiery woman.

"From the Carpathian Mountains of central Europe, she pushed and pushed. She was like a banker. She saved every nickel and then bought a bunch of row houses in Rockaway. She rented them at a premium because if they kept paying for five years, she gave them the house. She charged more for rent, but there was the prospect of owning the house. She kept a profit and put away some in a fund.

"People would come and ask to borrow from her fund.

These were people like her, immigrants. No bank would lend to them. She was their banker. I'm not talking like loan sharking. Her rates were decent. She used them to buy houses and sometimes businesses. Without any education, she just knew how to make money and be a good member of the community.

"She loved this country. Never wanted to go back to Hungary. She kept the family going. Not a baleboste, not a cook, but with plenty of chutzpah. And you my brother, who knew. You have her Hungarian genes," his sister explained.

"I thought it was going to be temporary. Now thirteen years later, I'm not quite free and I don't know what's going to happen next."

"You can't simply walk away," Esty always worried.

"Nu, you can't just quit?" his sister smiled at her guests.

"I'm here to check out the gambling possibilities."

"Everybody loves to gamble. Like the bootlegging. What a stupid idea to stop importing and making booze. The rabbis like a little whiskey after services," his sister explained.

"My idea is floating casinos. Take a boat filled with gamblers out past the international line. Bingo, let's play for money."

"I like it," his sister was encouraging.

A thin young man approached the house.

"Look who's here?" she screamed to her son.

"Uncle Abe and Aunt Esther. How nice to see you? Mama said you were coming down to Miami to escape the cold," son Bobby said.

"You look so handsome. Got a brown tan. Regular movie star," Esty gave him a hug.

"How's the tobacco business?" Goldy asked.

"Great. People like to smoke foreign cigars just like people like to drink whiskey."

"It's over. Prohibition is dead," Goldy said with a sad face.

"Now what Uncle Abe?"

"I don't know. Came down here to see my sister, you and your sister. Take time to think about the future," Goldy told his nephew.

"It's America, the land of unlimited possibilities. We got rid of the old and bad ideas. Now it's Roosevelt's turn to save the country. We're in good hands. Even in tough times people like a glass of whiskey and a good cigar."

"Abe is going to figure it out. I was talking about how much he's like our mother. Too bad you really never got to know her. She was a dynamo."

"Why do people call you Goldy? Is it short for Goldfarb? My Mama only calls you Abe."

"It's my golden brown, wavy hair and blue eyes. My Mama always called me that name," he ran his fingers through his thick, luxurious hair.

"I used to call him Goldy until Mama died," she stared at her brother. "Now I can't say that name. It reminds me of Mama. It's the one thing I miss the most about living here. It's not being able to go to the cemetery and see her," a small tear appeared. She brushed it away.

"Miami is an interesting place. I don't know, but people talk about gangsters down here," Bobby said.

"Gambling is here. All the other vices follow. You don't want to know what goes on."

"Your uncle is right. The less you know the better. As his wife, he tries to keep me as ignorant as possible about what he and the others do," Esty explained.

"Here's a story for you Uncle Abe. I'm in the shop. Two guys with fedoras enter. They tell me if I want to keep everything running smoothly, I need to pay them, monthly, protection."

Laila cries out, "Why didn't you tell me?"

"I didn't want to worry you," the son responded.

"You want me to find out what's going on?" Goldy offered his assistance.

"You already helped. I told these two guys, I was Goldy Goldfarb's nephew one of Dutch Schultz's guys from New York. He said 'I'm sorry,' shook my hand and left."

"Goldy, the Accidental Gangster. Your fame follows you here," his sister told them. They all laughed.

"How did you get involved with Dutch Schultz?" his nephew asked.

"It's a long story. When we both are older with lots of time to waste, I'll tell you."

"What's with the name Dutch Schultz? That's not his real name?" Bobby asked.

"No, Schultz was the name of a trucking company where he worked and its owner was a real thug. Dutch took it as his own after a 17-month prison sentence. Arthur Simon Flegenheimer was his original name. Dutch who loves publicity told people that his real name was too long for the newspaper headlines."

"Uncle, are you afraid of Schultz?"

"Bobby, a cautious man would be wise not to overly excite Mr. Schultz. He is known for his hot temper. Fortunate for me, I'm probably the only honest man who works for him. And he appreciates that."

"He's been indicted does that change what you do?" Bobby was hungry for information.

"Let's see. In a matter of months, Prohibition is dead. My long-time bootlegging boss is indicted for tax evasion because he never paid the government their share of his illegal bootlegging. So what am I to do?"

"Yes?" his sister asked.

"I don't know, but I will be calling on some associates here in Miami. I like the weather; we could stay for a few months. After Roosevelt's Inauguration, we'll all get a better idea of where the country's going. I am certainly not going on a bank robbery spree like those idiots, who must have a death wish."

"You think Schultz will land in jail?" Bobby was the most curious.

"So far he's avoided prison except for a stint when he was young. Of course, tax evasion got Capone. But, I think Schultz is smarter. His worst crimes are not as sensational although just like Capone he's hungry for the crowds. Wants to be loved."

"You'll need a new boss," Bobby told his uncle.

"No, he needs a way to get out from all of this. Enough with the Accidental Gangster. Let's go back to 1919 before Prohibition," Esty sighed.

"You can never go back," sister Laila spoke the obvious.

"I guess," Goldy grinned.

•••

After dinner, when Bobby left for his home and Esty went to bed, the sister and brother sat on the porch.

"I want you to meet someone," his sister said.

"Going to join you at some mahjong tournament?"

"No, this is serious."

"OK. Nu, who?"

"He is from a Zionist organization. He's just here in Miami for a short time. I told him a little about you. Less the Accidental Gangster and more about boats for smuggling."

"What are they thinking?"

"You should spend time with the man."

"OK. Smuggling people out of Europe to here, America?"

"I don't know. I mentioned Papa was from Bialystok. He said there was some Zionist group there. You were there a few years ago. Tanta Anat mention anything about Jews going to Palestine?"

"No, they didn't have any plans to leave Poland."

"This man I think is getting support from Baron Edmond de Rothschild. I'll arrange a meeting. The situation in Europe is bad and getting worse. U.S. government is anti-Semitic. We'll get no help from Roosevelt. Instead of those five children you took out, we need to take out thousands."

"I know how to smuggle whiskey and beer. I know how to make forged American documents. If I can help that's fine. Call him."

Sister Laila arranged a meeting with Fritz Schoenberg in her house. The bearded man came on foot. He was staying nearby at one of the smaller hotels.

Laila made the introductions on the front porch. She and Esty took a bag of food, two metal chairs, and went off to enjoy the sand and surf.

It was eighty degrees and both men felt the sun's brilliance. They faced each other, sizing each other up without uttering a sound. Laila had left them tall glasses of ice tea and her home-made cookies.

"My sister tells me you are from some Zionist organization."

"I am. We are supported by Baron Edmond de Rothschild to save our people. You have been to Europe. You understand the dire situation. The Nazis are going to rule. Hitler's stated purpose is to eliminate all the Jews. He is not joking."

"What can I do to help?"

"Your sister tells me you are in the bootlegging business. You smuggle liquor into America."

"That's all about to change. President Roosevelt is going to end Prohibition."

"So this makes this meeting prescient. You have boats and no cargo. I have precious cargo and lack transportation."

"Where are these people heading?"

"To Palestine. We will establish the first Jewish state in two millennia. The only way we can guarantee the continuation of our people is to establish a Jewish state."

"In the desert, among unfriendly Arabs, surrounded by British troops?"

"You are the smuggler we having been looking for. You have the resources and abilities to assist us."

"How about bringing them to America. Here in this country, they will be safe."

"The American government just put up more obstacles for European Jews to immigrate here. The answer is a permanent state. A Jewish state in the land where David and Solomon ruled."

"You got a plan on how we're going to get them from Europe to Palestine?"

"No, we need you. Someone who knows how to smuggle goods to places not so willing to accept the goods."

"People are a lot bigger than bottles of whiskey and beer."

"People are also a lot smarter."

"OK, but where in Europe will the people be picked up? There are many ports."

"I understand you have experiences with Antwerp and Hamburg."

"No, those northern ports are too long a ride to the Mediterranean Sea. There are German Jews you need to evacuate. Take them to Britain. They may be safe there."

"The point is to bring them to Palestine."

"I can't bring thousands or even hundreds on my boat. It's impossible."

"If you can help in any way that would be wonderful. We are not expecting miracles. But we need all the assistance we can get. You are a businessman and we are making a business proposition."

"I'm not looking for money. After having spent the last twelve years evading the American government, I don't want my boat confiscated by the British authorities in Palestine."

"We have places where the passengers can be brought. We

have been working on this since the fall of the Ottomans. The British government, while deeply anti-Semitic, is more sympathetic than the Americans. We are not bringing people to Britain, we are bringing them to a place largely inhabited by Arabs. The British hate the Arabs. Jews are preferable."

"You have a port where we can dock without harassment from the British authorities?"

"Yes, Haifa is a qualified port. The problem is to get the Jews out of Europe. We need you to do that."

"If I can dock in Antwerp, I can get people out. But it's a long voyage to Haifa. If you can bring people to southern European ports the trip is more manageable."

"What are you thinking?"

"Italy or Greece. If the trip is shorter and in calmer waters, we can accomplish much more."

"I will talk to my associates and find out more about travel routes."

"I have an associate here that I will discuss the project with. There is the possibility of a second boat."

"Do you mean Meyer Lansky?"

"Do you know him?"

"Of course not, personally. But we know about American gangsters. Their lives are followed in Europe."

"We are living in difficult times. If I can get more support, the trips are more likely to be successful."

"The British promised us in 1917 in the Balfour Declaration a 'national home for the Jewish people' in Palestine. We are going to make them stand by that proclamation. It is time for a new Jewish state. I would hope that you, Mr. Goldfarb, and your family would emigrate to Palestine. We need resourceful men. Men who are not afraid. I gather your business has made you an ingenious, fearless person."

"I don't know about fearless. But I love this country. I can't see giving it all up to farm in the desert. Seems like a harsh life."

"You are a man in the liquor business. We could use your talents to create a beer and wine industry. Jews since the beginning of time have made beer and wine."

"I know beer, not wine."

"Palestine is the future for Jews not America. I welcome your support. I will be here a few more days."

"Seeking money. I can make a donation."

"I'd rather that you bought land in Palestine. Then a few years from now you can decide if you want to start a brewery or raise grapes for wine."

"Why not? I own a hotel, a gas station, a pharmacy and a movie theater. A brewery in the desert. Who knows?"

"We know that we must get the Jews out of Europe. The sooner we start the more we can save. I look forward to doing business with you Mr. Goldfarb."

"I will call my contact today. Hopefully, I'll have some definite ideas before long. I do agree the Jews must leave Europe. I'm not convinced the Promised Land is in the desert in Palestine."

"You must visit. There is more than the desert."

"Are you by chance a relative of the composer Schoenberg?"

"A cousin."

"You see I'm not a barbarian."

"Mr. Goldfarb, I would never take you for a barbarian. We are after all Jews. We tamed and civilized Europe. To thank us they want to kill us and eliminate us from the earth. That's gratitude."

They met on a bench close enough to the ocean to hear the waves gently breaking onto the sand. It was sunny and bright. Miami Beach was at its best. Goldy wore a straw hat to keep his pale New York skin from burning.

"Goldy you enjoying the weather?" Meyer Lansky asked him.

"Beats the weather up north."

"Are you a lost soul? Prohibition about to end, Dutch, God knows where."

"A time to assess my options," Goldy said while waving away an irritating fly.

"Do you know where Dutch is?"

"Don't know," he quickly responded.

"Would you tell me if you knew?"

"No," Goldy's answer was empathetic.

"You're a good soldier. Dutch always said you were the only honest man he knew."

"I'm a bootlegger, but not a thief."

"Schultz was always a miserly boss. He got rich, but did you get rich? Me and Luciano, we always give a percentage to our boys. Not Schultz, he gave you all a teeny amount for all your efforts."

"I'm not complaining," Goldy answered.

"Nu, what are you going to do? Boss on the run. Prohibition gone. You have a plan? That's why you invited me here today."

"Casinos, floating casinos. Just day trippers. A few miles, just past the international line. Doesn't have to be only high-fliers. Good honest people love to gamble just like they loved to drink whiskey and beer.

"My plan, "Goldy said, "we go out into international waters around five in the evening. We stay out for three or four hours. Serve some buffet dinner and all they can drink."

"How do we get these people?"

"All the hotels here in Miami Beach. You give a little to the bellhops and the desk clerks. Let people know by word of mouth. All these good upstanding citizens from up north have money to spend."

"You have the boats?"

"Dutch has one freighter, which can be refitted. Rothstein had a second freighter. I don't know if it's still available. We're not providing hotel accommodations just a few hours out in the ocean."

"Who's going to refit the boats?"

"I got two Irish brothers. Best boat builders anywhere. I can have them take a look at the boat I've been using for the booze."

"Find out how much?"

"There's enough for Dutch's portion, your portion and a small amount for me," Goldy suggested.

"What about casinos in the desert?"

"I see the possibilities. Las Vegas is not so far from Los Angeles. All those Hollywood types like to gamble. But you'll need nicer accommodations. People aren't coming for the day."

"Alright I'm open. Get me some numbers. Show me how this is going to work and we'll keep talking. Anything else?"

"One more thing," Goldy's voice hesitated.

"OK?"

"A man approached me yesterday. He's a European from a Zionist organization. They are supported by Baron Edmond de Rothschild. They want to smuggle people out of Europe and bring them to Palestine."

"Europe is a dicey place for Jews. Hitler is a menace," Meyer nodded his head several times.

"I spoke to him about bringing Jews to America. But he's not interested in that immigration. He was talking about taking Jews from Antwerp or Hamburg, Germany to Palestine. That is a big trip. If I use my refitted freighter, it's a schlepp. I will help him. But I want a southern European port. Somewhere in Italy or Greece or Marseilles, France. Do you have any contacts?"

"I'll speak to Luciano. He has friends all over that part of the world. But I'll help you as best as I can. I agree Jews are in danger. They'd be better off if you smuggled them here to Miami. Here I got lots of contacts including the docks. We could bring them in."

"That could be a second plan. Zionists go to Palestine, the rest of the poor slobs come here to Miami. I read the newspapers and realize how lucky we are to live here as a Jew. That lunatic in Germany, Adolph Hitler, was just named Chancellor. That is a bad omen of what's to come."

"It's a dangerous world. Even in New York City there are

challenges. Casinos and human smuggling are good plans for you now. I gather you never were too interested in the numbers rackets in Harlem or shaking down people."

"I'm not so good with numbers. And look at me. Do I look dangerous?" Goldy laughed and Lansky followed.

"Dutch isn't a big man."

"But he looks dangerous. That's not my style."

"You know why I like you Goldy Goldfarb? I see a little Arnold Rothstein in you. You don't dress as well probably because Schultz doesn't pay you enough. But there's a classy side to you. Casinos that's your shtickloch." Lansky broadly smiled.

"My philosophy is that we have to move with the times. Prohibition is out, gambling is in."

"Gambling was always in," Lansky reminded him.

"Not gambling on a big scale for the ordinary joes and janes. The boats are just the beginning. But we have to remain inconspicuous. The G-men are looking to put bootleggers in jail. We got to be invisible. Meyer, you got the right contacts here in Miami so the boats go undetected."

"You are certain there's a huge appetite for gambling by the average guy and gal?"

"Yes. We are in the midst of a Great Depression. Just like people love to go to the movies, gambling is a distraction. Regular Americans don't want to go to dark basements to gamble. Make it attractive. Pretty girls serving drinks. Free food. The numbers rackets are for lowlifes in Harlem. This is much fancier."

"It's too bad you didn't really get to know Arnold. I know you would have appreciated one another."

"He was taken too young. It was a real shame what happened to him."

"Did gambling get Rothstein? Or was it your boss?"

"George McManus killed Arnold. You got to pay your debts."

Lansky put his hand on Goldy's arm, "Dutch doesn't deserve you. We'll keep in touch."

"It's always a pleasure to see you Meyer," Goldy left with a smile on his face.

A people yearned for normalcy. They were facing homelessness and desperation unknown until those days. On the fringes, the American fascists and communists plus the many anarchists proposed insurrection. Not even inaugurated and a hungry immigrant named Giuseppe Zangara shouted: "Too many people are starving" as he attempted to assassinate President Franklin Roosevelt in Miami on February 15, 1933. It was Roosevelt's calm in the presence of an assassin that restored the populace's faith in hope.

The nation listened on the radio to President Roosevelt's first Inaugural Address.

"This great Nation will endure as it has endured, will revive and will prosper. So, first of all, let me assert my firm belief that the only thing we have to fear is fear itself—nameless, unreasoning, unjustified terror which paralyzes needed efforts to convert retreat into advance. In every dark hour of our national life a leadership of frankness and vigor has met with the understanding and support of the people themselves which is essential to victory. I am convinced that you will again give that support to leadership in these critical days.

"We do not distrust the future of essential democracy. The people of the United States have not failed. In the end they have registered a mandate that they want direct, vigorous action. They have asked for discipline and direction under leadership. They have made me the present instrument of their wishes. In the spirit of the gift I take it.

"In this dedication of a Nation we humbly ask the blessing of God. May He protect each and every one of us. May He guide me in the days to come."

In twenty minutes Roosevelt outlined his plan. "Our greatest primary task is to put people to work."

Everyone in the larger Goldfarb family congregated in the living room glued to the words emanating from the radio. Only Silvie was missing as she continued her medical school studies in Baltimore.

"So Papa what are you going to do now that your bootlegging days are over?" Izzy innocently asked.

"I can become your helper. I don't know how to run the projector, but I can collect tickets."

"You would make a great ticket collector. Even sell popcorn. My major investor takes a small role in the business."

"I am invisible in all your businesses. The investor who lets those who know what they're doing run the show. I just collect the money," Goldy laughed.

"Papa, you're a good businessman. We all learn from you," Izzy spoke for them all.

"Just don't get involved with gangsters," Esty told them all.

"If it wasn't for Dutch Schultz, we'd have none of this. He's a hothead, but we've done alright with him," Zayde backed their boss.

"If you manage to stay on his good side. Now he's gone. I don't wish him ill, but if he never returned to New York, our lives would be less complicated," Esty said.

"Your mother and I will take a train to Los Angles and see my sister. We can discuss the movies. Get some more stars to parade down Central Avenue and stand in front of Izzy's movie house. We'll speak to Irving, the screenwriter, maybe he can get our movie theater first runs before any others. Like some bigtime downtown movie house in Manhattan. We got the stars once before. He has some pull. Movies and bootlegging, similar. All about connections."

"Are you really interested in the movies?" Hannah asked her father.

"This is the first time in more than twelve years that I don't have a tight schedule to follow. So I'm going to see my family."

"Really, Papa is that what you are going to do go traveling?" Gladdy asked.

"Well, I have time and I have never traveled west," Goldy told them.

"Where's Dutch?" Bluma, now known as Billie, asked.

"I don't know. He disappeared," Goldy snapped his fingers, "gone."

"Is he dead?" Hirsh whispered just in case his ghost haunted the Goldfarb house.

"I don't think so, but in his absence and with no booze to travel, I can consider my options."

"How are you so sure he's alive?" Zayde was cautious about

the future without Dutch.

"If someone killed him they would want the publicity. He's in hiding. That was a conscious decision to break away from the limelight and the government scrutiny."

"We can always use an extra pair of hands at the auto shop," Zev suggested.

"I am very handy with my hands," he showed off his nicely trimmed fingernails. He allowed Hannah to practice doing manicures on his hands.

"We still have the boats docked in the Bay," Izzy knew the location.

"I can always go back to fishing."

Esty was quietly listening and then spoke, "Until we know what's going on with Dutch, we cannot rest."

Zayde smiled, "Yes, the big unknown."

"What's to become of the freighter docked in Jamaica Bay?" Rivka enjoyed accompanying the booze on those cruises to and from Canada.

"I have an idea. I've been discussing it with Lansky. Floating casinos leaving out of Miami. Everyone likes to gamble," Goldy enthusiastically reported.

"Is there interest? I agree there is a huge market for gamblers not just high rollers." Zayde always liked the idea and said so when Goldy suggested it months ago.

"Will we all move to Miami? We could remodel some old hotel in Miami Beach. Redo it just like we did with the one here in Far Rockaway." Billie was dreaming of expanding the hotel empire.

"Nothing's certain. It's been weeks since I suggested the

idea to Lansky. They got this Commission that meets to discuss ideas. I'll just wait for an answer. Meanwhile, Esty and I are going to take a train ride to California. I'd like to see the Pacific Ocean."

Esty nodded her head.

"I want to go and meet the movie stars," Minnie jumped up and down.

Minnie was the slow one. She was always going to live with Goldy and Esty.

"Can I Mama. Please?" she cried.

"Yeah, why not," Esty said.

"I'll come here for the few weeks and live in this house and take care of all my girls," Rivka appointed herself the babysitter.

There were five girls living in the Goldfarb home. Izzy was the man of his own house with his wife and the first grandchild. Silvie lived in Baltimore. There were the three younger Goldfarb girls. Hannah and Gladdy were in school as well as the Polish cousins Sisel and Tzipi. Goldy was overwhelmed with the feminine touch. He was eager to leave his house. Polly, he wasn't going to miss, but Ruby Two he adored and the big canine loved him back.

The three were off to Los Angeles. It was a first for them all. Minnie was so excited to be taking this long train ride across the country. She wasn't retarded. She looked perfectly normal, but meningitis had robbed her of mental growth and development. She would remain a child forever.

Irving drove a magnificent car, a Chrysler CL Imperial

Phaeton. He picked the trio up at the train station. Goldy's mouth hung open at its beauty. The ladies tumbled into the back seat while Goldy took up the navigator's position.

"Welcome to Hollywood. It's everything they say. Goldy, you and your family will never forget this adventure. I guarantee it. I made arrangements for you to come to the studio. If we're lucky a few stars might be walking around. Next time bring Izzy and his family."

"I was looking for a little break for Esty and Minnie. I have some time available. I can take a real vacation," Goldy said.

"Things slow in the bootleg business," Irving laughed.

"They're dead. The Accidental Gangster, that's me. I have no business at all. I'm waiting for my next act."

"Hollywood, I'm telling you, this is the place where dreams come true," nothing could dampen Irving's enthusiasm.

"I believe you. Izzy's movie theater is packed, day and night, every day. People need escape and hope."

"And inspiration. We have it all in the movies. This Great Depression is depressing. The noise from Europe is disturbing. Burning books is the first act of a greater tragedy sure to come. In Hollywood we make people happy."

"I like happy," Minnie told them.

"When we go to the studio I will show you things you never saw before. What people see on the screen. My, my it takes so many people to make those illusions. There are camera men, hair stylists, costume designers, set designers. It takes a small Army to make a movie."

"I can't wait," Esty said with Minnie nodding her head in agreement.

"And the movie business is a Jewish business. I don't have to tell you about all the Jews in the business. Some of them changed their names. Don't want those Jew haters in the Midwest or South boycotting our movies."

"Some of the studios are a little shaky. Finances in trouble. One studio buys out another," Goldy commented.

"Yeah, changes are a big thing. Movies keep being created, but studio ownership is iffy. There is political support for the movie business. In a time of people begging for food, we provide fat bellies. Jobs and jobs for all kinds of workers.

"Has been an influx of foreigners to Hollywood. Smart people can see the smoldering embers and know there's an earthquake coming. The studios employ dozens of European refugees. Most are Jews, not all."

"And what's happening abroad with the Nazis. Jews everywhere should all be afraid," Goldy tempered the conversation.

"Oh yeah. We heard from plenty of those bastard Nazis after *All Quiet on the Western Front* was released. They objected to the truth. We make fun movies but also serious ones. If we can make you laugh that's great. Occasionally, we need to tell another story."

"I'm getting involved with a Zionist group to get Jews out of Europe and take them to Palestine."

"With your bootlegging boats?"

"New purpose. I have a new calling," Goldy told Irving.

"We got several German Jews working in the studios. Actors, but mostly writers. One just got here. Someone pulled strings. He's talking about the Gestapo, a German secret police. These are dangerous people. I mean your types are dangerous, especially your boss Dutch Schultz. There are just many more of these German gangsters. Book burning is their solution to killing ideas."

"If you know anyone, personally, I would like to meet them. I need to know as many ways as possible to get Jews out of Central Europe."

"Yeah, I know a writer. He was helped from some Jewish organization. I'll call him and set up a meeting at the studio. I'll take your ladies around the studio. Maybe, we'll run into some star. You can visit with this writer."

By 1933, for some it was clear. The new German government was systemically going to isolate and marginalize the Jews. Thirty-seven thousand (37,000) emigrated. In the early 1930's, the Nazis were not opposed to Jews emigrating. The problem was no country wanted them.

Who helped the Jews? Jewish groups around the world were involved in saving their landsmen. They saw the danger and reacted. It created European Jews wanting an exit visa to Palestine. Most other places were so limited through strict immigration policies. In the midst of the Great Depression, governments were unwilling to share their nation's bounty with aliens.

Edward, the new Hollywood writer, had grave misgivings about leaving his native Germany. Americans were barbarians. He was soon to learn that his own countrymen were more evil than the worst historical barbarians.

Goldy and the man sat in the dining hall of the studio. He

was tall with a pencil-thin moustache. The writer had leading man features although not an actor or director. Once the Nazi government closed the doors of universities, professions and most gainful occupations, Edward realized it was time to leave.

"I could have gone to Palestine without too much trouble. But I'm not a Zionist. I don't want to work on farms and raise chickens. I am a writer. I wrote for great German directors. This country is difficult to get into. Letters were written, people called on my behalf. Finally, someone said I could leave with my immediate family. My parents, my in-laws, they were not permitted to leave."

"Where does the journey begin for people seeking to leave Germany?"

"With money there are routes. No one put up a sign 'Jews Welcome.' Switzerland, as the land of neutrality, is one avenue. Spain and Portugal with enough bribes will take in a few Jews. The Swedes are open for business. What's a life worth? You realize all these countries are officially neutral."

"If I take people to Palestine, I need an easy port free from spying government agents and threatening guns?"

"German Jews are not leaving for Palestine by embarking on a ship in Hamburg. They must find themselves in other countries. The Italians are actually tolerant for fascists. Mussolini reportedly has a Jewish mistress. If there were relatively safe ports, I would choose Italy."

"Do most European Jews want to leave? Are they Zionists?"

"Germany is a bad place for Jews. Given a choice of Berlin or Tel Aviv, most would go to Palestine in hopes of getting to Britain, Canada and here in America. A stop point on a longer

225

journey. I sincerely doubt they actually want to live in Palestine, too snobby. I would describe it that way. If faced with death, of course, Palestine is acceptable. But not a desired choice."

"Do you have regrets about leaving?"

"I am writing "B" movie scripts. The work is shit, but I'm free to tell you that. So life is good here. They are not burning down synagogues or arresting Jews."

"I appreciate your time and your candor."

"My new friend Irving says you're a gangster."

"I'm the Accidental Gangster," Goldy proudly proclaims.

"You, might make an interesting story. Jewish gangsters. Are there gangsters like you in Los Angeles?"

"Of course. If you want, I can see if I can make a connection with Mickey Cohen. A former boxer, he has a very nasty reputation. But I work for another Jew with a thuggish reputation, Dutch Schultz. I can inquire if you're interested in meeting Mr. Cohen."

"Interested! Are you kidding? These are people worth writing about. Nothing like a gangster movie to sell tickets."

"I don't know Cohen myself. I can try and see if a meeting can be arranged. I'll introduce you as a screenwriter. Most of these guys love publicity. Being seen with celebrities. They think of themselves as celebrities."

"That would be wonderful if it can be arranged. Goldy Goldfarb, great name. You can be in my screenplay. How did you get that name?"

"From my golden brown, wavy hair. It was my mother's nickname for me. It just stuck."

"The public is fascinated by gangsters. The really violent ones robbing banks and killing cops, and those with style. Are you one of the violent types or the smooth talker?"

"I hate violence. As I said, my allegiance started by accident. Booze and gambling, people love their vices. Don't get too close to learning actually how things happen. Once you peel away the thin veneer and look underneath, you realize the business runs on ruthlessness, threats and bribery. You probably don't want any of your kids in the real gangster business. Trust me."

"I certainly look forward to seeing you again with or without Mr. Cohen."

"To the movies," Goldy offered a toast of ice tea.

"L'Chayim Mr. Goldy."

Goldy made a call to Meyer Lansky. Meyer called his buddy Bugsy Siegel, who then called Mickey Cohen. Mickey joined the two writers and Goldy for lunch at the studio. The gangster posed for several photos with the writers. Goldy declined to be photographed with Mickey Cohen. He still didn't know where Dutch was hiding. Goldy didn't want to irritate his boss by posing with a Hollywood gangster and potential rival.

On Bastille Day, he received a call from Lansky to meet in New York City. Serious-minded people were alarmed at the political events in Germany. It was purposely chosen as the date that Hitler outlawed all political parties except the Nazi Party.

July 14 was hot and mucky so Meyer chose a waterfront location. Coney Island was busy with thousands escaping the heat. Meyer had a favorite restaurant down the street from the amusement park.

"Did you like Los Angeles?" Meyer asked.

"My wife loved California," Goldy responded.

"Better than Miami?"

"It's not so hot there. No humidity. Pacific Ocean is ice cool. Seemed just like paradise."

"Mickey treated you well?"

"He was a perfect host. And my brother-in-law took him around the studio. But Mickey knows studio heads. When there's union troubles, I'm sure he gets a call."

"We left things unresolved from earlier. I wanted to clear things up. I've good news and bad news. What do you want to hear first?"

"We're Jews conditioned to bad news. What's the bad news?"

"I took your idea about floating casinos not once but twice to The Commission. Each time they raised objections. Each time it was rejected."

"Why? Everyone loves to gamble," Goldy's most salient argument.

"Because it's different and new. They don't like new."

"Prohibition is gone forever. This is a new revenue source. We have a massive coastline on both sides, Atlantic and Pacific, big oceans. Lots of space."

"Yeah, that's what I told them. But, they already have gambling sources of revenue right on land. Forget that shit that Schultz has with the schvartzes in Harlem. Gambling is already a big business in Miami and New Orleans. Why worry about the weather and the Coast Guard? They got boats and airplanes. Why risk it?"

"Because there's a big audience for gambling and exciting to be on the ocean and play gambling games."

"I'm sorry. I could not convince them. They're old-school. If business is successful and working, why change it? Reasonable? Yes?"

"It's a new stream of revenue. You got to be open-minded."

"I support you, but I can't go against The Commission."

"Lucky didn't like my idea? Is it possibly because I'm one of Dutch's guys? Immediately, somehow my idea is poison?"

"No, I don't think it has much to do with Dutch. Although, I will admit they will never be friends. That's not the same as forever not being business partners. They don't like it. And they're stubborn like dogs who can't let go of a bone."

"I am stubborn. I remain convinced it's a great idea," Goldy shook his head in despair.

"No, Lucky didn't like the idea. And his position was endorsed by others. We already got gambling on both coasts. We don't need boats. If we try something new, then Nevada is worth considering."

"People would rather start completely new in the desert than support gambling boats? I don't get it."

"Nevada is legal gambling. No more bribes and it's not far from Hollywood."

"We could have gambling boats off Catalina Island across from Los Angeles."

"It's not going to happen until more guys think it's worth the risk."

Goldy's frowning was depressing, "So? What's the good news?"

"The boats have a better purpose. I will personally support you having those boats refitted so they can take passengers. I agree it's time to get as many Jews as possible out of Europe. I will pay and Lucky also is in on it. He has contacts in the port of Trieste, Italy. That's not too far to Palestine."

"Oh, yeah, that is great news."

"You go to your Irish brothers and do what's necessary so you can crowd in dozens and dozens of people. Time is not on our side."

"OK. This is a worthier cause. Might put me in good stead with Hashem."

Both men laughed. Goldy's disappointment was tempered by the good news.

"You tell that German Zionist we have one boat."

"What happened to Rothstein's other boat? If it's in decent condition, we can have it also refitted. I can get together two crews. Men need work."

"I don't know where it is. You can find other sea worthy boats. I agree we need to get Jews from Antwerp to Miami or New Orleans. It's got to be a bigger push than simply what the Zionists want to do. Not just the German elite has to be moved. Get those boats ready. I see the newsreels. The Nazi scum has to be defeated."

"They don't call me Mr. Mensch for nothing."

A handshake sealed the deal.

Chapter 9
Dutch and the Law

The newsreels showed it again and again. John Dillinger shot to death on the streets of Chicago like a dog. He was only 31 on July 22, 1934. The image stuck in his mind. Dillinger had a death wish. After 24 bank robberies and gun shooting attacks on four police stations, the man was the number one target of G-men. Informers set him up.

Dutch Schultz saw what happened to Dillinger. He had no death wish. There were millions more to be earned. On November 28, 1934, Dutch walked into a police station and surrendered. The Albany cops were as surprised as the federal prosecutors.

Dutch Schultz was indeed a marked man. He was a major target of New York prosecutor Thomas Dewey. The prosecutor was forced to wait. The original indictment had been handed down on January 25, 1933. Dutch stayed in hiding while his business suffered. He would come to learn that Dewey was a Rottweiler, he never let go. He was determined to put Schultz in jail.

Schultz needed money for his legal defense, lots and lots of money. From his Fifth Avenue apartment, he counted as his income declined from $54,000 a month to almost nothing. He desperately required those Harlem rackets and shakedowns to produce more income.

Unlike his competitors, who offered those who worked for them a fair share of the earnings, Shultz was just cheap and greedy. It was one of his many shortcomings. It would prove to be instrumental in his downfall. None of these gangsters had any loyalty except to themselves. By squeezing dollars from his subordinates, he opened up opportunities for his competitors to steal away those down the ladder.

In April with the birds chirping wildly and the flowers starting to bloom, Schultz was ordered to stand trial for tax evasion. The unlikely city of Syracuse, New York was the location for the first trial.

Goldy was able to convince Schultz's lawyer Dixie Davis to investigate the political environment in Syracuse. The men both agreed that since Schultz was going to be tried by a jury of his peers, it was important to know their attitudes towards Schultz and gangsters. Davis was familiar with Syracuse since he graduated from Syracuse University Law School.

The city as most of the country, was still reeling from the Great Depression. It was especially hard on Syracuse's manufacturing base. The proud city had lost one of its most important industries during the economic downturn. The world-class Franklin Manufacturing Company closed the year before. It had manufactured automobiles since 1899. At its peak of production in the 1920's, more than 15,000 cars were produced each year. The plant, covering 34 acres, employed 3,500 people. But alas, it failed to see the future which Henry Ford did. The Franklin cars were too expensive to manufacture.

Zayde and Goldy watched from a nearby bench as the workmen constructed the new hotdog restaurant on the Boardwalk. The day was bright and sunny, but winter was near.

"I'm calling it Izzy's," Goldy said.

"Why not?' his father replied.

The husky men were being supervised by Hirsh. It was difficult to sink holes in the loose sand. The men sweated while Zayde and his son drank beer. They hoped to finish the building before winter set in. It was to be ready to open for the spring crowds. Visitors came to the Rockaway Boardwalk as early as March. It was the sun that first brought them on the subway to the beach. As the heat of summer intensified, it was the cool ocean water that called them for relief.

"What does Schultz want now that he's reappeared after all those months?"

"He wants me to be one of his runners in Harlem. Do I give a shit about that business? I have managed to find something useful to do right now."

"Yeah, what are you going to do about Dutch?"

"How would you like to take a road trip to Syracuse?"

"What's there?"

"Schultz's trial. I proposed to Dixie Davis, a real goniff, Dutch's lawyer, to go up to Syracuse and check it out. The jury pool is from the locals. How are they going to react to a mutt like Schultz?"

"OK, this sounds like a good plan."

"Davis actually went to law school at Syracuse. He knows lawyers who practice up there. He's familiar with the town, the stores, the people."

"Is this Davis a good lawyer?"

"Who knows? To be truthful," Goldy was practically whispering, "if Dewey gets him, a lot of people would be happy."

"Too bad Lansky and Luciano didn't see your business plan as viable. I like it. If I'm in Miami as a tourist, a boat ride that offers gambling. How could that be bad?"

"Well, no one else did. Now I got Schultz on my ass. I got to at least go up to Harlem and tell him I'm protecting his interests."

"What's going to happen to Dutch? You think Dewey is going to do to him what other feds did to Capone?"

"I don't want to be questioned by federal prosecutors. That's another good reason to avoid being in the city. This trial could take months. It's going to be pleasant, weather-wise. Get fresh milk from some dairy farm."

"I'll bring my fishing gear. We can make a holiday out of it."

The men packed a bag for two weeks. They had no idea how long the trial was going to last. Goldy's first job was to sort out public opinion. This was not a small city. Until the Great Depression, Syracuse was cruising along. The downtown was vibrant with plenty of cars and people shopping along its broad main street. Then the city was crushed after the stock market crash. It happened all across central New York State.

Americans are an optimistic bunch. Wars and economic downturns dampened enthusiasm, but always failed to destroy it. A New York City Jew gangster, how was he going to be received in Syracuse? Goldy started his investigation by shopping Main Street. The two men casually went from one shop to another checking out the merchandise.

Syracuse was hardly a tourist vacation spot, but visitors were welcomed. It quickly became obvious to the two observers that many of the shops were owned by Jews. Without heightened words or gestures, the men asked shop owners their expectations about the forthcoming trial.

"I'll be happy to see new faces like yours," the jeweler told Goldy.

"You expecting huge crowds?" Zayde asked.

"The press from all over the country will be here. That's always good for business."

"What about him coming from New York City, the palace of sin," Goldy suggested and everyone laughed.

"You mean being a Jew?" the shop owner quickly caught on.

Goldy leaned over the glass case, "We Yids got to stick together."

"You think everyone is happy with lots of visitors?" Zayde asked.

"All the store owners will be very happy. Let these newspaper guys and even cops from everywhere visit. They will be very welcomed. Look around. We are in the midst of the Great Depression. We need more business, more money, strangers with cash."

"I get it. You think Schultz will get a fair trial?" Goldy inquired.

"Better than in New York City for sure. You guys religious

at all?"

"Going to recommend a good kosher restaurant?" Zayde patted his tummy.

"No, I wanted to invite you to shul."

"Sure on Friday night. We can go," Goldy answered for his father.

"I'll introduce you to some members of the community. You can ask them what they think of Dutch Schultz's trial here in our city."

The two strangers accepted the invitation and attended Shabbos services in the orthodox synagogue in the Jewish section of the city. There they learned that the notoriety meant more people and more people spent needed money.

In a strange way, Schultz represented the antithesis of the Jewish stereotype. His appearance was brash. Jews were seen as mild-mannered and easy to threaten. Dutch Schultz was none of that. His Jewish brethren in Central New York State were proud of the guy. No one was seen as tougher. And embracing the gangster world was invigorating. No one was going to dig too deep to discover the ruthlessness and danger of their illegal world. It just seemed so romantic for a time when fun seemed dead.

At the gathering after the service, Goldy shook hands with a newspaper editor.

"Exciting times here in Syracuse?" Goldy asked between sips of kosher wine.

"We have never seen anything like this. The publicity will be good for our community. Look around. We need the money."

"Can he get a fair trial?" Goldy had to report back.

"He doesn't want a fair trial. He wants the jury to love him enough, to be grateful enough that he doesn't go to jail. There's hope if the city treats him well, he'll reciprocate with bringing business here."

"Do you expect him to be convicted?" Goldy asked.

"It all depends on how generous the populace finds Schultz and his men."

"Interesting. The longer the trial, the more money to be spent. How does the court system work here?"

"Let me introduce you to one of the community's best attorneys," the editor suggested.

A bald man wearing suspenders saw the editor's hand motion.

"This is Ben Abrams," the two men shook hands. The editor left the men to discuss other matters.

"I'm here following the Dutch Schultz trial. Do you know the courthouse intrigue?" Goldy and the man stared at each other.

"It's a big deal having this trial here."

"Are you with the County or federal court?"

"As a landsman, I can tell you that Jews are not wanted by the prosecutor's office."

"Do you represent clients at the courthouse?"

"I am a defense lawyer. I know the many actors in the courthouse."

"There's two ways to influence a jury. You can intimidate them. Sending threats. Or, much better you can supplement their income."

"Which path does Dutch Schultz intend to follow?" the lawyer asked.

"Do jury members get a small stipend for showing up for jury duty?"

"It is small," the lawyer replied.

"Well, Dutch can enhance that to make it worth their time to come to court."

"Bribery is a criminal offense."

"All we need is one juror to see Dutch's point of view."

"I understand. But this isn't New York City."

"Better. Dutch can easily illustrate his fondness for the people of Syracuse."

"Everyone is talking about it. A big-time gangster here to sit and be judged by his fellow citizens."

"Who sits on the jury?"

"It's mostly white men."

"No women? The women usually love Dutch."

"They're at home with the children and the housework."

"But there's nothing to prevent them from becoming jurors."

"No, it can happen."

"It needs a little push in the right direction."

"People of Syracuse are flexible given the harsh economic times."

"You are a man who understands. Perhaps you can quietly accept a retainer to assist us as we navigate the courthouse procedures."

"I can be persuaded."

After they shook hands, they joined the other men. Everyone finished their wine with a hearty shout of "L'Chayim."

Immediately at the conclusion of the service, Goldy called Dixie Davis. It took a minimal amount of convincing for Dixie to recognize the value of the services offered by Ben Abrams. All they needed was one juror.

Dutch played the part of an innocent man so masterfully. There was a woman on the jury. She appeared so stoic, no facial expressions at all. It was difficult to determine if she was the holdout. The couple of farmers in their overalls were not impressed with Dutch's supposed innocence. Thankfully, there was not one teetotaler among the group. The others, primary local businessmen, went home each day of the trial and counted the dollars Schultz was bringing to town.

The actual trial was short. It was after the concluding words from the lawyers that time stood still. The jury foreman announced they could not reach a decision. The frustrated judge told them to return to deliberations. Goldy thought he saw a small flicker of a smile on the part of the hardware store owner. They continued their deliberations. Lunch and dinner were offered each day to the jurors. The court provided the finest food most of the jurors had eaten since the Great Depression inflicted such pain. It was assumed it was courtesy of Dutch Schultz.

After a while the farmers needed to return to the field. It was springtime. Planting needed to be accomplished and they were stuck in a courtroom with strangers. They begged the judge. "Set us free." His distaste for Dutch was not even concealed. But, it was time to call it quits.

"Hung jury," the judge announced. Thomas Dewey's men were flabbergasted. Dutch was not going to get away with this. The judge ordered a new trial. He didn't need the prosecutors' arguments to reach that conclusion. Dutch's lawyers were able to convince a different judge that a new trial could not succeed in New York City. There was too much publicity about the case. Against the wishes of the federal prosecutors and an angry Thomas Dewey, the new trial was slated for the tiny town of Malone, New York. Truly situated in nowhere land – God's tuchus. The new trial date was set for July 1935.

Dutch was a semi-happy man. One trial done and the next to begin. These yokels seemed malleable unlike New York City hardened citizenry. Dixie Davis appreciated Goldy's efforts to assist the boss. He was seen as a loyal soldier while the other 100 men in New York City were grumbling and cursing Dutch's name. His legal fees were eating into profits designed for his soldiers on the ground.

Goldy returned to Far Rockaway. The family all had closely followed the trial. Most nights Goldy called Esty from the Syracuse hotel where he was staying. The New York City newspapers gave great coverage to the events in central New York. Dutch was continuing front page news. He wore his new suit and his hair was carefully combed. He looked like a successful businessman not a gangster.

On his arrival at his home, he was unexpectedly met by his Zionist contact. Esty never appreciated visitors who arrived on the front porch to see Goldy. They often were threatening-looking. This well-dressed man politely refused to discuss with Esty why he was at their home. His accent was obvious and his polished finger nails fit his demeanor.

"Esty, this is Fritz Schoenberg, my Zionist contact," Goldy kissed his wife before sitting down.

"I'll bring some tea," she told them.

"What brings you to New York?" Goldy asked.

"You do. I know you have been pre-occupied with your business. But these are urgent times."

"Now that the weather is warmer, we can begin again the transfer of people to Palestine."

"No, I'm afraid your Italian escape port is under Mussolini's Army. The Italians are going to attack more of North Africa. We can't have the boats shot at and possibly sunk by aggressive Italian forces. They will not need provocation to sink boats. Those waters are too dangerous for our people."

"You're going to give up?" Goldy demanded.

"No, but we have to rethink the routes. We all know war is coming to Europe. North Africa will be dragged into it. It may involve Palestine and Egypt. I don't want you as an American caught in this cross-fire."

"What about getting Jews out of Germany and here to America. You don't want to let innocent people die. The words from Hitler and the Nazis are terrifying. We have to do something."

"We are asking Jews in America to help us to increase immigration visas to at least let in more European Jews. We have not been successful."

"I don't know about words. But the boat is well-designed. I

can smuggle people into American ports in the south. The borders are more porous."

"I think you're correct. I want you if you can to check on Mexican and Caribbean ports. At this point it is essential that we save as many as possible. We are united in this mission."

"I know Miami. I don't know México. But, I'm sure I can find out about other ports."

"You are a brave man."

"They call me Mr. Mensch."

"A deserving name."

"Want to stay for dinner?"

"No, thank you. I have many more people to see. Someday, we will meet in Palestine when it becomes Israel, our homeland."

"You keep safe. We will be in touch."

Esty brought the tea and cookies, "He's gone?"

"Yes, but I'm hungry."

"Is there any hope for our people in Europe?" Esty sat next to her husband. She poured herself a cup of tea.

"Hope remains. We will try and find a way. I promise you that," he responded. He poured himself a cup of tea.

"What's next with Dutch?"

"It's on to Malone, New York."

"Where is that?" she asked.

"In God's tuchus. But, if we managed a hung jury in a city, a small town will be easier to control."

"Should I repack your bags?"

"No, the new trial doesn't begin until summer."

•••

Dixie Davis understood there were two ways to influence a jury. You can threaten them and their families or you can bribe them. The gentler method was applied with good results in Syracuse. Next stop on the legal trail was the tiny town of Malone, New York on the Canadian border.

The citizens of Malone had a great affection for bootleggers like Dutch Schultz. Much of their economy during the 1920's and early 1930's was based on bootleggers bringing the wholesome stuff from Canada to New York City. The end of Prohibition and the Great Depression crippled the economy. Farming was hurting. People couldn't afford to eat and the mills were closing for lack of viable markets. The hard times had descended on little Malone.

Now a new trial for a well-known gangster and bootlegger was at hand. Schultz's attorney James Noonan appreciated the courtroom insider view from lawyer Ben Abrams in the Syracuse trial. In Malone, Noonan needed a similar tactic.

Noonan sent Goldy to find local lawyers, who had influence with the locals. The investigator found no synagogue so that eliminated one source of information. Where was he likely to find names of attorneys? He simply took himself to the courthouse and looked at the directory. With little to no crime since the end of Prohibition, the Franklin County courtrooms were quiet.

Goldy accidentally bumped into a man leaving a small room near the main courtroom. "Sorry."

The man smiled, "No problem I wasn't paying attention."

"Tell me," Goldy spoke. The man was better dressed than the people on the street. "Are you a lawyer here?"

"I am indeed. Robert G. Main, folks call me "Bud." I practice here in the County courthouse."

"I'm looking for a lawyer."

"Have you been indicted for a crime?"

"Actually, looking for a pal, Dutch Schultz. He needs a lawyer. Maybe two lawyers."

"You have met the right man. I also have a colleague, George Moore. We know these courtrooms. We were born and brought up here in Malone. It's not much to look at now, but not too long ago it was a hustling place."

"Bootlegging was the name of the game. Right?"

"Yes, I mean who doesn't like to drink a beer or a glass of whiskey."

"Well, then you know that was Dutch's game. He's been indicted by US attorney Thomas Dewey for doing what everyone likes to do. Is that fair?" Goldy asked.

"I hear you. But my reading the newspapers says this is a tax evasion charge."

"It is. But, again he was making money for a product that most of American wanted."

"But he didn't pay taxes on that earned income."

"True, but if he announced to the world what he was doing, he'd land up jail anyway. Doesn't seem fair. Do you agree?"

"We'll have dinner and discuss the case. I am a man who knows people. George and I can help. Let's eat and now drink perfectly legal whiskey and discuss the law."

Meanwhile, Dixie Davis was trying to make a deal with the federal government. These invisible negotiations started in

1932. A cast of many revenue department lawyers was engaged with Schultz's attorneys to settle the charges. Prison time was not on the table. Money was bandied about. The payment of less than $100,000 was offered. There was federal government official Hugh McQuillan in New York and Ralph Smith in Washington, D.C. handling the case against Dutch.

The major sticking point was documents. Schultz refused to allow his lawyers to hand over any of his financial papers to the government. It was that stubbornness, born of paternal neglect that fueled his opposition. No one could convince Dutch that things would be forgiven with $100,000 and documentation.

Then after Schultz's offices were raided by G-men, the documents were found. That infamous black book recorded every one of Schultz's transactions. There were names, dates and exact amounts, to the penny. His entire bootlegging operation was exposed to the federal agents. He was caught red-handed with his black book.

Dutch needed one juror in Malone, New York, only one to deliver another hung jury. Goldy concluded that Syracuse was a testing ground. More money carefully distributed to locals was required. The population was so much smaller. Schultz had to conduct charm school in this farm town community.

He arrived three weeks ahead of his trial date to spread the goodness around. His advice givers were primarily his two new lawyers Main and Moore. Anyone with the slightest of influence recognized the local guys. People tipped their hats when they walked on the streets of Malone.

Schultz left the glitzy and garish behind. The suits were expensive but conservative. He vanished all frowns and appeared in public with a smile and neat twenty and hundred-dollar bills. Goldy knocked on doors with gifts from Schultz. The lonely physician got money for new equipment. The veterinarian received money to expand. Farmers got bonuses for their milk production. The local school and library got funds to update their teaching materials and much needed construction. The harsh winters were tough on the building maintenance. In the midst of the Great Depression, Schultz's largesse was mightily appreciated. There wasn't a corner of town that Goldy hadn't provided a gift from Dutch.

The newspaper reporters from all across the world photographed Schultz. His was a dazzling smile. The hotels were booked with out-of-towners. The restaurants all required reservations. Once again, bootlegging had saved the town from oblivion. No one was publicly quoted as saying how much the town depended upon bootleggers. The local pastor lamented after the trial what he alone admitted to, which was obvious. Money, above all else, drove the verdict.

Judge Fredrick H. Bryant was a former Malone resident and his decisions in the case were instrumental in the trial's outcome. The judge seemed not to favor either side, certainly, not publicly. It was reported that one of the jurors felt Judge Bryant had brought the trial to Malone to ensure that a bunch of dumb farmers were selected. Jury selection went forward without heavy discussion. The pool was limited to Franklin County.

It was Goldy's job to ensure that a jury of his peers understood the generosity of Dutch Schultz. He had only to convince one of the twelve jurors of Dutch's innocence. No surprise a majority of the jurors were farmers. The foreman was Leon Chapin a farmer from nearby Bangor. Goldy had no trouble learning the home addresses of every juror.

Defense lawyer George Moore arranged for the car Goldy needed to visit the desolate farmers. Goldy marked each location on a big map in his hotel room. He was looking for the most efficient way of meeting each juror's family.

At the farthest reaches of his campaign of generosity, Goldy was met by a slammed door in his face. Not deterred, he slipped an envelope with Dutch's Christmas present under the door. The note said think of this money as a family rainy day fund.

The next name on the list, Hollis Child a farmer from Malone. His wife was very polite. They sat on the front porch sipping iced tea. The weather was always a good topic for idle conversation.

"Those were good days when Prohibition was still around. I was never a teetotaler. Who doesn't like to sip a beer in hot summer and a glass of whiskey in the winter to keep warm," she said. She tucked the envelope into her pocket.

None of the other farmers' wives were as sociable, but no one rejected the envelopes. The daughter of school superintendent L.P. Quinn remembered when it was easier to buy school books for the children. Those were the good times when the school budget wasn't under so much financial pressure. Charles Bruce was one of the few men on the jury that had graduated from high school. He had a position in town as a manager. The baker's family, the Riedels from Malone, spoke about the need for new equipment. During tough times one had to be particularly handy to keep the old machinery working.

Goldy and Frank Lobdell's son talked about Saranac Lake. Dad was a guide to this beautiful recreational area. The problem was there were so few tourists. He had hoped for many more because of the summertime. Early July was so slow. But then the trial was scheduled for nearby Malone, its massive publicity had unexpectedly brought visitors to the lake.

Dutch was remanded to serve his jury trial time in jail. On July 23, 1935, the trial of the decade began. Dutch was able to dress nicely, no orange jumpsuit. His suit was well-tailored, not too much flash, tie knotted perfectly as he faced the jury of his peers. Only for one day was he forced to endure the jailhouse food of sardines, boiled potatoes and cabbage, tea and water.

The case presented by defense lawyers Moore and Main rested on a simple theory. They would claim that Dutch received poor tax advice. This led him to break the law and evade paying taxes.

One most unanticipated sideshow was the presence of lawyer Dixie Davis' girlfriend in the courtroom. A dazzling show-girl of ample chest proportions and brilliant red-hair, most eyes were glued to her and not anything the lawyers were saying. The distraction kept the jurors from paying close attention to the proceedings.

The defense called Edward Reynolds to testify. He was Schultz's tax attorney. In 1926, he advised his client that it was unnecessary to pay taxes on his bootlegging operations since the activity was illegal. It was a wonder that he kept his law license in New York. Not entirely believing that advice, Dutch sought the services of David Goldstein.

Mr. Goldstein testified at the request of the defense that in 1931 he told Schultz, Reynolds' advice was wrong. He then began an odyssey of trips back and forth from New York City to Washington D.C. and Albany, New York to rectify this acknowledged mistake. These trips continued until 1933, when US Attorney Thomas Dewey indicted Schultz for tax evasion.

On the stand over a course of days, Goldstein described his many attempts to correct a mistake made by another lawyer. In a well-modulated voice, Goldstein described his numerous meetings with high-ranking Internal Revenue officials. They were so close to an agreement. The exact amount to be paid was determined. It was not to be, Mr. Goldstein admitted on the stand.

The prosecutor, who was hand-picked by Dewey, Martin Conboy was angered by Schultz's legal team's refusal to hand over documents about his illegal income. A key prosecutorial item was Schultz's meticulous, hand-written black book. In it were details on every revenue source, the amount and date. To the utter frustration of Conboy and his government team, Judge Bryant ruled that the government had illegally confiscated the book. It was not to be entered into evidence. The jury was not to look at or have any access to that infamous black book. Conboy's head fell to his chest. His whole body folded into a giant fetal position.

Suspicion immediately fell onto Judge Bryant. How was it possible for him to come to this conclusion? That black book was the core of the prosecutor's case. Without it, the case rested on poor Dutch's ill-advised tax lawyer's conclusion. Goldstein had dates and the names of government officials, who he had contacted. It appeared that Schultz's new legal team had made earnest attempts to rectify the bad information. Dutch wasn't indicted for bootlegging itself. He was in jail for not paying taxes on his ill-begotten funds.

Meanwhile, a whole different set of negotiations was unfolding. So confident were Dutch's rivals and enemies that Thomas Dewey had finally got their man that plans were created to take over Dutch's empire. In Manhattan, Lucky Luciano and Bo Weinberg, Schultz's top lieutenant, were discussing how to divide up the riches. The meetings were disguised as a means of protecting Schultz's rackets and extortion games in the most probable case that he was convicted. Enough people knew about the black book to know its value to the federal prosecutors. It may have been that one of Schultz's men tipped off the feds to the exact whereabouts of this book.

Bo Weinberg gave the job of telling the boss about this new agreement to Goldy. He was brought back to New York City to meet Bo in a storefront in Harlem. A table was set for two.

When Goldy walked in he saw Bo. The big man yelled out to a waiter, "Get the man a steak."

In Goldy's mind, Bo was not up to the job of boss. No one asked him for an opinion. Luciano was already a boss of bosses. How was Bo going to fit in with the Italians? He lacked the long history that Meyer Lansky possessed. But typical of all gangsters, Bo never recognized his own shortcomings.

"I want you to go back to Malone. Dutch trusts you. Tell

him that to protect his interests, Lucky Luciano and me are figuring how we can do that best. Charm him. I know you've
been working hard on getting him off. We find that unlikely."

"He doesn't trust Luciano. It looks, smells and tastes like a
conspiracy. A takeover." Goldy said what seemed so obvious.
Dutch wasn't the smartest man in the rackets business, but he
had good instincts. He knew a bad deal. He knew they were already counting him out of the game. Dutch was going to resist.
After all, he had killed Jack Diamond to earn his place at the
big man's table.

"There must be someone in control. Otherwise, all those
runners will be thinking they would do better by locking out
the bosses."

"You think he's going to believe me? You think he's going to
understand what's going on? His lawyers have convinced him
that he's going to beat this trial just like the last one. He doesn't
see himself as a loser."

"He always says you're the only honest guy he knows. He
will trust you. You can convince him it's all for the better," Bo
insisted.

"But what are you two really doing? Dividing up the spoils?
Where's Dutch going to land up after the trial if he wins?"

"Dutch is not going to be so lucky. This time Dewey's got
him. It was pure luck that helped him."

"I think it was more than luck."

"I forgot you were spreading the wealth around."

"It worked."

"It's not going to happen twice."

"You are neglecting to understand that the people in Malone are more beaten down than those in Syracuse. A few bucks here and some more there can change minds. We only need one juror."

"You my friend are naïve. Dewey is not letting this go. Dutch is going to jail."

"What happens if you're wrong?" Goldy asked.

"Every time he goes on trial, he takes more and more money. If he keeps being indicted there will be nothing left. He's taking all the money for those lawyers. And you," Bo's finger pointing threatening close to Goldy's head.

"I'm not taking anything for me."

"I know. Goldy you are an honest man."

"I hope this works because Dutch has a mean streak and a bad temper. You don't want him to think you're stealing from him."

"You tell him we're protecting his businesses. And you don't want to know what we're going to do. You are merely a messenger. He goes to jail for ten years, you will benefit. I know because he's the cheapest son-of-a-bitch in the business. We all should have gotten rich. Na, he's the only one with a Fifth Avenue apartment. What do you got? A little house in the Rockaways. Is that fair?"

"What if he thinks I'm lying? That I'm part of some conspiracy to rob him of his businesses?"

"He will believe you. I'm not telling you exactly what's going to happen. I want you to tell him we're just protecting his interests. We are all thinking about what's good for him. That's what you tell him, Mr. Mensch."

"OK, I hope you know what you're doing." Goldy's stomach grew queasy. It was not going to be easy to convince Dutch. Goldy didn't believe a word from Bo's lips.

"It's the business that needs to be protected. One person does not matter. We've all worked hard to protect what's ours. OK?"

"I'm off to Malone to see the boss." Goldy unenthusiastically told him.

Bo slipped a wad of money into Goldy's hand. At first, Goldy pushed Bo's hand away.

"Take it. You've been a good solider. Buy your wife a mink coat," Bo gently slapped him on the shoulder.

Goldy arrived while the jury was deliberating. He visited Dutch in jail. It was impossible to have an undisturbed conversation. In the evening of August 1, word came from a court officer to Dutch that the jury was deadlocked.

"I told them all, I was going to be freed," Dutch told a small audience waiting with him in the county jail.

"See, you're always right," Goldy saw no reason to tell Dutch anything about what Bo and Luciano were doing in New York City. It seemed like another hung jury.

An hour later the same man came back to say there was only one holdout, John Ellsworth, a self-righteous farmer, who gained little from Prohibition. He seemed unimpressed with the favors Goldy gave to his wife. He just hated the government.

Goldy went back to his hotel. He called Bo to tell him the news.

"What did he say when you told him about what me and

Luciano are doing?"

"When I heard the jury was deadlocked, I saw no reason to tell him anything."

"You think it's going to be a repeat of Syracuse?"

"Good chance. How long are they going to let the jury deliberate? These farmers want to get back to their fields. It's summertime, busy time." Goldy reported.

"Thank you for not saying anything. No sense making him crazy now. Hopefully, he'll never find out about our plans. When's this trial going to end?"

"I bet we're back in town by the end of the week."

"I'll let Luciano know. We'd better be prepared for Dutch's return to business."

The next day the judge called all the parties to the courthouse at noontime. Dutch was feeling very confident. He wore his nicest suit, the one with the wide lapels. He attached a flower to the lapel. The tie was solid blue. He said he knew it was going to be good. He had a feeling, those inner instincts told him luck was coming his way.

"Order in the court," the bailiff announced.

The twelve jurors took their seats. The judge appeared in his black robes. The courtroom was filled with reporters from all around the globe. People stood as the judge took his seat.

"Has the jury reached a verdict."

Foreman Leon Chapin rose from his seat, "We have your honor."

"What is the verdict?"

"Not guilty," Chapin's eyes turned to the large audience.

Judge Bryant slammed his hand against the hard wood.

"Not guilty?"

"Yes your honor," Chapin repeated himself.

"Your verdict is such that it shakes the confidence of law-abiding citizens in integrity and truth. It will be apparent to all who followed the evidence in this case that you have reached a verdict not on the evidence but on some other reason. You will go home with the satisfaction, if it is indeed satisfaction, that you have rendered a blow against law enforcement and given aid and encouragement to people who would flout the law. In all probability they will commend you. I cannot," he stormed out of the courtroom.

The room erupted with applause. Everyone present wanted to touch Dutch as if he was a magic amulet. Goldy waited for the adoring crowds to give the man more space.

"Do you want me to give you a ride back to the city?" Goldy asked Dutch.

"No, Rosencrantz will drive me. Deliver a dozen cows to Chapin."

Chapter 10
Dewey and Dutch

Immediately, Conboy delivered the bad news to Thomas Dewey. The US Attorney's face turned beet red. If he was capable of completely exploding into a million pieces he would have done so. He smashed the telephone receiver on his wooden desk. Several tiny pieces broke off and flew in the air.

"I promise; I will get that son-of-a-bitch. He's not going to get away with breaking the law."

It was the moustache that drew you to Dewey. Many men of the era wore them. But his seemed to be completely symmetrical reflecting a part of his personality. The exactness of his investigations were lauded by other law enforcement.

Short men often felt inferior. It was certainly a distinguishing feature of both Dewey and his principal target Dutch Schultz. Why Schultz the press asked of Dewey? Why this gangster when there were so many to select? If publicly Dewey had proclaimed, he was going to expunge the criminality inside New York City civic society, Schultz seemed not the worst of the bad apples.

Dewey sensed a vulnerability in Schultz. He recognized his ruthlessness and persistence, his love of money, so greedy that he paid his associates poorly. Dutch's avarice was his weakness.

Dewey was going to capitalize on that aspect of Schultz's personality.

Loyalty was an essential ingredient in maintaining a criminal empire. Dewey heard through his many informants that Schultz's one hundred associates felt maligned by their Boss. He had drained their coffers to pay for his legal defense. There was a shortage of compassion for their situation.

Tax evasion was a dead issue after the Malone trial. Schultz couldn't be indicted for a crime he had just been acquainted of days ago. Prohibition and the accompanying bootlegging were finished as sources of criminal activity for the special prosecutor. Those dozen years of illegality were legal history.

The new focus by Dewey and his fellow assistant prosecutors was on the numbers rackets. Harlem was the base of Schultz's activities where he often went head-to-head with African American entrepreneurs. His most serious competitor was a black woman originally from Guadalupe named Madame Stephanie St. Clair.

Similar to booze, gambling was always going to be a type of entertainment for the masses. Law enforcement attempted to crush it, but it remained an addictive sin. The numbers rackets were a form of a lottery. In Schultz's numbers rackets a bet as small as a penny was accepted. Men and women both white and black played the game. People in Harlem created new lives out of their numbers rackets' winnings.

A bettor chose three numbers from 000 to 999. The winning number was the total take at a racetrack of the Win, Show and Place bets the previous day. Schultz, ever so greedy, fixed the numbers minimizing the chances of anyone actually winning. His accountant, the brilliant mathematician Otto "Abbadabba" Berman, instantly calculated the least likely combinations of numbers from the Win, Show and Place categories.

With bootlegging dead, the numbers rackets were the target of Dewey's attention. Schultz was still his number one project, to bring him down. Since Schultz played by his own rules without regard to acceptable standards, complaining informants hustled to the Woolworth Building to make a statement. With an army of prosecutors, investigators, and stenographers, Dewey mapped out his attack on Dutch.

Goldy had never told Dutch about Bo Weinberg's instructions. When Dutch returned from Malone, it was obvious that his criminal allies had turned on him. Believing he was a doomed man looking forward to decades in prison, they took his businesses.

Goldy met with Dutch at a Jersey City restaurant where he aired his grievances.

"Goldy, my man, you are the only honest person I know. I can't be seen in Harlem. That little bastard Mayor La Guardia is after me. Dewey won't let me back in New York. What have I got, shit," his boss lamented.

"You're exaggerating Dutch. These kind of businesses need daily attention. People were afraid you were distracted with the trial."

"Who's side are you taking?" Dutch's tone of voice grew harsh.

"You can build up your business again. Here across the

river you can control Harlem. It's only the Hudson River that separates you. The gambling goes on."

"You going to help me get back in the game?"

"Where would I fit? I'm not a bookie, I'm too old to be a runner. I'm not an enforcer. I can't push around your competitors. I know you hate St. Clair but she has allies. There's so much money to be made. You will quickly get back with Otto's magic math. This was only a bump in the road."

"You know who turned on me?" Dutch slammed his hand on the table. The wooden object shook in fear.

"Don't think of them as enemies. They thought they saw an opportunity. Someone had to run the operation while you were rightfully busy defending yourself."

"It was Bo. He convinced me that he would take care of things for me. But what was he doing. He and Luciano were dividing up my territory. Those sons-of-bitches. I'm going to get it all back. Bo, we came up together. Him and me. Treated him like a brother. What's he do? He and Luciano are carving up my businesses. It's not the black bitch who was stealing my business, but my supposed friends."

"I think you're not quite seeing the big picture," Goldy 's voice was calm and soft.

"You taking their side?" Dutch's voice grew rougher and his eyes stared intently at Goldy's face.

"No, of course not. Forget what happened yesterday. Today, today what are you going to do? Guys like Bo, all bosses have men like that. What he did to you was not disloyal. He was saving the business for you."

"I'm going to kill Bo and if I find his brother, George, I'm going to kill him too."

Goldy realized these were not idle threats. Dutch never mis-used language when it came to a violent decision.

"May I suggest," Goldy waited for Dutch's reaction.

"Yeah, what?"

"Your real enemy is Thomas Dewey. He is the one who wants to see you in jail. Whatever happened when you were busy with the trial, that's done. The future is figuring out Dewey's next move."

"What do you hear?"

"It's going to be the numbers rackets. You got to protect your business. It won't be just you he's after. But he wants you because you fooled him. You embarrassed him by the acquittal. You made jackasses out of those prosecutors. You are the win-ner. They, for all their legal knowhow, lost to you. A guy who never finished school. Don't forget your great victory."

"You're right, Goldy. I'll try and make peace with The Commission. I got to remember the big picture, staying in business for the next fifty years."

"Figure out some kind of arrangement. There's enough people who want to make bets that the money's there for all of you. Temporarily, you're here in Jersey. Doesn't have to be for-ever."

"Goldy, I forget how sensible you are. What are you going to do?"

"I'm still trying to convince the right people that gambling on boats is a good business."

"OK, but when I call, you come."

"Dutch, you're the boss."

•••

Bo Weinberg was eating dinner at a Manhattan nightclub on September 9th. It was the last time anyone saw him alive. Despite Goldy's arguments for peace, Schultz never responded well to good advice. The next day, George, Bo's brother met Schultz in Jersey.

Schultz told George, "We hadda put a kimono on Bo," mob talk for his feet are wrapped in cement being eaten by fish in the East River.

Did Schultz actually shoot Bo or was it Rosencrantz, his loyal bodyguard? All that mattered was he was dead. But Schultz had sense not to go directly after Luciano. He always wanted to be the man's friend. His admiration was spurned like a maligned lover. That only made Schultz more determined.

Immediately after the meeting with Schultz, George found the backstairs of the Woolworth Building. He walked up those out-of-sight stairs to the office of Thomas Dewey. There he found a willing audience. Oh, George had tales to tell. Afraid for his life, George figured how valuable his stories were to prosecutors. In exchange, he expected a new identity far from the streets of New York City.

Goldy told Schultz to focus on the future. In Dutch's mind that was a world without Thomas Dewey. With Weinberg dead and Luciano out of his league, Dutch planned for a new assault with a new enemy. He called the man everyone feared Albert Anastasia, founder of Murder, Inc. and associate Lepke Buchalter.

"I need a job done," Dutch told Anastasia, "you're my man."

"What?" Anastasia was first and foremost a businessman. A hitman for hire; he needed a target.

"I want you to trail Thomas Dewey, the prosecutor. I know he lives here in Manhattan. I want to know every step he takes during the course of a day."

Dewey, a man of habit, repeated his every step, every day without exception. His movements were easy to trace. Although he was surrounded by other men during an ordinary day, there were small moments in time when he was without police protection.

Anastasia observed the routine. At 8 a.m., Dewey walked out into the street down the block to a local pharmacy. There he made several telephone calls in a booth inside the store. The prosecutor used this public phone booth because he considered the possibility that his apartment was bugged. Inside the pharmacy, Dewey was unprotected.

The plan followed the man's routine. The hitman would be inside the store before Dewey arrived. Dewey walked in and was shot with a silencer. The hitman would pivot and kill the pharmacist. No witnesses and the shooter quietly walked out the door.

After four days, it was clear that Anastasia had a plan, which he explained to Dutch.

"It's doable," he reported, "just let me know when."

Dutch had an impulse to follow Anastasia's plan, but do the murder himself. He had to pay Anastasia as it was. His thinking wasn't quite solidified when he went to meet The Commission to inform them of his plan.

Their permission was necessary although Dutch hated any

form of authority. The whole purpose of The Commission was to provide oversight. It was the organized part of organized crime. The membership was comprised of the biggest names in illegal activities.

Dutch stood before the tribunal and offered the plan he and Anastasia had worked out. There was heated discussion. The group previously had oked the murders of fellow gangsters. The special prosecutor, this was an extraordinary action.

These were familiar names to anybody knowledgeable about crime in the 1930's. Long-time friends from the gutter, Charles "Lucky" Luciano and Meyer Lansky were the original organizers. The Jews, Jacob Gurrah Shapiro and Lepke Buchalter, were members as well as Italians Frank Costello and Vito Genovese. Lansky, Luciano and Costello were pals from their days working for Arnold Rothstein.

The man accustomed to bare-knuckles racketing in the garment district, Jacob Gurrah Shapiro approved of the plan to kill Dewey. He was also under assault by the special prosecutor. That was the single vote. No one else supported the idea, fearful that by killing Dewey, the entire U.S. government would be after them all. It was bad for business.

Dutch stormed out of the meeting furious with his brothers in crime. He had been a good boy. He went to them for permission. They refused him. It wasn't bad enough he had those trials that ate into his financial reserves. His business was in shambles. He was searching to make money stuck in Jersey. Those bastards had no idea what a sacrifice he had made.

He called Goldy to complain, "They refused permission for me to kill Dewey. That's what you suggested."

"No," Goldy frantically argued. "I never suggested you kill Dewey. He's your enemy but also the special prosecutor."

"That's what The Commission cowards whined about. I got a right to protect myself," Dutch moaned.

"Dutch, I would rethink that plan. Remember The Commission torpedoed my idea for the floating casinos. I would suggest caution. You need these guys."

"Anastasia is going to do it for me. He knows how. He didn't get to be the boss man of Murder, Inc. without a set of balls."

"Let them think about your plan. Anyone support your idea?"

"Gurrah Shapiro. He knows about muscle. Those garment guys shoot and then worry about the consequences."

"Maybe he can convince others to side with you. Blow steam and then relax. Don't be so impulsive. Let Gurrah talk to his fellow Commission members. Speak to him."

"You can wait until they like your casino boats. I'm not a man who waits."

That was the last time Goldy spoke to Dutch Schultz.

Chapter 11
Chophouse Massacre

Luciano was beyond livid. Dutch had flaunted his position in the organization. Again and again, it was Schultz who failed to listen to reason. He defied all orders. It was him against The Commission.

Luciano turned to Lepke, "Take care of him."

Lepke knew what that meant. He returned to Brownsville, Brooklyn to assemble a team. It was methodical and planned like a business organization, not emotional and hot-headed. Schultz had acted out for the last time. Lepke chose a dependable trio to carry out Luciano's orders.

The two best hitman got the assignment Mendy Weiss and Charlie Workman. The lookout and driver was Seymour Schechter. Since he was forbidden to enter New York City by Mayor LaGuardia, Schultz had relocated to Newark, New Jersey. Across the street from Schultz's office was an ordinary Chinese restaurant. The Chophouse offered standard Americanized Chinese food for unsophisticated palates.

The usual group of Schultz associates were dining together that fateful October 24, 1935 evening. There was Otto, the math mind, Bernard "Lulu" Rosenkrantz, bodyguard and chauffeur, and Abe Landau, all-around muscle man.

Weiss and Workman had assassinated people before. They weren't afraid. These were the brazen men who gave other people aggravation. Seymour stayed in the car. His main function was as the look-out and fearless getaway driver.

Weiss and Workman saw the men eating. Oblivious to other diners, the duo entered the restaurant with their guns blazing, bullets flying everywhere. Frightened restaurant patrons leaped under tables. The white-coated waiters fled to the kitchen. One woman screamed.

Lulu and Landau feared no bullets. Despite being repeatedly hit by the two assassins, they kept firing their guns. Bullet casings lined the floor of the restaurant. Otto was immediately dead. His big body was an easy target. Lulu's body finally dropped on top of the table while Landau's bullet-ridden body slumped into a chair. Neither man was dead.

Weiss looked at the damage they had done, "Where's Schultz?"

The main target was not at the table. It was then that Workman started for the restaurant's bathroom. With a gun in each hand, his fingers on the trigger, he stormed into the bathroom. Schultz must have heard the noise. He was prepared but Workman was just a little faster. Shultz, bleeding from the gut, emerged from the bathroom. He kept firing but his limp body stumbled with the bullets striking the walls of the restaurant. Eventually, he fell to the floor, but he was still alive. Despite the obvious carnage, the target was still breathing. And as incredulously, even the two henchmen were still alive.

Workman charged out of the restaurant only to find that Schechter had driven off with Weiss. There he was with smoking guns and no ride. An angry hitman actually walked back to New York City across the Hudson River. And as a good employee of Murder, Inc., he filed a grievance against Schechter. Seymour's poor performance netted him an important demerit. Sometime after the messy shootout, he was murdered by his employer.

The horrified owner of the Chinese restaurant called for an ambulance. Landau and Lulu seemed the worst victims. The first ambulance took them to Newark Hospital. A delayed second ambulance took Schultz to the hospital.

Landau and Rosenkrantz died shortly after they arrived in the hospital. But not Schultz. He was still very much breathing as he was taken to a hospital room.

Goldy got a call, "Schultz was shot."

"Is he alive?" Goldy asked remembering how many attempts were made on Legs Diamond before his ultimate demise.

"Yes, he's in a hospital in Newark."

"Who's responsible?"

"Luciano and Murder, Inc. If I were you, I'd disappear for a while."

Goldy knew what to do. He calmly walked into the living room.

Esty asked, "Who was that at this hour?"

"Schultz has been shot."

"Is he dead?" she asked.

"No, but it's time for you and the children to take a little vacation. I want you to get to that bungalow colony I bought in the Catskills."

"When?"

"Now, right this minute. Pack some things, food, blankets, there's no heat. You got to go."

Zayde walked into the room, "What's happening?"

"Schultz has been shot. You need to take Esty and the kids and leave. Now. Take Rivka and Miriam. I think Moishe will be safe at the drug store. The boys in the garage should be OK. Bluma is fine in the hotel. Call Izzy and tell him to go with his family to his in-laws."

"They're going to kill you," Esty started to cry.

"Don't cry. I will be OK, but no one should stay in this house. Take the dog, Polly and the cats. Evacuate right now."

"I should go with you," Zayde said.

"No, I want you to protect the family. I will be fine."

"Where are you going?" Esty wiped her eyes.

"I'll be fine. Just get some things and get out of here." Goldy demanded.

"Where are you going?" Zayde asked.

"I'll be OK. I'm leaving now. Papa, you and Esty are in charge."

"Goldy, Goldy, how did this happen? You're not a murderer or a gangster," Esty stopped her tears. She realized she needed a calm head.

"You play with bad boys, sometimes things unravel," Zayde offered his appraisal of the situation.

"I'm going," Goldy kissed his father and hugged his wife.

Goldy had a short-term plan. He had a place to hide out for the next week or so without constantly worrying about the family. Everything depended upon whether Schultz lived. If he was dead, perhaps Goldy could make an arrangement with Luciano. The Accidental Gangster really wanted out. If there was a way to achieve that goal. He wasn't going to ask Hashem for forgiveness and promise to be a good boy if he somehow got out of this mess. He wasn't blasphemous. The only thing that could save Goldy and his family was Goldy. It was that simple.

He got into his car and drove north, much further than the Catskills. The car was on its way to Indian country. It was a long ride by himself. Along the route, he started making future plans. The big "what if" was Schultz's health. He was still driving the next day. At a gas station, there was a phone booth.

"What's the word?" he asked a bookie he knew.

The deep voice replied, "He's dead. Tough son-of-a-bitch it took more than a day to kill him."

He hoped that the voice on the phone didn't hear Goldy's sigh of relief.

He got back inside his car to complete his journey. He drove another hundred miles. When he got to the end of the paved road, he drove for miles on a dirt and gravel path. Finally, a fence appeared guarded by a sole soldier with a rifle in his arms.

Goldy stopped the car and got out, "You recognize me?"

"It's Goldy man," he replied and lowered the gun.

"Is Chief around?"

"He's by the main house. We can drive there," the guard jumped into Goldy's car.

It was another twenty minutes and the man whistled as

they passed deep forests of pines and flowering trees.

Goldy remembered the main house built of pinewood.

"Look who's here?" the guard pointed to Goldy.

Chief got off his chair, Goldy opened the door of the driver's side. The two men embraced.

"Who are you running from? Federal police?"

"No, far worse, Murder, Inc."

"We'll have to hide you in the cabin furthest in the Canadian woods and hide the car," Chief slapped Goldy on the shoulder.

"I appreciate your sanctuary. I really do," Goldy hugged the man.

"What happened?"

"Schultz was murdered."

"Who did it?" the guard asked.

"It was Murder, Inc. He never listened. Always so pig-headed. So irrational. It's a miracle he lasted this long," Goldy told them.

"We heard about the trials. Got off. No prison."

"Lot a good it did. Instead of being grateful, he started talking about doing something really stupid. He wasn't being paranoid. He had enemies, plenty of them. But no one would have killed him if he just didn't act so stupid."

"And you my friend as his associate you think those guys are going to go to war with Schultz's soldiers?" Chief asked.

"I don't know, but I sent my family to hide and I need some time to figure out my next move. I don't think anyone wants a war, but Schultz wasn't the only maniac."

"You can stay here forever. We will always remember how

you helped us. We made a lot of money helping you with the booze. Twelve years the money flowed. Too many of us, me included, didn't save for the future. That's not your fault. You warned me that the money wouldn't last that I should build some business. I wasn't thinking about tomorrow."

"You guys are doing better than some people. In the cities, on the dust bowl farms, people, children are going hungry. You all look well-fed."

"We hunt deer and rabbit. We eat the flesh, use the skins. We can fish in the lake. We are better off than some. Let's celebrate your arrival. We'll have a party for you Goldy Goldfarb."

"I got to have a plan. Now that the booze is gone, I'd like to say good-bye to my gangster days. I need a way to get out entirely. I want no part of Schultz's numbers rackets. I'm hardly the guy to shake down restaurant owners for protection money."

"Well, if you want to spend the rest of your days just fishing, you can do that here."

"My wife and children like city life. I do appreciate the offer. Yes, I do. You have no idea how truly grateful I am to know you all," Goldy shook hands with all the men standing around.

After a week, Goldy had formulated a plan. There was no point in simply hiding for the rest of his life. Ten years ago it was easier. Now, it was unsafe for Jews to return to Europe. The Nazis were more powerful than ever. There was the Caribbean. Esty liked warm weather. He spoke no Spanish but others had escaped to Mexico and South America. Money bought politicians and residency papers. He wanted to go back and live his former life; the family enjoyed their former lives.

Goldy, Chief and four braves drove two cars to where the family was hiding in the bungalow colony in the Catskills. Chief insisted that Goldy needed security. He was reluctant to put his Indian friends in danger.

"Me and my braves, we are soldiers. We all served in the Great War for both Canada or America. My braves are unafraid. We faced more dangerous enemies than American gangsters. In those trenches, hand to hand fighting, gas, rats, barbed wire. We are not afraid. We all voted," Chief reported.

When they arrived at the bungalows, they were met by a small army. His father was holding two pistols as if he was starring in a western movie. There were the boys with rifles, Hirsh and Zev. Izzy was carrying a hand gun. Even Bluma was pointing a rifle at the approaching cars. Rivka held a gun as Goldy signaled it was him.

"Oh, oh, wait a minute. It's Papa," Izzy said while Goldy held his arms up high.

"Oh, Goldy," Esty ran to her husband. She showered him with wet kisses. He held her tightly to his chest. A tear formed in the corner of her eye. He kissed away the wet spot.

"I'm alive and I'm here with my posse. Meet Chief and his braves," Goldy pointed to the Indian party.

Zayde shook hands with Chief, "Great to see you," the older man said.

"We remember how good you and your son were to us. Treated us as business partners. We were equals. That means a lot to us," Chief explained.

"Chief and his guys are going to stay with you while I take care of this problem," Goldy told his new army.

"I'll go with you, " Zayde said.

"I go with one of my braves to protect you, help you. The others will stay with your family. We know how to use guns," Chief said.

"No, no, you won't. I'm going alone," Goldy announced.

Esty pulled at his jacket, "You cannot go alone," she cried.

"I know what I'm doing. I'm going alone. If I show up with an army it will be bad, seen as a threat. I go alone, I can have a reasonable conversation."

"Who are you planning to see?" Zayde asked.

"I'm going to see Lepke," Goldy told them.

Esty started to cry, "The madman, the murderer. I'm going to be a widow."

"Everything is about business. And money. I'm going to offer him money to set me free. I know what I'm doing."

"I don't look good in black. They will kill you," Esty insisted.

Every face showed concern. There were no smiles or laughter, deep frowns from everyone. No one believed Goldy.

"You have a death wish?" his father asked his son.

"I'm telling you. Money will make it better. I'm going to be alright. Trust me."

For this matter, no one trusted his judgement. But once Goldy had made an important decision, it was impossible to change his mind.

"Don't worry," he told his family, Chief and the four braves. The Indians understood his stoic stand. A brave sometimes must do the impossible to prove his manhood.

Goldy kissed and hugged his family members one by one. The youngest girls and Minnie, they were confused by all the discussions.

Esty had finished crying. It was her fate to be a young widow, "I will always love you."

"I am not going to my death," he tenderly kissed his wife's face. His lips moved around its oval shape. No spot was left untouched.

His father hugged him so tightly, he thought his ribs would burst.

Rivka accepted his foolhardy plan. She whispered in his ear, "You're never coming back alive. You want to be the sacrificial lamb, to save us. We'll bury you next to Mama."

He looked behind only once. His eyes scanned their faces through his car mirror. Only Minnie danced and waved. Ruby Two, a spitting image of her namesake German Shepherd, howled. Polly could be heard screaming, "Papa going, Papa going."

He drove off completely satisfied his plan was possible. Goldy never lost confidence that he would succeed despite the family's reaction. They never understood the minds of gangsters. Having never shared shots of whiskey and salutations of joy at the results of a big hit, his family was clueless how they operated. Even the most-trigger happy like Dutch Schultz above all, respected money.

He had to get money, lots of cash. Gangsters loved being feared and feeling respected; it was an ego trip. But greed. It was the most powerful aphrodisiac.

He drove all night to his hiding place. There he kept the treasures he earned, always in cash. The stock market and the banks, they took money, promised wealth and then crashed.

No one was around, but the gate was open. Goldy walked into Washington Cemetery in Brooklyn, so serene. It existed before Brooklyn became part of New York City. Two generations of his family were buried side by side.

He parked the car. With an empty carpet bag in his hand, Goldy walked to his mother's grave. The limestone marker was cold to the touch. He placed a pebble on top as he offered the traditional Jewish prayers for the dead. He wiggled part of the limestone monument and pulled open the compartment. A hidden trap kept the cash bills unsoiled and dry.

"Oh Mama. I don't know that if you were alive, you would have approved of what I have become. I know it was certainly not what you expected. But I am still your golden boy. Me, Goldy, with the lovely curls. All the mothers wished their little girls had my curls. I was your oldest and only son.

"Oh Mama, you know I would never have put Papa in danger. I love him just as you loved him. Your American you called him. You were so proud that he became a citizen. You loved this country, but it took many more years for you to completely abandon the country of your birth.

"Oh Mama, someday I will get to Hungary. I will. I am not going to die. The others they may think so, but I know. I have your determination. Your zest for all that life can offer. I am not finished with life. I have many more years left to see more of the children marry and have their own children. I will be a grandfather many more times.

"Oh Mama, I am the businessman you wanted me to become. You thought the fishing boats were silly. But I have now a pharmacy, a car shop, a Kosher hotdog stand on the new Rockaway Boardwalk. It's not Atlantic City, but you would love it, just love it. Best of all, I have a hotel. It bleeds money, but it is absolutely beautiful. And I have a young cousin who found a new life coming to America. Her taste is exquisite, you would approve. She is a granddaughter of Tanta Anat.

"Mama, Mama, you always disliked Anat. You called her stupid and small-minded. And she is. She had the opportunity to come to America. She refused. Her daughters refused. The Nazis will do terrible things to Jews. You were right to leave Hungary and never return. All those letters you wrote to her pleading with her to come to America.

"I miss you Mama. But I am a good son. I have become the Accidental Gangster. It's only been a piece of my life. I will give away this money so that I can return to a normal life. It's not fair to Esty and Papa that we always have to look over our shoulders. I will change it all. I promise.

"Mama, people actually fear me because of my associations. Imagine, a Jew who is feared. I must say, I do enjoy carrying a gun around. It's like I'm part of a western movie. I'm not sure if my part is the good guy or the bad one.

"Mama, who would have thought there were Jewish gangsters. The man who I called boss for fifteen years, Dutch Schultz, a Jew. He was a terrible human being although his mother loved him. I know you still love me. I have never killed a soul. I didn't choose a dangerous path it chose me. It was

Dutch who sent his boys to find me. It was the boats. You never liked the boats. The government also hated them and seized them. I no longer own any boats.

"Mama, me and Rivka are going to go into business together once I have settled this problem. I will buy my freedom as slaves bought theirs. Then sister and brother will open a detective agency. We will help men and women find out about their cheating spouses. You know how much Rivka loves to gossip. She has been practicing trailing people. She follows random people on the street to learn how not to be detected. If war comes she can become a spy.

"I must go Mama. My family needs me. I have a responsibility to protect them. I will return to you as I often do. I tell you what's in my heart. I can't share my true feelings with anyone but you. Always that was so. Me, your golden boy. Rest securely, I will solve this problem. No more the Accidental Gangster. Schultz is dead and I will buy my freedom.

"Mama, what I have really learned from playing this role is not to fear anything. Perhaps as you told me many times, we should all fear nothing but the judgement of Hashem. He will look positively on my accidental life. There is a place with the angels for someone like me. I am not finished with life, not yet."

The headquarters of Murder, Inc. was in Brownsville, Brooklyn. This was a lower class neighborhood largely occupied by Jews and Italians living in close proximity to each other. It was an economic step-up from the filthy tenements of the Lower East Side. Here the garbage was collected by the city. The fire department came if called. The police only arrived for their regular bribes.

Goldy knew the candy store where the members of Murder, Inc. hung out waiting for a call for a hit. Ideally, the murder should be smooth, no police, not too much blood. It was imperative not to accidentally murder innocent people walking on the sidewalk or patrons in a restaurant.

It was the golden locks of hair that was his most distinguishing physical feature. He opened the candy store door.

"Hello," Goldy said to the woman behind the luncheonette counter. She probably had some warning system under the counter. In a few moments, a burly man stepped out of the rear darkness and towards him.

"Goldy Goldfarb," he said to the man, "you know me."

He nodded his head, "What do you want?"

"I'd like to speak to Lepke. Is he here?"

A man of few words, "Why?"

"If he has a few minutes, I'd like to talk to him."

The man eyed the bag Goldy was holding.

"What's in the bag?"

"For Lepke's eyes only," Goldy replied.

The man and woman exchanged facial expressions. Goldy thought he saw a nodding head motion.

"No guns," he said.

Goldy handed over the gun resting in his waistcoat. The man grabbed the gun and pointed to a back room.

The area was much larger than he expected. Behind the backroom where he was standing was a set of dark curtains leading into a deeper space.

When the curtains were parted, Goldy walked into another room where he saw Lepke at a desk. A small group of men were standing around. No one was displaying a gun, but certainly every man was carrying one.

"What do you want Goldy Goldfarb?"

"Can I speak to you alone?"

Lepke was not a trusting soul. Anyone who made his living killing people had reason to be constantly suspicious.

The two men stared at each other. Goldy had no reputation for being a dangerous man or a foolhardy one.

Lepke waved to his men and the three men slowly rose from their chairs and left.

"Now is that better? Why are you here?"

"I have a proposition for you and The Commission."

"I'm listening."

Goldy put the bag on Lepke's desk. It was spotless not what Goldy had expected.

"There's $25,000 in the bag. All the cash I have. I offer it to you and The Commission. I want out. I'm finished with the business now that Schultz is dead."

"You were a loyal soldier Goldy. He left behind a bunch of profitable businesses."

"No, I'm ready to get out. I don't have much, but it's enough. I was never a greedy man."

"Unlike your boss."

"I could complain. I'm sure many complained about Dutch. Not me."

"Didn't he promise to make you rich?"

"He did, but he said lots of things. I'm not going to bad

mouth him."

"You never said anything bad about him to me or anyone else. You don't want revenge? Get even? Want a split of his businesses?"

"Dutch never personally wronged me. But he did some really stupid things. I understand that."

"He wanted to kill Dewey."

"That was one of his stupidest ideas. I understand that he was hot-headed. When he wrapped his mind around an idea, it was hard to dissuade him."

Lepke touched the bag's zipper, but never opened it, "This is a peace offering?"

"You can say that. This is all I have. It's yours and The Commission. I just want out. I can go back to my fishing station."

"Didn't the G-men seize your boats?"

"They did, but I can buy another. I got my little fishing station. I got twelve row boats. I'll sell bait as I once did. It's a simple life. It's all I need. I don't want any trouble. I can quietly just disappear. Forget you knew me."

"Tell me Mr. Mensch, before he died did Dutch tell you where he hid the seven million?"

"I wasn't with him when he died."

"Where is the safe with the seven million?"

"I don't know. I heard the rumors just like you."

"The most persistent rumor was when he thought he was going to prison he had a waterproof safe built. He dug some hole and buried it."

"I heard the same story. I was told the G-men were in some

tiny town, Phoenicia, in the Catskills digging holes looking for it. He never said anything to me."

"Well who helped him dig the hole?"

"I heard it was Bo Weinberg, poor devil. No one's seen him in weeks. He's probably dead and unable to share any secrets. Maybe, he told his brother George," Goldy presented an explanation.

"George ratted to the G-men. Maybe that's why they're digging holes in Phoenicia."

"I'm sure that information, if George had it was worth quite a bit. George could have negotiated a deal for protection with that valuable information."

"A snitch is still a snitch. You can figure when his brother disappeared, George thought that Dutch had killed him. If he had waited for us to act, there was no need to go to the G-men. We could have handled it."

"I'm not a treasure hunter. I'm a fisherman. That's all I want to do. You will take the money. It's all I have to give. Consider it my exit fee."

The missing money was still on Lepke's mind, "Think. Where are all the places that Dutch liked to travel. He would never have trusted just anyone to bury that safe."

"I don't know. If I had seven million to offer you, I would do it. It's a mystery. Dutch takes it to the grave."

"Lots of people are still dreaming about that safe."

"Not me. I want my freedom. You're a Yid, like the slaves from old Egyptian times. Set me free."

"I'll bring it to Lansky and Luciano's attention."

"I would appreciate that. I don't want any trouble. It's been a great ride. I want to grow old in my own house."

"Don't fool yourself Goldy. This life changes you. I bet your neighbors are afraid of you. That's a good thing. In this world, being nice is not the way. Let them fear you. You spent more than a dozen years working for someone who was never nice. He was feared and he loved it."

"Maybe. What he really wanted was to be accepted. He always felt himself to be the outsider."

"You knew him better than most."

"He did all kinds of crazy things. He converted to Catholicism just recently. And why? Nothing to do with his new bride was a Catholic. He wanted to make nice to Luciano. He always wanted to get closer to him. So he thinks by converting it was going to change things. He's still dead."

"Not many people attended the funeral."

"I understand it was his wife, a sister, a priest and his mother. She still loved him. Brought a tallit and placed it over his coffin. They buried him with it."

"Once a Jew always a Jew," Lepke chuckled.

"Any help you can lend," Goldy asked as he watched Lepke grab the bag.

The meeting was Goldy's gamble that he would be able to escape his gangster days.

It was an empty house he returned to that afternoon. Polly wasn't shrieking as he entered. His beautiful Ruby Two wasn't welcoming him with a gentle bark and lots of tail wagging. It was quiet. Esty wasn't making sounds from the kitchen. Pots and pans were silent. The cats weren't sleeping on his favorite chair.

An old newspaper was on the dining room table. President Roosevelt announced a new program to heal the Great Depression. Two workers on the gigantic Hoover Dam project on the Arizona and Nevada border were interviewed. This government work saved them from starvation. His family never starved. Before there was bootlegging, there was fishing.

Goldy drifted from room to room. It wasn't a big house, it just felt that way. He found kosher salami in the icebox. Homemade bread was hidden from view in the metal breadbox. He turned on the radio while he ate his sandwich, washing down the dry bread with beer.

He waited for news. His eyes scanned the front street. If he was a marked man Lepke would send three men. The getaway car needed a driver and two gunmen. One would enter through the front door and the other the rear door from the backyard. He found a second gun. He placed one in each hand.

The phone rang. Goldy didn't recognize the voice, "Meet Lansky in Coney Island. You know the restaurant." The phone went dead.

With both guns wedged in his waistband, he drove to Coney Island.

Goldy motioned to Lansky's bodyguard as he entered the Italian restaurant. Quickly, he walked to Meyer's table. The Man signaled for him to take a seat.

As Goldy sat down, the bag appeared. He hoped Lansky couldn't see how fast his heart was pounding. He willed away the perspiration forming under his armpits.

"Not necessary. We are all friends," the other man pushed the bag towards Goldy.

"I'm glad," his heart slowly returned to normal at the words of encouragement.

"I ordered spaghetti and meatballs for us. I know no cheese for you," Lansky said.

"I'm surprised you remembered. The last of the Kashrut rules I follow from my Mama. No meat and milk. And no bacon, no pig," Goldy felt a sense of relief. It could be short-lived. The guns were still in position.

"You were a loyal soldier to Schultz. Better than he deserved. Your game was bootlegging. It's gone and so is he."

"I just want out. It's been a crazy ride. I understand why Dutch had to go. I'm not looking for revenge. I'm not looking for a piece of his rackets. I'm not a muscle kind of guy. You guys can split up his empire."

"Did he promise to make you a rich man?"

"He did. I'm not a rich man. But I got enough. I was a fisherman and I can return to fishing. I got a little bait and tackle shack. It's fine."

"Didn't the government seize your boats?"

"They did," he tapped the top of the bag, "I can buy another."

The food arrived steaming hot. The waiter poured a glass of red wine for each man and a shot glass of whiskey.

"Schultz always said you were the only honest man he knew. Right Mr. Mensch?"

"I tried to be an honest broker with Dutch."

"How did the Beer Baron of the Bronx land up with a

solider fisherman from the Rockaways?"

"I don't know. He never really explained. I didn't ask him too many questions. I think it had to do with the miles of fairly isolated beach of the Rockaways. No police boats or much commercial ship traffic. It was a good spot. Every night the booze could land on another stretch of beach."

"I'm still proposing your idea of floating casinos to The Commission. I'll let you know if they change their minds."

"Call me for the casino gambling and booze. I like those sins. I'm too old to be running the numbers rackets."

"You were close to Schultz," Lansky said.

The small hairs on Goldy's arm stood up; again, he felt pressure on his heart.

"I was one of many."

"Let me ask you. What do you know about the safe with seven million dollars in it?"

"I don't know anything."

"Schultz might have confided in you. If it had all that money in a waterproof safe someone had to help him bury it. You're not the guy for that job. But did he say anything? Some hint of where he buried it?"

"Not to me. I heard that before the Malone trial, Schultz was afraid he would be convicted and spend many years in jail. It was Bo Weinberg who probably helped him."

"You worked with both Weinberg brothers. Some hint about the location of the safe."

"Bo's disappeared. Maybe, he absconded with the loot."

"We both know Schultz killed Bo and George fled to the federal prosecutors."

"I did hear that the federal guys are digging up around Phoenicia, New York, near some bungalows. It's some small town like Malone," offered Goldy.

"You think George told the G-men that's where the safe is?"

"Maybe. George never told me."

"Essen Goldy," Lansky started to eat. Goldy whirled his spaghetti around the fork and then helped by a big spoon, dropped the pasta in his open mouth. He learned how to eat spaghetti from watching Luciano.

"This is good," Goldy told his host.

"If you should find out any information or remember some little detail about that money, you'll let me know. There will be a finder's fee for you. No questions asked."

When the meal was finished the men shook hands. Goldy drove home to the Rockaways, the beach and the clean surf. He called the single phone in the main cabin of the bungalow colony.

Zayde answered, "You're alive."

"I am and you can all come home."

"You're sure it's safe?"

"I do because I know what they want from me. I don't have it, but I'll look."

"What is it?"

"The location of the supposed safe with seven million dollars that Shultz buried."

"Does it really exist?"

"I don't know. Dutch could be a prankster. Might only be Dutch's last laugh at his enemies including the government," Goldy answered.

Chapter 12
Medical School

Silvie was her father's daughter. Both were indisputably polite but tough and fearless. And they were determined people. A Jewish girl who wanted to be a doctor had many hurdles to overcome. Hunter High School and Hunter College in Manhattan had prepared her for the wide world but not for the anti-Semitism and misogyny of medical school.

He was the only Jewish guy and she was one of only a handful of women in their first year of medical school at Johns Hopkins. The school was located in Baltimore and was one of the few to accept women. The quota for Jews was limited but he had great credentials having graduated from the University of Pennsylvania, an Ivy League college.

Silvie had fewer options in pursuing her medical education, but Baltimore was a perfect place. It was not too far from New York City and more importantly, she was able to live with her cousins. Cousin Blanche worked for President Roosevelt's government while Cousin Ike worked on the docks at the Port of Baltimore.

Her father occasionally visited her in Baltimore. The cousins refused to accept any money for taking in Silvie. It was a family's obligation to take care of their own. Besides Goldy had secured Ike's job at the port. Italians and a few Jews ran all the ports across the east and west coasts.

Goldy liked to rock on his cousin's front porch in Baltimore. The house itself, one of a dozen attached in a row, sat high on an incline. It was at least 25 steps to the front door. Just walking up and down the front steps was adequate exercise for anyone.

He waved to her as she started her hike up the steps. Her medical school books were bulky and heavy; and she strained as she walked. He went down to greet her and carry some of her textbooks.

She kissed him and he returned the gesture. "Papa so nice to see you."

There were four rocking chairs on the porch. She dropped her book bag and sat down. "Oy."

"My Silvie working so hard. Even the walking is a burden."

"Papa what are you doing here?"

"Just checking to see how my baby girl is doing."

Then Cousin Blanche appeared with a tray of freshly made cookies and lemonade.

"Essen," she said as she poured out the lemonade. She sat in the third chair.

"I'm now working in the hospital. The first two years I only spent in a classroom. This year we get our practical experience with real patients not cadavers."

"Wonderful. My daughter the doctor," Goldy held her hand.

"She's got a fella," Blanche announced.

"Really?" her surprised father responded.

"Yeah. His name is David and he goes to medical school

with me."

"A Yid?" her father asked.

"Yes, he is. We members of the tribe have to stick together."

"I invited him to dinner so you could meet him," Blanche said. "About time her Papa meets her boyfriend."

Silvie pointed a finger at her cousin, "You knew Papa was coming so he could meet David."

Blanche's peach-colored skin turned a bright red.

"Is this serious?" Goldy looked at his grown-up daughter, no longer a child or a teenager but an adult woman.

"He is the love of my life."

Goldy whistled. "Really? I should meet this boy. And your mother what does she know? How long are you together?"

"Since the first day of medical school. We looked at each other and we just knew."

"My daughter the romantic. How is it Cousin Blanche knows about him and not your Papa?"

"I have spoken to Mama about David."

"But your Papa? No word to me," he felt his face get red. He tried to suppress his anger. "Does he have one leg? Misshapen eye? It took all this time for me to find out."

"No, no," she gently touched her father's cheek. "But I want you to like him. I knew he was the one but we had to get to know each other better. I had to find a way to tell him about your former business. And Dutch. I wanted Cousin Blanche to arrange this dinner when you visited me in Baltimore."

"I could hate him. But I love you so. I would learn to like him. What do you see in him? What makes him so special?" Goldy knew this was extraordinary. Silvie never had a serious beau in high school or college.

"He wants to save the world. More specifically, he wants to save the Jews," she answered.

"Oy," he immediately responded, "he's a Zionist."

"Yes and I told him about you helping to get the Jews safely out of Europe."

"And what did you tell him about Dutch?"

"That took some time. He really had to know what a good person you are. Bootlegging was only a part of your life."

"It's the part that pays for your medical education."

"He's a German Jew. I know you don't like them," Silvie said.

"No, it's not that at all. Dutch was actually a German Jew."

"Papa, Papa," she shook her finger at his nose. "Don't lie."

"It's them who call us kikes. That kind?"

"His father is also a doctor. They live in the Midwest. Not so friendly with bootleggers and Italians."

"I'm sure during Prohibition they got their booze from Canadian Jews working with American gangsters."

"He is a nice boy," Cousin Blanche felt obligated to defend David. He always brought something for her when he came over for dinner.

"It was an instant attraction the moment we met at that first day of medical school. I just knew," Silvie giddily replied.

"And him? Did he know?"

"Yes, yes. It was mutual."

"And this Zionist business?"

"Yes, he has an acquaintance from Europe. We have met him several times. We will be going to Palestine after we graduate. Jews must have a homeland of their own," she announced to her father.

"You want to live in a desert surrounded by hostile Arabs who hate you. The British are all anti-Semites. This is the land of opportunity, America. You want to give this up for some crazy idea about a Jewish Homeland."

"You must read Herzl. He knows what Jews need. We must have a land of our own. The British promised us," she defiantly told her father.

"I know. I have read his plays and his writings. But he's been dead for thirty years and there's still no homeland."

"It will happen if enough people believe it can happen. You smuggle Jews out of Europe right now. I know some go to Palestine."

"I do, yes. But the first thing I ask them is do you want to go to America? America is the safest place on this earth for Jews. Certainly, not Palestine."

"The future is a free Jewish Homeland in Israel," she slammed her hand on the chair's arm.

Her startled father jumped from his chair.

"Let's prepare for dinner," Cousin Blanche took Silvie's hand and led her into the house.

As Goldy sat shaking his head a tall, young man started walking up the stairs. He waved to him.

His arms were filled with flowers and candy. "Mr. Goldfarb, I presume?"

"David," Goldy took the flowers from his arms.

The young man sat in the chair closest to Goldy.

"I'm so glad to finally meet you. I love your daughter. I

want your permission to marry her."

"And take off to Palestine where you'll both be killed. If not by British soldiers, then by angry Arabs. Is this the life you want for my daughter?"

"You have been to Europe recently. I know you smuggle out Jews. Some you take to Palestine. We cannot as Jews be so beholden to goyim who hate us. Hitler means to exterminate us. He is not making idle threats."

"Yes, yes, get the Jews out of Europe. But bring them here to America, to Baltimore to New York."

"Americans don't care if Jews die in Europe. This is an anti-Semitic country. We must have our own homeland."

"War is coming to Europe but not here in America. Jews can be safe here."

"We have a mutual friend Fritz Schoenberg," David informed his future father-in-law.

"Yes, we work together to get the Jews out of Europe. We need ocean liners so thousands can leave not my freighters that handle a hundred souls. We need the support of politicians and officials in the Roosevelt administration."

"You have made my point. American politicians do not want to help the Jews of Europe. We must save our own people by bringing them to Palestine."

He looked into the eyes of his future son-in-law. "Foolish words." As Goldy began to speak he heard his daughter.

Silvie called them into the house, "Dinner is served."

Goldy cornered his cousin after dinner. "So many Zionists here in Baltimore? Nu?"

"A hotbed of Zionist activity in America right here in old Baltimore," she answered.

"Why? Is it because there is a large contingent of Hungarian Jews here? It's because of Herzl, the Hungarian Zionist?"

"I don't know. But Henrietta Szold is from Baltimore."

"Who?"

"The woman who founded the Jewish woman's organization Hadassah. You heard of Hadassah?"

"So?"

"Szold is living in Palestine making a difference among our people living there. Her goal is to recruit doctors, nurses and medical supplies to Palestine to fix the health care. Palestine is a pretty backward place. With Jewish brains and determination, she is going to change that."

"What does that woman have to do with Silvie?"

"Hadassah is the link. That's what got Silvie interested in Palestine. They need doctors. I think it was actually your daughter who got David involved."

"Oy, my activist daughter. What am I going to do?"

"You should work with Hadassah and bring Jews from Europe to Palestine. I know you work with some of your gangster friends to do that but you should work together with people who have pure intentions."

Goldy knew there was no point in arguing with the love birds. They talked social niceties around the dining room table. After dinner, Goldy drove his soon to be son-in-law back to his dormitory at the medical school. He stopped on his return to a telephone pay box on the street.

"Esty, you knew? I'm the Papa and I'm the last one to know. I bet Rivka knew about this David."

"Oy. She called me just around when Dutch was killed. I didn't want to worry you with everything going on."

"I'm the Papa. I should know first," he insisted.

"Well, you met him. What do you think?"

"A German Jew. Does he know about Dutch?"

"Silvie has managed to keep most of the details from him. Now that Dutch is dead, what is there to know."

"Well, I can only imagine what his Jewish doctor friends are going to think about this wedding."

"Blanche and Ike only say nice things about him. He's polite. He brings gifts when he visits," Esty reported.

"My cousins are going to be the judge of our daughter's second most important decision."

"What's first?" Esty was certain of his response.

"Medical school of course. She's going to be a doctor. We can set her up so good either in Far Rockaway or even Manhattan. If he wants to be a fancy doctor."

"Goldy, all they talk about is Palestine. They are Zionists."

"Blanche says she made him a Zionist. It's all about Hadassah."

"She wants to make a difference."

"That is a problem. Worse, David knows Schoenberg. Two Germans what can you expect."

"So what should we do?" Esty implored.

"Nothing. We do nothing. You know inside that cool head is a stubborn mule our Silvie. You reject him. What happens? They run away together. Elope. No," Goldy knew his daughter's temperament.

"We have to invite his parents to dinner at our home in Rockaway," Esty was making plans in her head.

"Blanche says his parents visit him in Baltimore but she and Ike have never met them. Silvie has met them. She has gone to dinner with them."

"You start talking to her about the future. A wedding, we'll have it at the hotel. Billie will do something real nice just like Izzy." Esty was going to talk to Billie the next day.

"What do they think about their son's Zionist views?"

"I don't know?" Silvie never said anything to her mother.

"Izzy's parents admired my gangster connections. I'm not so sure these two will have the same attitude," Goldy remarked.

"It's not so important now," Esty was relieved that Dutch was dead and Goldy was still alive.

"This is not what I wanted for my Silvie, a German Jew Zionist," her anguished father said.

"I know. You hate him already."

"My sainted mother, a Hungarian, who first entered into this country through the Port of Baltimore, hated those German Jews. You look around and wonder but, Baltimore, the "Charm City" as my mother sometimes called it, had the second largest Jewish population in America. And the German Jews have been here a long time."

"He's not from Baltimore," Esty said.

"He thinks like a Baltimore German Jew with their social clubs and debutante balls like the goyim."

"She loves him," his wife responded.

"It's those German Jews who owned the garment factories. Everywhere. Here, New York. And they treated their Jewish brethren from Eastern Europe like serfs."

"That was the past. Now we have to think about the future," his wife said.

"We must figure out somehow to keep them both in this country."

"I have heard her say why should she go to a medical school that has a quota of Jews attending. Why not a class full of Jews."

"They haven't graduated yet. You work on her about a nice office. She loves us. Does she want to be so far from us?" Goldy had not formulated a real plan.

"I don't know what we can do to change her mind either about this David or both of them going to Palestine."

"OK. Let's go along with their plan. I'll go talk to The White Shul rabbi about another wedding."

"We must try and get them to forget about going to Palestine. She knows what you're doing. It's dangerous to get there. It's worse to live there between the Jew-hating British and the angry Arabs."

"A Zionist. She has some of my mother in her. She was a Hungarian who talked about Herzl and Zionism."

"War is coming back to the world. Hitler, Mussolini, all terrible for the Jews. You can't let them go to Palestine. Surely, they'll be killed," Esty was distraught.

"You always said I would be killed working for Dutch. He's dead and here I am. The Accidental Gangster is still planning and scheming. I'll try and figure something out."

• • •

Before Goldy left Baltimore, he went to meet a connection. Gus was from the docks. The Port was visible and shining in the night light as they talked.

"I need for you to do me a favor."

"Dutch is dead but you Goldy were always a good soldier. What can I do for you?"

"I want you to follow someone."

"You want me to threaten him. Rough him up. Not too serious?"

"No, no. I want you to follow him. Get a camera and take photos of the people he meets. Be inconspicuous. You know what that means?"

"He shouldn't see me or my camera."

"That's it. Here's his name and address." Goldy handle Gus a piece of paper with David's information.

He read it and then put it in his shirt pocket.

"You want a report every day?" Gus asked.

"No, no that's not necessary but we speak at least every week. This is important to me."

"Don't worry the job is in good hands. I'll keep watch and let you know."

"Also, you got friends in the police department?"

"Yeah, I got contacts."

"I want you to have him check to see if this guy has ever been arrested. Does he have traffic tickets?"

"Not a problem."

"I want you to find out if he's attended meetings of the Community Party. I'm sure they get together somewhere."

"I can do that."

They shook hands and Goldy slipped the man a fistful of twenties.

"Not necessary. Keep the money. Pay me after the job is done. If you're satisfied."

Goldy hoped he didn't have to do everything. It would be far more difficult for him to be inconspicuous in Baltimore.

Chapter 13

Spring 1936?

Lansky never called. Goldy wasn't feeling entirely secure that he was free of his former life. Shortly after the Coney Island meeting, he started noticing that black cars followed him. When he went on errands, he saw a man in a black overcoat behind the steering wheel. The cars weren't flashy but seemed powerful. The frowning face belonged to either a G-man or someone sent by The Commission. Goldy started paying attention to the driver. It was not the same guy every time. He was being watched.

Goldy looked over his shoulder every time he walked up his front steps. His stalker never came close enough to alert Ruby Two or Polly to impending danger. All through winter, Goldy felt prying eyes on himself. He considered confronting the driver; he changed his mind. So far it was only annoying not threatening.

One day in early spring his shadow disappeared. Goldy walked into his house and went out the back door looking for the black car and the man in the dark overcoat. He found no strange cars in the neighborhood. He traveled to the kosher meat market to buy chickens driving very slowly. His eyes checked every cross street. No one was trailing him. Two weeks passed and he had no strangers watching him or the house.

"I think whoever was watching us is gone," he told Esty.

She walked to the front room and spied the street behind her drapes. No one but neighbors had cars on the street.

Zayde walked into the room, "Looking for your mystery man?"

"I think they're gone. I haven't seen anyone for two weeks," Goldy explained.

"Here's why," Zayde threw down the daily newspaper.

Esty read the front page story. "I see. The government agents arrested Charles "Lucky" Luciano in his hideaway in Hot Springs, Arkansas. Lucky ain't so lucky after all. Got him on a bunch of prostitution charges. He and Lansky have bigger problems than finding some lost treasure buried by Dutch Schultz."

"Let me see," Goldy took the newspaper.

"He's in a heap of trouble. Got some woman prosecutor. What's her name?" Zayde asked.

"Eunice Carter. Seems she got some of these prostitutes to rat on Luciano. Doesn't look like some slap on the wrist," Goldy reported.

"Maybe it's true. That's why we don't have a shadow watching you. They need muscle to go after these women willing to testify. I'm glad I'm not one of them," Esty said.

"I'm thinking Luciano's guys are gone. The G-men who were watching me, they gave up fast. Not Luciano and Lansky they kept up the surveillance. Not now. I could be a free man," Goldy smiled.

"Think they're still tapping the phone?" Zayde had immediately noticed the clicking sounds starting in November of the last year. He warned his son to avoid saying anything important.

"Have you heard anything in the phone lines?" Esty asked.

"No, it's been quiet. My son, I think more important events have overtaken treasure hunting."

"Shall we go treasure hunting? Where's a map of the Catskills?" Goldy asked.

Esty looked through a desk drawer, "I found one."

"What are we looking for?" Zayde asked.

"Dixie Davis was Dutch's lawyer. He came from Tannersville in the Catskills. The G-men were digging holes in Phoenicia, also in the Catskills. And I don't know why. Perhaps as a joke, he buried the safe in Cairo where Legs Diamond had a place before he was killed by Dutch."

"Should I put a couple of shovels in the trunk of the car?" Zayde was smiling.

"You're not really going digging in the dirt in some tiny hamlet in the Catskills?" Esty was confused.

"No, of course not. We're going snooping. We'll ask around these towns about Dutch. Did they see him there last year? If it happened at all, he must have done it before the Malone trial, last July. "

"Should you talk to his lawyer that Dixie fellow?" Zayde asked.

"Oh no. I don't trust him. We have nothing better to do than go on a treasure hunt. We 'll leave Sisel and Tzipi with Rivka."

"I bet your sister would like to come along. She still has it on her mind that you two are going to go into the detective business," Esty added.

"She can come but who's going to look after the girls, Sisel and Tzipi?" Goldy liked the idea of his sister joining them.

Esty said, "Bluma can watch them. They can all stay in the hotel along with Gladdy."

It was decided. No one was more excited than Rivka. It was their first detective job. Find Dutch Schultz's millions was the assignment. Confident they were no longer under watchful eyes, the four adventurers went to the Catskill Mountains of New York State.

Their bungalow colony was in Sullivan County where most Jews vacationed. The three most likely towns where Dutch buried the safe were in nearby Greene County, northeast of the Jewish Catskills. They made a perfect triangle. Cairo was not in the mountains but on the way into the Catskills. The roads were narrow and windy, and dangerous to drive in the snowy wintertime. Springtime was the best time for this venture.

"If we find the money what would we do with it?" Rivka asked.

"If we actually find anything, I'd give it to Lansky. I'm sure he will give us a generous finder's fee. If we kept the money, you better call the funeral director to measure our coffins. Money, that they all understand. Everyone greedier than the next fellow," Goldy added.

"He was such a cheapskate, Dutch. It's better that his

money be forever hidden," Esty never liked the man.

"Oh, just think of this as our mystery case. Where would Dutch bury his loot? And who knows the location besides the dead Schultz? He didn't bury a huge safe by himself?" Rivka was asking all the logical questions.

"Does Lansky and friends think you helped Schultz bury the safe?" Zayde posed the question.

"No, I'm not too big a guy. They think Schultz confided in me and told me the location."

"Well, too bad he didn't," Rivka was so pleased with the journey.

The four had such fun chasing after any leads to Dutch Schultz's presence in the tiny hamlets of Greene County, New York. If people knew something, they were quiet. With Schultz's death, Goldy thought someone would be willing to speak. The barber mayor of Tannersville said nothing. The newspaper editor in Cairo was speechless. The Phoenicia blacksmith plead ignorance. They all suffered from collective amnesia.

Goldy returned to his bait shop. He sat on a chair in the sand sorting his fishing lures. He paid his young cousins Sisel and Tzipi a few coins to go clamming. He used the clams as bait. There were few customers but he kept a fresh supply of bait.

He heard the car pull up. She was visiting the bait shop for the first time in years.

"So Papa, I find you at your favorite spot," Silvie said to her father. She found another chair and placed it in the sand.

He hugged her as she sat next to him.

"Silvie my girl," he tapped her hand, "my doctor, soon to be a bride."

"Oh Papa, sorry you never found that treasure chest. The idea was right out of a pirate movie."

"It was fun chasing after leads. I never really expected to find anything. Dutch was a prankster."

"Maybe all those quiet towns people dug it up once they heard Schultz was dead. They followed him when he came to bury it. Hiding in the woods. They kept their distance. Waited even after the news of Schultz's death expecting someone like you to claim it."

"Interesting theory. You want to join your Tanta Rivka and my private investigation company?"

"I thought you wanted me to be a doctor?"

"You and David can look at some properties I picked out for your future home and office. You can practice together. Wouldn't that be swell. One is right by the ocean not far from Izzy. The others are in more commercial locations."

"I know you still can't accept our plans. David and I have a whole different scenario about practicing medicine."

"We can go into Manhattan if you want something classier." Goldy was still not going to concede.

"No, Manhattan is not an option. Please Papa. We have other plans and we have been talking about this for a long time. I know you hear my words but you refuse to accept them."

"What? I will do anything to set you both up in a practice."

"You can help us. In fact, Papa, you are one of the few people on this earth who can actually help us."

"What do you want me to do?"

"We're going to Palestine. You cannot stop us. Stop trying. Please. Help us get there in one piece."

"Palestine. A Zionist. That's so dangerous!"

"Papa dangerous? Really? Who lived a dangerous life? Who walked around with a gun? Who disappeared out of the country to get away from the police? Who hid on an Indian reservation to avoid being killed by other gangsters? Who?"

"I was an Accidental Gangster. It's over. I have this bait shop and my twelve rowboats. Tanta Rivka has this idea for our PI business. I think it's a bit nutty but why not?"

"I know you want to protect us. Keep us from harm. That's not me and it certainly is not you."

"Is it wrong to want to keep you and David safe?"

"Do you know how frightening you are to others. They don't know my real Papa, the sweetest guy in the world," she took his hand and held it.

"I'm scary? Me?"

"I guess you were blind. The neighbors thought it strange that when other fathers went to work they usually left around 7 or 8 in the morning. That was the time you and Zayde were coming home. Then there was the police coming by to question Mama. The neighbors were petrified. I can tell you that no child in school, probably no teacher, would ever make any of us unhappy."

"My hours were a bit strange but afraid of me. No, can't be?"

"Oh yes, especially after they heard Minnie tell them that you worked for Dutch Schultz. He was a feared hombre."

"I think you're exaggerating."

"When I went to college. People always ask what does your father do for a living? I'd say he's a businessman."

"I am."

"I couldn't tell them you were a bootlegger so I said you owned a hotel."

"I do, very legit."

"As David and I got closer, I told him you worked for Dutch Schultz. I was there when he told his button-down surgeon father. The man's jaw dropped. But then he started thinking about his son, the brilliant surgeon, married to a gangster's daughter. His mother must have just finished reading Fitzgerald's novel *The Great Gatsby* and she asked about Mama's diamond rings."

"I must say, although Dutch promised me, it never happened. I never got rich."

"But his father went from 'Oh, my God' to alarmed about marrying into the family of a killer. Papa you were better than any contact in Washington, D.C. You got things done."

"Better to be respected and feared than ordinary, I guess," her father replied.

"One of my friends told David that both Dutch Schultz and Meyer Lansky attended Izzy's wedding. Of course, Dutch is dead. They were wondering whether Meyer would attend our wedding."

"I can ask him," Goldy held onto his daughter's arm. "Forget the wedding. What's with this Palestine? You can end up in jail by the British or worse get killed."

"I know you can make this happen. You have been working

with Zionists to get Jews to Palestine. My Zionist friends told me you have been doing this for some time. You never mentioned this important work you have been doing to save the Jews of Europe. You and Lansky."

"Because I know what's happening, I know how dangerous this is."

"You can get me and David there safely. I know you can," his daughter's voice softened.

"If you go to Palestine, I'll never see you again."

"You and Mama will come to Palestine. We will have a modern state of Israel. A place where Jews don't have to be afraid. Help me Papa."

Goldy exhaled a big breath. Shaking his head, "I will call my Zionist friend Fritz Schoenberg. It's a mistake. You could have a nice practice right here in Far Rockaway."

"Papa, you never took the easy way, why should I."

Meyer Lansky did attend the wedding of Silvie Goldfarb and David Gordon. He handed them an envelope filled with American dollars and British pound notes. Against all the pleas of mother and father, the new couple journeyed to the new city of Tel Aviv. For Silvie, it was a loving reminder of home in Far Rockaway with its sand and beach.

Goldy became Abe Gilbert and Rivka Stein became Rebecca Sullivan. The two started their private investigation business. The lost loot of Dutch Schultz never was far from their thoughts. Most of their cases involved wronged husbands and wives. Sisel and Tzipi went from clam diggers to operating the bait shop and its twelve rowboats.

Epilogue
Some People Get What They Deserve

Chophouse Massacre Assassins

The killers of Dutch Schultz did not have happy lives. The driver of the gateway car Seymour Schechter, who sped away too quickly, was killed by Murder, Inc. for his incompetence and cowardice. Along with Schechter, Emanuel "Mendy" Weiss was in the getaway car. But he had participated in the Chophouse Massacre and as a result remained a loyal member of the hitman squad for Murder, Inc. He did become a familiar figure in the gangland murders of the 1930's and 1940's. Finally, the police caught up with him, and in 1944, he was executed by New York State authorities. It took the federal prosecutors years, but Charley Workman was eventually charged with Schultz's murder on March 27, 1940. He then spent the next 23 years in prison.

What Happened to the members of The Commission?

Lucky Luciano

The boss man that Schultz envied and loathed, Charles "Lucky" Luciano spent his last days in exile in Naples, Italy. He died a relatively old man for a gangster at age 64 in 1962.

In April of 1936, he was arrested and charged for operating a string of 200 brothels in New York City. His sentence was harsh. He was ordered by the courts to spend between 30-50 years in prison. He was saved from this plight by his old friend Meyer Lansky in 1943. With connections with the U.S. Navy, Lansky convinced the U.S. government that Luciano could serve as a spy in his native Italy. After the war, his sentence was commuted by President Truman. He was deported and spent the rest of his life in exile in southern Italy.

Lepke Buchalter & Gurrah Shapiro

For Louis Lepke Buchalter life came to an end in Sing Sing Correctional Institution in Ossining, New York at age 47 in 1944. Lepke was one of the founders of Murder Inc. He was responsible for the murders of as many as one thousand people either by pulling the trigger himself or ordering the murder of someone else. He was electrocuted with his underlings Mendy Weiss (one of Schultz's killers) and Louis Capone.

His claim to fame was as a labor racketeer with other Commission member Jacob Gurrah Shapiro. They started in the garment industry as shakedown artists. The money came from two sources. Lepke and Gurrah got paid by the factory owners for not burning down their businesses. And they also got paid by the union workers for protecting them against having their teeth knocked out. Their business grew from the garment industry to trucking, dry cleaning and trash removal. It was a lucrative enterprise earning the two long-time friends five million dollars a year. Shapiro joined his pal in Sing Sing dying of natural causes in 1947.

Frank Costello

Frank Costello was a protégé of Arnold Rothstein along with Luciano and Meyer Lansky. He was one of the very few gangsters of the era to die in peace. Italian-born, Costello survived an assassination attempt in 1957 orchestrated by Commission rival Vito Genovese. He gave up being a boss, handed it over to Genovese, and retired from the business, dying of a heart attack at age 82 in 1973.

Vito Genovese

A vicious rival, Vito Genovese started as Luciano's second in command in the narcotics and racketeering businesses. Indicted by the special prosecutor in 1937, he fled to his native Italy. There he became best buddy with Italian fascist leader Benito Mussolini. He was returned to the U.S. to face murder charges in 1946. Somehow the witnesses kept getting murdered so he was freed. With a ruthless hand, he emerged as the boss of bosses. His favorite sinful business was narcotics. In 1959, his luck ran out and he was sentenced to a federal prison in Missouri for fifteen years where he died in 1969.

Meyer Lansky

Meyer Lansky, real name Meier Suchowlanski, was a true patriot born on the fourth of July in what is today Belarus in 1902. His empire was the glamorous world of gambling. He controlled casinos in London, Las Vegas, Cuba and the Bahamas. The scrupulous gambling games he created, assured gamblers that they could lose, but the games were never rigged. By 1936, he controlled casinos in New Orleans, Florida and

Cuba. He convinced The Commission to allow his boyhood friend Benjamin "Bugsy" Siegel to open a casino in Las Vegas; (gambling was legalized in Nevada in 1931). That didn't end well for Siegel, who was killed in 1947. However, mob-controlled gambling in Las Vegas flourished for decades. He developed elaborate ways of avoiding paying his taxes by transferring ill-gotten funds to Swiss banks. In 1934, the Swiss government enacted banking laws that assured the client of complete anonymity. At one point he purchased a Swiss bank. In 1970, he fled to Israel to avoid federal tax evasion charges. Two years later the government convinced the Israeli government to extradite Lansky. His was acquitted of charges in 1974. He then spent the rest of his life in peace in Miami Beach, Florida dying of lung cancer in 1983.

Harriet Goodman Grayson is a proud graduate of Far Rockaway High School class of 1966. She is a graduate of Queens College. She holds a Masters in urban planning from NYU and a Masters in urban sociology from Denver University. She has worked as a planner for the City of New York and the state of Colorado. Faced with governments' lack of interest in plan-

ning, she transferred her skills to become a Strategic Planner for a variety of insurance companies. Later she would marshall her experiences to become a grants writer and events planner for non-profits and local governments.

Other non-fiction books by Harriet Grayson: "Guide to Grants Writing for Non-Profits," "Guide to Grants Writing for Local Government" and "Special Events Planning for Non-Profits."

Books are available on www.amazon.com and www.oceanbreezepress.net

Sasha Perlov Murder Mystery Series by Anastasia Goodman, (Harriet Goodman Grayson's pen name).

Loose Ends

Sasha Perlov is a man of conflict. Striving to secure the beach communities of New York City now destroyed by Storm Sandy and haunted by the world he left behind in Russia. As a NYPD detective, he finds himself driven by passion for a woman whose

husband has been found dead on the living room floor. It is Sasha's duty to find out who is responsible for his death. As a modern Inspector Javert, Sasha never gives up on a case; he hates loose ends.

The son of a Jewish dissident and the grandson of the Hero of the Battle of Stalingrad his tortured past never leaves him. The tangled web of history follows him to America–the New Jerusalem. Sasha's life is controlled by the contradictions that never leave him.

Death and Diamonds

This Sasha Perlov mystery continues the exploits of the Russian-born, NYPD detective. Sasha's Russian cultural and language skills place him in the middle of the murder of a young diamond merchant. The jeweler is a member of an exotic Central Asian Jewish community more Persian than Russian called the Bukharians. The group is linked by international police to Colombian drug dealers.

Sasha's investigation takes him from the streets of the New Jerusalem (America) to the original Old City as he seeks informants and contacts. How did a young scholar, father of five children, living in Brooklyn, NY become a diamond courier and for whom? His life seemed so ordinary until he started taking more and more trips to Israel meeting an enigmatic Ubecki multi-millionaire real estate developer. And what of the ties between this Ubecki and an evangelical Christian US Defense Department analyst accused of stealing classified documents from the US government and handing them over to representatives of the state of Israel.

Spies, couriers, hush money and money laundering figure in this mystery novel. What the police originally label a simple street mugging becomes a case of international intrigue.

The Terrorist

The year is 2004 and the terrorist attacks are still fresh in our memories. Protestors against the Iraq War line the streets of major cities. Sasha Perlov, Russian-born NYPD detective, is requested by the US Attorney's NY office to interrogate a potential terrorist. Is a Muslim woman picked up by US immigration in Long Island a terrorist? Why is she in the company of members of the infamous MS-13, experts at drug and human smuggling? Is a Latin gang and foreign terror group creating an alliance?

History, intrigue, and the effect of political turmoil converge to challenge Sasha as he attempts to seek the truth. Join Sasha as he fights the enemies within and outside of our borders—to protect the country he loves.

Books are available on www.amazon.com and www.oceanbreezepress.net

Based on True Events
Rockaway Riptides

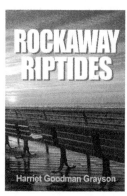

It is a coming of age story for all ages and all times. The turbulent 1960's were when rioting and protesting happened across the country. In a sliver of a peninsula jutting off of Long Island, the Rockaways felt protected from the raging currents. Living in an isolated part of New York City, the citadel that nourished and sheltered the young people was Far Rockaway High School. Built of the sturdiest materials in the 1920's, the tribal tendencies of its residents and the tempestuous winds of war in southeast Asia, were kept under control by its teachers and administrators. Rockaway Riptides captures this period of instability as seen through the eyes and experiences of the senior high school class. Tragedy and triumph shape the lives of these young people during this difficult period in American history. Relive how young and old faced the twin whirlwinds of a war 10,000 miles away and a racially and ethnically divided city.